HELL HATH NO FURY

DARK DESIRES BOOK 2

M.L. MOUNTFORD

Spyros

Enjoy

M / Mountford

For my amazing husband and two wonderful daughters.

1

LILITH

He was dead. I sensed he was no longer connected to me. As he'd failed to complete his training, our link was still active. I could sense his energy, yet it had just been snuffed out. I wasn't upset by it. He had been a means to an end.

Daniel's life had little consequence to me, as long as he had succeeded—as long as she was gone.

"Is it done?" I spoke into my phone.

"We are waiting for confirmation, your Majesty," the voice responded.

"I want to know immediately," I said before I hung up.

If Daniel had succeeded, there was no doubt in my mind that Louis had killed him. I was very aware of that when I'd sent him in there. His death had been unavoidable.

I wanted Louis. I cared about nothing else.

I waited, and it felt like hours, but it was mere minutes until my phone rang again. "Speak," I commanded.

"Your Majesty, Daniel is dead." I knew that already. There was hesitation down the line—the person didn't want to say any more.

"Tell me, child," I spat.

"The girl lives. She was the one to kill Daniel, not Lucifer as we first believed. She is aware of Lucifer's true identity now, though, your Majesty." The voice was small, and I could hear the apprehension through the line.

I didn't answer. I simply hung up the phone.

Then, I screamed, louder than I'd ever screamed before. It wasn't fear that ripped through me; it was unadulterated rage. The windows in the old warehouse shattered all around me as I continued to scream from the bottom of my soul.

The man who was tied to the chair next to me tried to cower. He was unable, though, as he was bound tightly. He was no one, just a plaything.

I stopped screaming. I'd genuinely forgotten he was there while I'd been lost in my rage. I turned to face him. He was panting with pain; blood trickled from his ears, and I assumed his eardrums had burst. Tears streamed down his face, soaking into the gag forced into his mouth.

"Shhh, it'll be over soon," I said soothingly while stroking his face. I yanked him out of the chair, breaking his bindings and holding him in front of me. In an instant, I savagely bit into his neck and felt his warm blood drip from my mouth and down my chin. I unforgivingly drew and drew before I finally ripped out his throat and dropped his limp body to the floor. The rest of his blood flooded from his torn-out throat, pooling beneath him. The crimson of his blood glistened in the moonlight, and I felt strangely soothed by the sight of it. There had been no reason to kill him other than me being pissed off.

I looked into his glassy eyes as he bled out in front of me; it wasn't a pleasant way to go, but I was not in a *pleasant* mood. He would have felt it—he would have suffered. I wanted him to be in pain. I wanted someone else to feel anguish like I was—it wasn't fair I was going through it alone.

I licked the blood from my lips, tidying up as I looked down at the man's corpse at my feet. It was a waste, really.

I gave it little further thought.

She *knew*. All was not lost. The little tramp knew that he was the Devil.

Luke, that's what Tess had thought his name was. He'd had many names over the years, but he would always be my Louis. He was special to me, and I to him, despite what he might say. We shared things no one would understand; we had been there at the beginning.

He said he was through with me, that it was a mistake, but I knew those were lies. He loved me as much as I loved him. We needed each other; that was why he'd done what he did all those years ago.

Louis was mine—he had been for all eternity, and no one else could have him. Especially not some little human whore. I would destroy her, and then he and I would be reunited and remain together for the rest of time.

Just because she knew who he was, though, didn't mean this was over. Louis had a way of being persuasive; he could twist and manipulate everything. It was his skill. He could sway her. Sway her straight back into his strong arms, arms that didn't belong to that little bitch.

She was human, so he had to know it couldn't last. She was so fragile and finite. Her life would end, since she was not immortal like us. What could he possibly want from her?

I wasn't prepared to take any chances this time. Whatever he wanted from her, he wouldn't get it. I wasn't going to let anyone else handle this. She couldn't return to him—I wouldn't allow it.

If I wanted her gone, I'd have to do it myself.

He'd know I was involved by now. I hadn't wanted to get my hands dirty. Now, I had no choice. I could snap her neck like a twig—it wouldn't be a hardship for me, and now I *really* wanted to.

I'd have to kill Tess myself.

2

LUCIFER

Shit, shit, shit.

"Tess, wake up for me, Tess." I leaned over her, checking her pulse. "Come on, baby, stay with me."

Thank fuck, I thought when I finally found a pulse. I pulled her to me, cradling her unconscious body. She was alive, but I wasn't convinced that she was okay.

She'd taken quite the beating from that motherfucker. I still couldn't quite believe that she'd killed him. I'd stood open-mouthed and wide-eyed as I'd watched her end him; shock and disbelief had surged through my body.

Another emotion darkened my mind: anger. I was absolutely livid, both with Daniel for nearly taking her from me, and with myself for not being able to protect her from something like that—someone like *him*.

Irrationally, I also felt a tinge of anger that Tess had snuffed him out. It was precisely that, though, irrational. She'd had no other choice. What the hell had I expected? She was fiercely independent, and I knew she'd done it so she'd be free of Daniel forever.

But it galled me immensely that I hadn't been the one to

dispatch of him. I'd have annihilated him, made him suffer and pay for everything he'd ever done.

Not immediately, though. He would have died, but first I'd have taken him to Hell and prolonged his agony. I'd have delayed his inevitable death with long, drawn-out, painful torture. I would have made him pay for every single thing he'd done to Tess.

He would have suffered before I eventually peeled his skin and flesh from his bones. Then I would have staked him through the heart, centimetre by excruciating centimetre, until I watched his body decay in front of me.

As it stood, though, he was gone. His soul would never be mine. He'd simply ceased to exist when Tess had impaled him. No one knew *what* happened to vampires when they died; they were simply gone.

Though Tess had robbed me of my time with Daniel, I couldn't begrudge her her vengeance. She had seen a way out, and she had taken it. I couldn't blame her for that.

Looking down at her now, I felt only concern. I had to get her to a hospital so that she could be checked over. She was bloody, bruised, and still unconscious. I stood gently, ensuring I kept her body close, protectively pressed up against mine.

I portaled us to a hospital, the best in the city. It was important to me she had the best care, the best doctors.

As I made my way to the desk in the emergency room—Tess still cradled against me—the nurse saw me, stood, and moved toward me.

"What happened?" she asked, her eyes studying Tess's unconscious body.

"She was attacked, I brought her straight here." It didn't matter what I said—I fully intended to make everyone forget she'd ever been here.

"Follow me. What's her name?" asked the nurse, moving

through the waiting area to a long room with multiple curtained cubicles. I answered her questions as we moved, then stopped behind her when she motioned us through one of the curtains.

"No, we'll need a room, a private one," I said matter-of-factly. I wasn't rude, but it definitely wasn't a request—it was an order.

The nurse shook her head and turned to face me, but immediately stopped when her gaze met mine. She could feel the power that radiated from me. I'd been told it was oppressive, like every fibre of your being was heavy. As if your body was having an internal battle within itself, a fight for dominance that would only ever end one way.

It didn't take long for the nurse to submit; there wasn't much fight in her. I assumed she was coming to the end of a long shift. Her body and mind felt tired, weary, and she surrendered to my control quickly. She nodded and moved from the cubicle.

I once again followed her as she led us to a private room. It was comfortable enough—as comfortable as hospital rooms could be. I gently placed Tess on the bed; she'd not once moved since I'd cradled her against my body. The gentle rise and fall of her chest against my body was the only evidence she was still alive.

The nurse began to check Tess over. "Sir, I'm going to have to fetch a doctor to assess her. She has some nasty-looking wounds." She returned five minutes later with a doctor. Thankfully, he seemed to have just started his shift, and he was bright-eyed and bushy-tailed, ready to go.

They both glanced at me as I stood next to Tess's bed. I was holding her hand—not willing to leave her side. "Sir, I'm afraid we must ask you to leave while we examine her, if-"

"I'm not leaving," I hissed in the doctor's direction. There was no way I was leaving her alone, not now—maybe not ever.

"We really must insist. We've got a lot of tests to do. Sarah here will show you to the waiting room." He motioned for the nurse to escort me out of the room.

I'd love to see her fucking try, I thought to myself.

I turned my focus on both of them, eyeing them both. I fed them my influence like waves rippling through the room. I felt when the power hit them.

I rarely used my powers of persuasion, I didn't need to, but this time I had to. Both nodded at me and began to check Tess over—I let out a grumble when the doctor asked me to move so he could assess some wounds on Tess's face. I reluctantly agreed and moved to a seat in the corner of the room. I wouldn't leave, but I would let them work.

They cut off her clothes, exposing more wounds and gashes on her torso, arms, and legs. Her beautiful skin, which was usually ivory, soft, and supple, was now varying shades of blue and black, and dried blood seemed to be everywhere. She looked utterly broken. I noticed there was heavy bruising on one side of her ribs, and I was pretty sure she'd once again cracked at least one of them.

I watched as the doctor opened Tess's eyes, looking into them with a small light. "Tess, can you hear me?" She didn't respond, lying perfectly still.

"Pupils are equal, round, and reactive to light. I want a CT head scan, though, make sure she has no head trauma. Actually, make that a full-body CT scan." He moved a machine closer to Tess's bed and squirted some clear liquid on her discoloured stomach. He then moved a wand from the machine across her stomach and up over her chest. A snarl threatened to leave me as his hand moved closer to her breasts. I knew he was helping, but I didn't like him touching her at all.

"Ultrasound looks clear, but we need some X-rays. Looks like she has some damage to her ribs that we should check on. It could lead to a possible pneumothorax," the doctor said to the nurse while scribbling notes. "How did she sustain these injuries?" He turned and cast a quick look at me before going back to his notes.

I once again tapped into my powers as I said, "That's not important, and there's no need to contact the police." I didn't need anyone asking questions about this—it was for me to deal with, personally. Both he and the nurse nodded in agreement.

"Sarah, if you could arrange those scans. We also need to run some blood tests. I'll be back soon. If anything changes, contact me immediately."

The nurse hooked Tess up to several machines that beeped rhythmically before taking blood and leaving us alone in the room.

As I looked at her—now covered in a hospital gown, unresponsive, and looking like an empty shell—I thought back to how close I'd been to losing her. All because of Daniel.

It wasn't just Daniel, though; it was Lilith as well. She would die. There was nothing that could prevent that now. She had sealed her own fate. Despite her constant interference in my life, I'd allowed her to live. Not anymore. She had finally gone too far.

Tess had vanquished her demons by taking Daniel's life, and now I would do the same. Lilith was my responsibility, and I'd nearly allowed her to take something so important to me. *Someone* so important to me.

In such a short space of time, Tess had become essential in my life. I had feelings for her I'd never had for anyone before. I loved her, or at least that's what I thought this was.

What had started as trying to get one up on Daniel had

developed into something real. Feelings for Tess had slithered into me, wormed their way into my heart and taken me by surprise. Looking at her as she lay utterly helpless, I knew that I'd do anything to keep her safe.

But now that she knew *who* I was and *what* I was, would she still want me? She'd already said we were done before she passed out, but I had to at least try to win her over. I needed to show her I wasn't what she thought I was. Sure, I was the Devil, but I wasn't *all* bad.

If she didn't choose me, it didn't matter. I'd protect her regardless. Until her final days, never again would anyone harm her. She was under my protection, always.

That was what you did for the ones you loved.

3

TESS

Beep, Beep, Beep.
Oh, God.

I felt like I'd been hit by a train. My limbs were like lead weights, and I was unable to move. Everything hurt. *Everything.* My head was pounding, so much so that I could feel my own blood pumping with every painful heartbeat. Every single part of my body hurt.

What the hell happened?

I wracked my brain for anything that could explain why I felt like I'd gone on a date with a steam roller, but I drew a complete blank. There was only pain.

Beep, Beep, Beep.

I knew I wasn't at my place—I could tell it wasn't my marshmallow-soft mattress—so where was I? I had to open my eyes, see where I was, but it was a struggle. The darkness soothed my aching head, and I didn't want to risk making the pain worse. I needed to know where I was, though.

I forced myself to open my eyes. I was right, the light was harsh and made my head throb harder. I squeezed my eyes shut to force away the blinding light.

Come on, Tess, you can do this.
Beep, Beep, Beep.

I once again slowly peeled my eyes open, and the light wasn't such a shock this time. As they adjusted, I realised they weren't that bright. The lights in the room were dimmed, giving off a gentle glow. As I looked up, I saw a plain white ceiling with the odd sprinkler here and there. I continued to try and focus, to assess where I was. There were white walls and a closed wooden door.

Beep, Beep, Beep.

I turned to see where the slow, rhythmic beeping was coming from and spotted several machines, illuminated with numbers and lines. I took notice of the wires and followed them to find they were attached to me.

I'm in the hospital. But... but why?

I moved my gaze from the wires and monitors hooked up to my arm, to my other hand, which was being held—by a large, male hand. I traced my gaze up an arm, to a body, and up to the face of a sleeping man. He was slumped back in a chair which had been pulled close to the bed. He was asleep, yet his face looked anything but peaceful. He looked troubled. As I studied him I felt calm—soothed, even—by his presence.

Luke.

I continued to watch him sleep. *Had he brought me here? What happened?* Despite his pained expression, he was still handsome. A warm, fuzzy feeling spread through my body, easing some of the pain that had taken root in my very being.

He looked awkward in the hospital chair, his frame too big to fit into it comfortably. His position was stiff and actually looked painful. I wasn't sure how long he'd been here. I wasn't sure how long *I'd* been here.

The stubble on his face was more pronounced, darker, and thicker than usual. He had slight bags under his eyes, and his hair was dishevelled—like he'd constantly been running his hands through it. It was clear we'd both been here a while.

His clothes were casual—black sweat pants and a tightly fitted black tee that showed the outline of his muscular chest. I loved running my fingers along his chest, absentmindedly following the curves of his pecs.

I looked down to find I was wearing a hospital gown— one of the ones that always gaped open at the back, exposing your ass to anyone behind you. The blankets from the bed were tucked up under my arms, essentially cocooning me in. *Real sexy.* I had some bruises on my arms, but they weren't the cause of my discomfort; I couldn't see the rest of my aching body, but I knew from the pain it wouldn't look good.

What happened?

Why am I in the hospital?

And why do I feel like I took a beating?

The last thing I remember was getting ready to go meet someone. I'd got dressed and was heading to my bedroom. *Who was I meeting?* An anxious feeling rose through me. I felt uneasy, sick. Then I remembered.

Daniel.

I was getting ready to go meet Daniel. But I'd never left my condo. He was there, in my place, waiting for me.

I killed him.

Oh, my God. I killed him.

I'd plunged a piece of wood through his heart, a heart that had been changed forever. He wasn't the Daniel I'd known. I didn't think it was possible, but he'd been crueller, darker, more twisted.

I was overwhelmed when the recollection of everything that had happened with Daniel slammed into me. Him breaking into my home, him throwing me into various pieces of my furniture, him telling me he was a vampire, and then him proving it to me. And me killing him, watching as he faded into nothing before my eyes.

I should have felt guilty, even upset at what I'd done. I'd taken a life, but in all honesty I felt relieved, at peace with the knowledge that I no longer had to live looking over my shoulder. I'd unburdened myself of a dead weight that had been dragging me down for years. If my body hadn't been so messed up from the beating I'd say I'd have felt lighter. As it was, though, I felt like my body was fused to the bed. Like I was one with the mattress. Like it had somehow melded to my body.

Luke's hand twitched, pulling me from my thoughts and making me once again focus on his sleeping face. His expression remained troubled. His forehead was crinkled, and his eyes scrunched together.

Wait, Luke was there too. He tried to help me.

He must know that I killed Daniel. If he knew then why is he still here? Why didn't he call the police or leave me to deal with it all myself?

Then the realisation hit me like a freight train.

He knew what Daniel was—he knew, and he didn't care. He wasn't scared by a vampire, because he was, in fact, something worse. Much worse.

Luke was the Devil.

I knew it sounded crazy, but it was the truth. I felt the painful truth in my bones. Luke was the Devil.

The pain swelled in my body, not only from my injuries but also from the betrayal of what had happened. He'd played me. I was nothing to him other than an arrangement, and maybe a fuck just for the hell of it.

He'd told me he loved me, but how could he? Was he even capable of that? I highly doubted it.

I gasped and snatched my hand from his grasp, then tried desperately to force my limbs farther up the bed, away from him and his touch. I hardly moved, but it was enough to startle him awake.

His eyes, still heavy, focused on me and he smiled.

Is he fucking kidding?

"Red, you're awake. You gave me quite the scare," he said in a gentle tone. He adjusted himself in the chair and leaned forward, attempting to take my free hand.

I recoiled from him, in fear, anger, and repulsion. *"Don't fucking touch me,"* I hissed. I didn't want him anywhere near me.

"Tess, please. Don't be like this."

"Get out. Now!" my voice dripped with venom. I wanted him gone. Away from me. Now.

"I'm not going anywhere. You need to let me explain—"

"I don't need to do shit. You, however, need to get out of this fucking hospital room and leave me alone. I don't want to see you ever again." Tears pricked at my eyes, but I refused to let them fall. I wouldn't give him the satisfaction of knowing he'd gotten to me. Knowing just how much he'd broken me.

"I'm not leaving, Tess, I suggest you get used to that." He settled himself in the chair and continued to watch me.

"Luke… Lucifer… Satan, whatever the fuck you're calling yourself, I don't want you here. Leave."

He interlaced his fingers and placed them on his knees as he remained in the chair next to my bed.

Fucking stubborn prick.

"Fine, then I'll go," I said, pulling back the blankets on the bed. I forced my legs from the bed. They were heavy, like two dead weights, but I had to get out of there. He hadn't moved; he was still sitting in the chair.

I planted my feet on the floor, and once I steadied myself, pushed off the bed. I stood shakily—and my legs immediately gave out. *Shit, this was going to hurt.* I expected to hit the floor, but it never happened. Soft yet strong arms cocooned me and prevented me from hitting the cold hospital floor.

He lifted my body and held me tightly against his. Like I was a bride he was about to carry over the threshold. I desperately tried to push him away, hitting out at his chest and arms. But I was weak, and he was too strong.

"Put me down now!"

I don't need saving. Especially not from the Devil.

4

LUCIFER

She was fighting me, hitting, and scratching at my chest. She was too weak to do any damage, and the blows hardly even registered. I desperately wanted to hold her, show her I would protect her and keep her safe.

But that was the last thing she wanted.

"I said put me down, Luke!" she demanded.

I gently placed her back on the bed, and she pulled her knees up to her chest. The movement caused her to wince and it was clear she was hurting, and my presence was making it worse. But I couldn't bring myself to leave.

I thought about sitting on the edge of the bed, but seeing her curled up, defensive, like I was a threat to her, made me think twice. I instead moved around the bed, heading to the chair I'd been occupying.

"Don't sit; just leave." She watched as I ignored her and sat down. "What do you want, Luke?"

"To make sure you're safe," I said softly.

"You don't have to worry about me anymore. You have what you wanted. Daniel is yours. I'll eventually be yours too. Until then, leave me the *fuck* alone." Her voice was angry, but it was also laced with uncertainty, and something else.

It was fear.

She was afraid of me. It was like a sucker punch, and it took me aback. I didn't want her to be scared of me. Of everyone, she was the *last* person that should fear me. "I won't hurt you, Tess. You don't have to be scared." I heard my own voice crack from the emotion.

"Are you kidding me? Of course, I should be scared. You're the Devil. You are the actual fucking epitome of a *bad* guy. Whatever was between us, it's done. There's nothing more to say, so you should leave."

I sighed, pinching the bridge of my nose. How could I explain this to her, explain it so that she understood how I felt. I wasn't used to all of this; emotions like these were new territory. They were unnerving.

"Tess, I'm not going anywhere. Not until I know that Lilith is no longer a threat. I can't have her hurting you. I wouldn't forgive myself if anything happened to you," I said gently.

"It's too late. Look at me. *Look at me*. I'm already hurt and you did that. You and Daniel, by having a pissing contest about who I belonged to. Like I was some piece of meat. It would have been easier if you'd both just measured your cocks, and left me out of it." The fear was still there, but her anger had taken over. "You don't care about me. I don't think you actually know the meaning of that word. All you know is darkness. You filled my head with exactly what you thought I wanted to hear and it was all lies—"

"I never lied about anything. I may have omitted some parts of my life, but I never lied to you or about how I feel about you. I love you, Tess. I do." I leaned towards her, and she flinched back again. I felt an ache in my chest, and I knew I had to do damage control, show her how I felt.

"Don't, Luke. I don't want you anywhere near me. *Ever.* You may not have lied, but you weren't honest. I don't trust a single word that comes out of your mouth, and I need you to fucking leave." Her nostrils flared and her eyes narrowed; her knuckles had gone white with the tightness of her grip on the sheets.

"We can talk about all of this later. You need to rest now. It's important for your recovery and—"

"You're not listening to me. I can't rest or recover while you're here. For all I know, as soon as I go to sleep you're going to drag me to Hell with you. Take my soul and add it to your collection. I might not even wake up."

Was she serious?

"You're being ridiculous. I've told you I wouldn't hurt you—"

"And I've told you I don't trust you, Lucifer." She said my name with so much contempt it hurt.

Neither of us said anything. We stayed silent, as we each considered the other's position, but neither of us willing to relent. I wasn't sure how long we stayed like that. It wasn't until the doctor arrived that we both snapped our attentions away from each other.

"Ms. Adams, you're awake. How are you feeling?" It was the doctor who had broken the tension between us.

"Like I've been to Hell and back," she said, glaring in my direction. "When can I leave?"

The doctor picked up Tess's notes and examined them. "Well, according to the X-rays, you have a couple of broken ribs, but they didn't cause any internal damage. Your CT scan shows no internal bleeding anywhere, which is good. You'll be pretty sore and tender for a while, though, due to the level of soft tissue damage. Can I ask… how exactly did you come by these injuries?"

Tess began to speak, but I cut her off, once more feeding

my influence to the doctor while I said, "We've already discussed this, Doctor. Now, when can Tess leave?"

He shook his head as if clearing a fog that had taken up camp there. "Of course, sorry. You should be fine to leave once we get your discharge papers sorted, Ms. Adams. Shouldn't be long now." With that, he left the two of us alone again.

Tess immediately turned to me and spat, "What was that? What did you do to him?"

I rubbed my temples with my fingertips. *How the hell am I going to explain this?*

"I used my influence."

"What? That's all you're going to give me? You dismissed him like it was nothing. I *want* him to know what happened —maybe that way he'll make you leave." She was still huddled up on the bed, the farthest away from me she could possibly be.

"Tess, I made him leave. No one will know you've been here or what happened. I thought that was best for you, considering you're the one who killed your ex-boyfriend." She flinched at my words. I admit that I could have been gentler in my delivery, but I was starting to get pissed off. *Can't she see I'm doing my best?*

"What, so it all just goes away? As simple as that?" she asked.

"If you want it to. I can make everything go away, Tess. Will you let me?" She had no choice, but I knew she'd now hate to be indebted to me.

She sighed heavily as if the realisation that she couldn't do this alone had finally dawned on her. "Hurry up and deal with Lilith so I can move on with my life. Without *you* in it." She glared at me, finally coming to terms with her current predicament.

"Tess, I will always be there—" I held my hand up to stop

her from interrupting me. "I know you don't believe me, but I love you. If you don't want to be with me, then I'll have to deal with that. But I will never leave you unprotected. You're too important to me for that. I will kill anyone who hurts you and I'll be with you, always." I tried to keep my tone as calm as I could, but the thought of her being in danger shook me.

I could see her cheeks had become wet, but she didn't make a sound. I watched, unsure of what I should do. I shifted my weight in the chair, waiting for her response. I was about to move closer to her when she spoke.

"I can't be around you." More tears stained her beautiful face and my guts twisted. "I need you to go, please," she begged.

"Emma is on her way. As soon as she gets here I'll leave. There will always be someone with you though, Tess. If you don't want it to be me, one of my people will be shadowing you until we've dealt with Lilith," I said in an adamant tone. Conrath, it would be him. He'd served me well with Tess so far, and he already knew all of the details.

"Fine," she whispered while readjusting herself in the hospital bed. She shuffled farther down and stretched out her legs. Then she turned her body away from me slightly. She could still see where I was, but she didn't have to look at me.

I never once took my eyes off her; I was relieved that Daniel hadn't inflicted any serious injuries, though I was pissed at him and Lilith for putting Tess and me in this position. I didn't know if I could repair the damage they had caused, but I'd do my hardest to try.

5

TESS

I SHUFFLED myself off the bed and gently planted my feet on the floor. It was freezing cold against my bare skin, and it sent a little shiver through my whole body. Before I even had the chance to stand up properly, he was there.

"Where are you going?" he questioned, holding his hand out for me to take.

"To use the bathroom, if that's okay with you?" I replied, ignoring his hand and standing while still holding onto the bed. He didn't move from in front of me.

Once I'd managed to steady myself, I took a tentative step forward. He was shadowing me like a parent would a baby learning to walk. "I'm fine, but it would be easier if I didn't have to walk around you," I said, glaring at him. He held up his hands and backed away, once again moving to sit down.

"Let me know if you need any help."

Is he kidding? I'm pretty sure I can take a piss on my own.

I turned to him, giving him a sarcastic smile. "I'll manage."

I didn't even need to go; I just wanted a minute alone, away from his constant gaze. Away from him studying my every movement, and fussing every time I winced—which was pretty constant. Whatever painkillers they had given me were *definitely* not strong enough. A bottle of whiskey might do the trick: numb the pain and make me forget everything, including that I'd had sex with the Devil.

In all honesty, I was hiding.

I was hiding in the fucking bathroom.

Glancing at myself in the mirror, I realised I looked like shit. My hair was greasy and lank. I'd been cleaned of the blood that had covered my face and neck, but my reflection was awful. I was bruised, with dark black circles under my eyes. A dressing covered the mark that Daniel had left on my neck.

I moved my eyes down to study my arms, where I found grab marks, and I could see multiple finger-sized bruises where Daniel had held me tightly. I knew the majority of the damage was on my torso—hidden from view. To fully take in the extent of my injuries I had to look under the absolutely fetching blue hospital gown I was modeling.

Once again focusing on my reflection in the mirror, I gently lifted up the gown. Thankfully I still had on my underwear, no bra though—I assumed they'd cut it off.

Daniel's newfound power had clearly made him even more heavy-handed. No wonder I felt like I'd gone ten rounds with an MMA fighter. I was covered in bruises of multiple sizes—the largest being that on the side of my ribs. I shouldn't be surprised. That was Daniel's favourite spot. Hurt like hell, and it didn't show.

My body was in bad shape.

In reality, all of me was in bad shape. Everything ached and felt broken—including my heart. I'd let my walls down, allowed someone else in, and it had turned out like this. I'd thought he was different, and we'd connected on a level I'd never experienced before. I'd felt so at ease with Luke, like I could be totally honest and open. I was my snarky, smart-mouthed, awkward self with him and he'd stayed, in fact, he kept coming back. Wanting to know more about me, but not being pushy or overbearing with it.

Now I knew why. He'd needed to keep me close if he was to get Daniel's soul. I was nothing to him, despite what he was telling me now. He was a good actor, though, I'd give him that. I nearly believed him, but how could I? He'd had years to practice his skills of manipulation and deception… many, many years of practice.

I was nothing to him, a bump in the road. That feeling should relieve me. That I was insignificant. That I was nothing. I didn't feel relieved though, I felt sick to my stomach at the thought that I meant nothing to him. I was being ridiculous. *He was the Devil!*

"Tess, are you okay in there?" he said from just behind the door.

Tears had once again started to fall, but I wouldn't let him know it. "I'm fine. I'll be out in a second," I snapped.

Tucking my hair behind my ears and smoothing the hospital gown, I readied myself to face him. So, I steeled my expression and took a deep breath before opening the door and stepping back out.

Except the room was empty. He'd gone.

I was flooded with mixed emotions: relief, but mainly loss and longing. Despite everything, I did still care for him. I knew that was ridiculous and absurd, but it was how I felt. I'd get over it, but at that moment I thought I'd break.

I shuffled back to the bed and positioned myself on it, pulling the covers over my legs and settling in. That was when I saw him. He hadn't left—he was outside of the room talking to a sobbing Emma. They looked to be having an animated conversation, with Luke gently rubbing his hand up and down her arm in a reassuring manner. The sight of it made me bristle.

I watched the two of them talk and wondered what Luke was telling her. I doubt it was the truth, but I was curious as to what he'd fabricated. What elaborate lie he'd come up with? I suppose I should know if we were to keep our stories straight.

Emma turned and caught my gaze. She held up a hand to wave and gave a half smile. Luke turned when he realised Emma was looking at me. He said something to Emma, and she walked away.

Where is she going?

He slipped back into the room and opened his mouth, but before he had the chance I cut him off. "Where'd Emma go?"

He sighed deeply and moved to stand at the end of the bed. "One of my people is downstairs, in the lobby with some things from your place. I asked Emma to go get them so you could be ready to leave," he said, his voice steady.

I dodged his penetrating gaze for as long as could; time seemed to move slowly but I knew it had been a lot longer than it seemed. I wanted to avoid speaking with him but I knew I needed to ask what he'd spoken with Emma about.

"What did you tell her?" I asked. "I need to know."

"Emma thinks you were jumped on the way back from your run. She's quite upset, but I'm sure she'll be fine. I've been very vague; however, I told her everything is in hand but that I'd like it if you could stay with her for a while and she has kindly agreed."

"Do I get any say in this?" I knew the reply before he even started to speak. "Don't bother."

"Tess, this is all for your benefit. I'm not doing this to piss you off. It's to keep you safe."

"If it wasn't for *you* I wouldn't need protecting would I, Lucifer?" I said his name with loathing.

He ran a hand down his face. "I know, but here we are, and I'm trying to make things right." He moved to the door and opened it, then returned to the end of my bed. Someone else walked through the door and closed it behind them. The figure loitered behind Luke. Waiting.

Hold on, what the hell is this?

An uneasy feeling pumped through my body, and I stilled. Focusing my attention on the pair.

"Tess, this is Conrath. He'll be your protection from now on. Wherever you go, he'll go." He was deadly serious. From behind him moved a man, shorter than Luke, with a small but graceful build. It seemed odd describing a man as graceful, but that was the first thing I thought of. There was a fluidity to his movements. He had a shaved head, but my eyes were immediately drawn to a large, hooked, almost beak-like nose.

"Ms. Adams," Conrath said as he inclined his head in acknowledgement.

"Hello," I replied. I once again loaded my voice with loathing. "Luke, I don't need a bodyguard, I'll—"

"Conrath will be with you twenty-four-seven, unless you'd prefer me to stay?" he said, raising his eyebrows.

"Fine," I replied. Conrath nodded at me, and then turned to Luke and did the same. After that, he slowly left the room, closing the door behind him.

Great bodyguard he is, I thought to myself.

As if reading my mind, Luke said, "He's very good. You won't even know he's there."

"I'm pretty sure I'd know if someone was following me," I said snarkily.

"He's been watching you for months, Tess. So no, I don't think you would. Anyway, he stays. If he needs me at all, he'll let me know, and I'll come straight away." As he spoke he held on to the end of the hospital bed, which made the muscles in his arms flex. It nearly distracted me from what he'd just said, not quite though.

I held a hand up in the air. "Hold on. He's been watching me for months? Because of the deal you had with Daniel?" *Of course, he had.*

He was about to reply when the door was again opened, and Emma rushed in. She dropped a bag on the floor and rushed to my side.

"Em, I'm fine. It looks worse than it is. Honestly," I said, trying to reassure her.

"Tess, you are not fine. Look at you. Absolute motherfuckers, I'm gonna kill them when the police find out who did it." As she painfully clutched my hand, tears began to fall down her cheeks.

Before I had a chance to respond, Luke said, "The police will be in touch soon, Red." He gave me a knowing look.

"Em, can we leave, please? You know I hate hospitals." I gestured for her to pass the bag so I could change out of the God-awful hospital gown. She placed it on the bed next to me.

"Are you sure you want to stay at my place and not with Luke?" she asked, looking between the two of us.

"Yes," I said quickly. "Luke has some business overseas to attend to, so he'll be gone for a while. Unfortunately, it can't be helped. I'm fine so there is no reason for Luke to delay his trip." *That ought to keep him out of my hair for a while.*

Luke moved from the end of the bed to stand in front of me and leaned down to cup my cheek with his hand. He looked me in the eyes and placed a gentle kiss on my lips. I flinched, not from pain, but from confusion.

"If you need me, Red, you let me know straight away. A car is coming to pick you and Emma up and will be waiting outside. I love you." With that, he stood up straight. "Take care of her, Emma. She's very precious to me." He turned and left the room.

I couldn't help the sob that erupted from me, ripping

Emma's attention from the door that had just closed. It was a vicious sob, one that I didn't think would end. Now that he was gone I could let everything out—all of the emotions that had been bottled up.

"Hey, shhh. It's okay, Tess. Everything will be fine," she soothed.

No, I don't think it will be.

6

LUCIFER

I STOOD IN THE SHADOWS, camouflaging myself so I wouldn't be seen loitering outside Tess's room. I didn't want to leave—I wanted to stay with her more than anything—but she didn't want me there. At least that was what she'd said—her body language told another story.

She was just coming to terms with everything that had happened. As soon as she did, I knew she wouldn't want to be with me—she probably wouldn't even see me again. The thought of never being with her made a heavy feeling settle in my chest. Like there was a lead weight attached to my heart, dragging it to the pit of my stomach.

She looked so fragile curled up in the hospital bed. Like a porcelain doll that had seen better days; the cracks were starting to show. Despite all of that, she looked beautiful to me; she always did, even when she was telling me to leave her alone.

Emma was perched on the side of the bed, her back to me. She hugged Tess and then immediately stopped as Tess flinched at the contact. Emma smoothed her hand over her friend's face soothingly. No, she was wiping away tears. It was then that I caught sight of Tess. She was sobbing, tears streaming down her face and dripping on to the blankets.

Fuck.

I wanted to rush back in, pull her on to my lap and hold her close. Whisper to her that everything would be okay and make all her pain and fear disappear. But I couldn't do that. Not until Lilith was gone and Tess was no longer in danger. Not until every threat had been eliminated.

I had to prove myself to her, prove that I was worthy of her. It was the only way I'd have any chance of making things right. However, I had absolutely no clue how to do it. This was all new territory for me, a path I'd never taken. I would most definitely need help.

I was aware of Conrath's presence as he came to stand beside me. "Sir, the car is here," he said.

"Thank you, Conrath. Make sure you never let her out of your sight. If you lose her, I want to know immediately. Do you understand?" I glared at him. I had no reason to be pissed with him, but at this moment in time I was livid with everything and anyone that wasn't Tess.

"I'll have eyes on her twenty-four-seven, Sir. You have my word." I believed him. Conrath had been shadowing Tess for so long I think he'd come to feel protective of her. I knew he would do his best—whether that would be enough against Lilith was yet to be seen.

"Go with them in the car, and make sure they get to Emma's safely. Let me know when they arrive. I have an urgent matter that needs my attention."

With one last, longing look at Tess, I turned and headed to the front of the building. After that, I made my way across the road and skulked back into the shadows. I knew Conrath would stay with her, but I needed to see her get into the car with my own eyes. It felt like an eternity before the three of them appeared; Emma was helping Tess walk to the SUV, and Conrath was carrying the bags, ushering them to the vehicle. Emma helped Tess slide into the large black SUV and followed her in. I watched as Conrath looked around and then nodded to the shadows where I stood before climbing in the passenger side. The vehicle took off through the busy New York traffic, and I watched until it was out of sight.

I portaled back to the living room of Tess's condo. I began to stalk through the rooms as I followed the damage that had been caused by Daniel.

I linked Bee. *I need you at Tess's place, now.*

I didn't need to turn to see who opened the door; I summoned, and she came. "What happened here?" Bee said as she came to stand next to me, glass and furniture crunching under her feet as she walked.

"Daniel happened." She was now standing next to me in the bedroom as I stood looking at the spot where Tess had staked Daniel. Nothing was left of his body, no dust or ash, just the stake.

"I take it he's dead?" she asked as she nudged the stake with her foot.

"It was Tess," I said in a whisper.

"Wait. What?" Her eyes shot up to my face, and she waited for a response.

"Tess killed him. I didn't get the chance." I'd so wanted to be the one that did it. I was desperate to torture and kill the smug prick for what he'd done.

"But that means she—"

"I know exactly what it means. I don't need reminding," I said, probably harsher than I needed to. She held her hands up in surrender.

"How did he manage to find her and avoid us? What am I missing?" she asked perplexed.

"He was a vampire," I replied with a snarl, as I clenched my jaw, hard.

"What? Who the fuck turned him? I can't imagine anyone wanting to be his sire—from what you said he was a prick with a bad attitude. Who'd want to deal wi—wait. Lilith," she said, her eyes widening and her nostrils flaring. There was absolutely no love lost between Bee and Lilith. They hated each other, always had. Lilith saw Bee as a threat and Bee hated Lilith for what she'd done.

I proceeded to fill her in on all of the details. How Tess had taken the brunt of Daniel's anger and that he'd been sent her to kill her so I could be Lilith's again.

"She is one crazy bitch, I've always said it. You should listen to me more," she chastised.

"Bee, now really isn't the time for this, we need to find Lilith and put an end to this."

"Let me do it, please. I can deal with this while you take care of Tess. By the sounds of it, she's in bad shape," she said.

"No, Lilith is mine. This started with the two of us, and that's how it'll end. Besides, Tess… doesn't want to see me," I said quietly.

"Why?"

"She knows who I am. Daniel told her, and she made me show her," I said as I pinched the bridge of my nose.

"Shit. I suppose she was going to find out eventually," she said matter of factly, like everything hadn't just gone to shit. I turned toward her, staying silent, just looking incredulously at her. "What? I'm just saying. If you're serious about her, you were going to have to tell her eventually. Now that she knows, you can get it all out of the way early. Figure out if she can move past it."

I continued staring at her, unsure whether or not she was deliberately trying to piss me off. "Are you fucking serious? Yes, it would have come out eventually, but not like this. I could've eased into it. This way she's just been blindsided."

"Look, Lucifer, I don't mean to sound like a bitch, but it's best you find out now if she can deal with this before things get deeper. If you'd both gotten more invested and *then* she found out and couldn't handle it, well... that would be worse. This has been like ripping a band-aid off," she said calmly. "How is Tess?"

My gaze shot up to meet hers. "How do you think she is?"

"Okay, okay. Let's move on. What do you want to do about Lilith?" she asked. "I still can't believe she's been this stupid."

"As per usual I don't think Lilith was thinking about anyone other than herself and what *she* wants. I want everyone on this, Bee. *Everyone.*" We needed to be smart about our actions. Lilith was the queen, and it was unlikely any vampire would give her up, but there were plenty others she'd pissed off over the years who would gladly contribute to her demise.

"We have a few vampires I could talk to. See if we can flush anything out. If you kill her though, you know it'll cause outrage. The vampires will be in an uproar."

She was right. If I were to kill their monarch, it would bring a whole host of trouble to Hell's door. There were no other options though; Lilith had overstepped for the last time, and she wouldn't get another opportunity. I'd rip her heart from her chest with my bare hands and watch her fade in front of me. Tess was off-limits, and Lilith had pushed me too far this time.

"We'll deal with that when it happens. I'm sure we can appease them in some way. If need be, I'll just remind them of who is really in charge. If that doesn't work, I'll kill them all. They live on borrowed time anyway," I said in a nonchalant manner.

Bee nodded her head in agreement. She wasn't a huge fan of vampires; she saw them as leeches, which wasn't far from the truth. After all, that was how they came to be. "What about this place? Is Tess coming back here?"

"No, she'll be staying with Emma for a while—Conrath is with them. But I want a larger security detail with her at all times. Can you arrange that?" I asked, moving through the debris of broken and shattered furniture. I noticed Tess's blood in various spots throughout her place and clenched my fists with each drop I saw.

"Consider it done," she replied, noticing from my coiled body and clenched fists just how tense I was.

"I want this place put back to how it was. There needs to be absolutely no trace that anything happened or that Daniel was ever here. It has to be perfect, Bee. *Like. It. Never. Happened.*"

"I have this. Go, find Lilith," she urged.

I nodded and moved to the door. I needed to regroup and formulate a plan. One thing was sure, though, Lilith would suffer.

7

TESS

I smoothed the sheets on Emma's bed and then opened the curtains, illuminating the small room with golden sunshine. It looked like a beautiful day, bright and sunny—not at all like how I was feeling.

I winced as I lifted my arms to tie my hair back from my face—I knew it would be a few weeks until my ribs fully healed. That meant no running, swimming, or self-defence. In all honestly, though, those were the last things on my mind. I hadn't left Emma's place for a week. She'd tried to persuade me to meet her at the bar, or at least go for a coffee with her—I did neither.

I just wanted to hide, curl up in a ball, and try to figure out the multitude of emotions that swirled within me—I was no further forward with figuring out the cluster-fuck that was my life.

Making my way to the bag in the corner of the room, I stuffed my possessions inside, preparing myself to leave Emma's. It was time I went home. I walked into the living space where Emma was asleep on the sofa. She stirred as she heard me enter the room.

"Hey, babe, how are you?" She arched her back like a cat as she stretched out on the sofa. Because I was hurt she'd insisted I sleep in the bed and that she would take the couch. I'd tried to argue with her, but it was pointless. She was adamant that "someone in my condition" should be sleeping on a proper bed.

"Not too bad thanks, Em. Look, I'm going to head back to my place today, get out of your hair."

"I think you should stay a little longer," she replied as she sat upright, patting the couch next to her. I made my way over and cautiously sat down. "You're still pretty banged up."

"Honestly, I'm good, I think it's best if I try and move on, get back to normal." *Whatever that looks like now.*

"You aren't putting me out, you know. You're not a burden, and I don't want you to think you have to leave. You can stay as long as you like. You know that, right?" She held my hand gently, supportively.

"I know, but I need to go home. For me." *For my own sanity.*

"Give me half an hour to get ready and I'll come with you," she said.

"No, Em, I'm gonna catch a cab and go now. I just want to be home, in my own space." It was a lie. I didn't want her coming because I didn't know what state the condo was in, and that would raise too many questions. Questions I didn't have any answers for. At least not any I could share with her.

"Babe, are you sure? I'm not at the bar till later. I can come with you."

I squeezed her hand reassuringly. "I'll be fine. I'll talk to you later," I said, gently pushing myself off the couch.

"You better, or I'll be over," she said with a mischievous smile.

I picked up the bag and made my way to her door, letting myself out. Getting in the elevator, I pressed the button for the lobby and wondered how easy it would be to grab a cab. I was caught in my own mundane thoughts paying little attention to anything. When the elevator stopped and the doors opened, a familiar sight was waiting for me. I recognised him, but I couldn't remember his name.

I let out a sigh. "Can I help you?" I said coolly. I wasn't in the mood for this.

"Ms. Adams, I have a car waiting for you. I assume you're returning home?" he replied, his tone soft. His large, hooked nose took up the majority of his face, and it immediately drew my attention to it.

"I can get a cab, thanks."

"I must insist, Ms. Adams. It's my job to protect you, and I take that role seriously."

"You mean it's your job to keep tabs on me, and you don't want to piss off your boss. Can't say I blame you, really."

He remained stony faced, the epitome of composure. My outburst had had little effect on him, and I knew I had little choice in the matter. "Where's the car?" I said, deflated. He walked through the lobby of Emma's building, then held the door open for me.

As I stepped out onto the sidewalk, the sunlight hit my face, and I noticed just how warm it was. This was the first time I'd been outside in a week. The fresh air felt good against my skin. I let my eyes slide closed as I took a few deep breaths.

A cough made my eyes snap open again. The man was gesturing towards a large SUV. It looked to be the same one that had picked us up from the hospital. He once again opened the door for me, and I slid in. He made his way to the other side of the car to join me, positioning himself next to me.

"To Ms. Adams' condo," he said to the driver. I couldn't make much of the driver out as I was positioned directly behind him. I did, however, study what I could see of his face in the rear-view mirror. He had black, sunken eye sockets and his eyes looked like they'd glazed over. He slowly nodded his head.

Chatty.

"What's up with Lurch?" I said, gesturing to the driver. "Cat got his tongue?"

"Not cats, no. That would be the work of the angels," he replied, not a glimmer of amusement in his voice.

I turned to him wide-eyed. "What?"

"Enoch here had his tongue cut out by the angels. How long ago was it, Enoch, a hundred years? More?" Enoch grunted and slowly nodded his head.

"But… but they're angels, why would they do that?" I said, looking between Enoch and my shadow.

"Because they can be cruel bastards when they want to be. They aren't always light and love. In fact, they mostly aren't."

I was missing something. I had to have been. "What did he *do?*"

"What makes you think he did something? You're assuming that because we're on the Devil's side that we're bad?" He shook his head and turned to look out of the window.

I honestly wasn't really sure what I should do or say. I didn't think I could make this less awkward, but I felt like I should try. These two men had done nothing to me; in fact, they were risking themselves to keep me safe.

"I'm sorry, this is all very new to me. I'm not very religious, but what I do know is what I've heard. Heaven and the angels are good, Hell, and everything associated with it, is bad. I honestly meant no disrespect." I turned my attention to the driver. "I'm sorry about what happened to you, and I didn't mean to be insensitive." He nodded his head again.

I can't believe I'm in this situation, apologising to—I don't know, a demon? Fuck my life.

"My apologies, Ms. Adams, years of assumptions have made us all a little bitter. Enoch here was captured by archangel Michael and some of his soldiers. They tortured him for information about Hell and our master, but Enoch would yield nothing. He remained silent. So as a punishment, they silenced him forever and sent him back battered and bloodied. To add insult to injury, they pinned his tongue to his coat. But, apparently *we're* the bad guys."

I clasped my hand over my mouth as I let out a gasp. *Holy shit.*

"These, however, are matters you needn't concern yourself with. We're here," he said as he grabbed my bag and slipped out of the SUV. I leant forward in my seat, closer to Enoch.

"Thank you for the ride. I really am very sorry." His sunken eyes met my gaze in the rear-view mirror, and I saw him incline his head towards me. I jumped back when the door next to me opened. My shadow was gesturing for me to get out. I smiled at Enoch, then slowly stepped out of the car.

I looked up at the familiar building. *Shit, I don't have any keys.* As if the man read my mind, he waved my keys in front of me. "Lucifer asked me to grab them when I collected your other items for the hospital," he said as he dropped the keys into my hands.

"Thank you."

We slowly made our way up to my condo. I stood outside my door, summoning the courage to enter and witness the carnage Daniel had caused. This had been my place, untainted by him and his darkness. Now… now I wasn't sure how I felt about it. Would I still feel at peace here?

Only one way to find out.

I slid the key into the lock and, taking a deep breath,

turned it. I was about to push the door open when I heard him speak. "Should you need to contact me my number is in your phone, Ms. Adams. I'll be close by if you need anything."

"Thank you," I said, pushing open the door and stepping into the condo. He moved forward and placed my bag just inside the door. He nodded his head and began to walk away.

"I really am sorry for what I said. I didn't know."

"It's forgotten. Now get some rest, and remember I'll be close by if you need anything," he replied with the smallest of smiles. It was hardly there.

"I'm sorry, I've forgotten your name," I said, sheepishly. I knew I'd been told at the hospital but I was hardly in the right frame of mind to take on board any new information.

"Conrath, Ms. Adams. Now get inside, it's not safe to loiter." He once again began to move.

"Please, call me Tess." He kept walking.

Determination took over me as I fastened the many locks on my door, and then closed my eyes before I turned around to study the damage. *You can do this, Tess. It won't be that bad. You've done this before.*

I forced my eyes open and moved into my living area—and was immediately surprised by what I found. Instead of the expected carnage, broken furniture, and my own blood, I was met with an immaculately tidy space; there was no sign of the horrific events that had unfolded here. I made my way through each of the rooms, and all were the same. Impeccably tidy.

I moved to the kitchen to grab a water from the fridge, only to be surprised by its contents. Instead of finding a fridge full of out-of-date and spoiled food, it had been fully stocked. There was fruit, vegetables, meat, cheese, milk, and a massive selection of other delicious-looking food. I moved and checked the cupboards that had also been filled.

I grabbed a water and moved to the living area. On the way I noticed a note on the table.

R<small>ED</small>,
 G<small>LAD YOU'RE HOME SAFELY</small>.
 X

I already knew he was responsible before I set eyes on the note. Of *course*, he was. He hadn't wanted me to come home to that. He'd eradicated all evidence that Daniel had been here, or that my ex had smashed up my place in the process. In all honesty, I was glad Luke had done it. The thought of having to clean up my own dried blood and the wreckage of my life was too much.

I instinctively picked up my phone and texted him to say thanks. The phone immediately buzzed—the Devil was calling. I could ignore it, but he knew I was home and that I had my phone. Despite everything, he'd done this for me: cleaned my place, so I didn't have to. I answered before I could think better of it.

"Red, how are you?" he asked tentatively.

I tried to calm my racing heart. Just the sound of his voice had butterflies in my stomach fluttering and my core throbbing. *Fuck.* "I've been better. I just wanted to say thanks for my condo."

"Conrath informed me you'd be heading home today, so I wanted everything to be perfect for you. One less thing to worry about."

"Thank you for sending Conrath and Enoch to pick me up. I appreciate that."

"Of course, Red. I know you don't believe me when I say this, but I only want what's best for—"

"Don't. I'm not getting into that. I just wanted to say thanks." I heard him sigh through the phone. I don't know why, but I didn't like it. I didn't want him to hurt. "How long will Conrath be with me?"

"He and the others will remain with you until Lilith is found." When he spoke her name, his voice changed its tone—it dripped with loathing. He hated her. I wanted to know what their relationship was, though it was none of my business. He was nothing to me now—I just had to convince myself of it.

"Fine."

"Red, I know you don't like this, but it's for your protection. Lilith is dangerous, and she wants you dead. I *need* to make sure that you are safe."

"I'm not your problem anymore, Luke. What I do or what happens to me is *none* of your concern."

Another deep sigh rumbled from him. "Red, I know this is all my fault. You're on Lilith's radar *because* of me, so until she is found my people will always be with you. If you won't let me protect you, then they will. Whatever you believe, know that my feelings are true and they haven't just gone away because you're mad at me."

Is he kidding? Making out like I'm some petulant child who has no right to be pissed off with him.

"I have good reason to be mad, *Luke*." Before he had the chance to reply, I hung up the phone.

Seriously?

It turns out that despite having been alive for millennia, the Devil was just as clueless about women as every other man.

8

LUCIFER

I WAS CONSTANTLY ON EDGE. The thought of not knowing where Lilith was, coupled with not being able to be with Tess, had me wound tight. I'd been to see Tess, not that she knew I was there, though. Wherever she was I'd make sure I was there too, just to catch a glimpse of her—see that she was safe with my own eyes.

Conrath and the others had kept me updated, but it wasn't the same. She'd warmed to Conrath, which made his job much easier. He said she was generous with him, was always polite, and would always check in with him. It was clear when he spoke of her that he did so with affection. He'd come to care for her, which made him the perfect person to carry on protecting her.

I felt jealous of him, though. *How pathetic is that?* He was allowed to be close to her, see her daily. He'd talk with her, be able to see her, yet I watched from the shadows like some fucking stalker or peeping Tom. I knew he didn't have those feelings for her and it was more of a fatherly relationship, but it still irked me.

There had been no word on Lilith; she was lying low. In

truth, I hadn't expected anything else from her. She'd wait, plan, and then only act when she had the advantage. Lilith was smart, always had been. Even at the start.

I sent a link to Conrath to check in on where Tess was. He let me know she was at her place; she'd been out earlier, but he expected that she'd be in for the night now. Good, I didn't want her out unnecessarily.

After that Bee linked me telling me she'd be with me in five minutes. She was on her way to my circle with the witch. The one that would try and help me solve the mystery that was Tess.

Bee had discreetly searched for someone who was up to the task, asked some loyal friends and had some informal "chats" with various people. After several positive testimonies, she finally came across Gabriela Morales. Bee said the woman was up to the task, but the final vote was down to me. I'd decide after I met her. I wanted to assess her in person—put her through her paces.

I took up a seat in the living space and made sure I looked especially menacing. Yes, I needed something from her, but this wasn't your typical business transaction. If she was as good as Bee said she was, there wouldn't be a problem.

The click-clack of heels told me that the two of them had arrived, and sure enough, Bee walked into the room, the witch following behind her. I knew she'd have been honoured to be invited into my sanctum, a place reserved only for me that very few others had seen. She'd know that and hopefully appreciate the sentiment that came with it.

She was not at all what I'd expected. Most in her position would be following Bee meekly, cowering behind her and averting her eyes, only staring at the floor until spoken to. Not Gabriela. She walked with an air of defiance like she would not be intimidated. Her head was held high, and she looked around, taking in her surroundings.

Bee made her way over. "Lucifer, may I present Gabriela Morales. I believe she may be of service to you." She moved and sat down on the sofa, leaving the witch standing in front of me.

She bowed her head low, but her eyes remained on me. *Ballsy.* I liked her immediately. I moved my gaze to Bee, who smirked at me.

"Tell me about yourself, Ms. Morales."

She remained standing, despite Bee sitting on one of chairs. She knew exactly what was happening. "Please call me Gabriela, Sir. There is much to tell, perhaps you could tell me what exactly you'd like to know?" She had a thick Spanish accent, and her voice was low and husky. Ordinarily, the rolling of her r's would've made my cock twitch, but it didn't stir at all. The accent made sense when you considered her beautiful skin tone and thick, dark hair, which she wore in loose, shiny curls. She was beautiful, and I could appreciate that. But Tess's ivory skin and emerald eyes outshone everyone else's beauty.

I gestured for her to take a seat. "Where are you from?"

"I was born in Águilas, in Spain—"

"When?" I asked.

"You shouldn't ask a lady her age," she replied, her lips quirking into a smile. "I can promise I am qualified for whatever task you need me to complete. I've been practising magic for over four hundred years. I'm adept in many techniques. Whatever you want, I can do it." She wasn't cocky with her abilities, just confident she could get it done.

I looked at Bee, who was still smirking. She loved this—when people held their own against me—amused when they weren't intimidated by my presence. In this instance, I was also impressed. I didn't want someone to pay me lip-service, I wanted results. She believed she could achieve them.

"I assume you will have heard by now that I want a

human. The matter relates to her." I leaned forward in the chair and laced my fingers together. "Is that a problem?"

"Why would it be?"

"Many of your sistren believe that she is not worthy of me—that they would be a more suitable candidate for me. What is your take on that?"

She eyed me and raised a brow. "All due respect, Sir, you're not my type," she said. Her gaze quickly flitted to Bee. "Your business is your business. I am loyal to you and the way of things."

I really did like this witch. I had a feeling Bee did as well, but for different reasons. A grin spread across my face as I met Bee's gaze. She shook her head, dismissing me. "Did Bee tell you what I need from you?"

Bee's eyes widened and she replied before Gabriela could. "You told me not to mention any specifics. She knows only what you told me to tell her." Bee clenched her fists, her eyes now attempting to bore a hole directly through my skull at the thought she'd let slip more.

Gabriela shook her head, so I pressed on.

"The human is immune to me. I can't read her, and none of my powers are effective on her. She is a void to me. I've probed deeply… but I cannot break through—"

"You suspect magic is responsible?" Gabriela asked.

"That was my initial thought, but the more I know of her, the more I think it's just who she is. Her mother is human, but her father…"

Gabriela looked between Bee and me. "So you want to know who her father is. More specifically, you want to know *what* her father is?"

Very astute, Bee had done well in sourcing Gabriela. She would be the one to uncover answers and hopefully quickly. "Yes, it's a matter of urgency. Is that something you can do?"

"I can. Unfortunately, it will take some time." Not at all

what I wanted to hear. She continued on. "I will have to use some dark magic, and that is not a quick process." Gabriela worried her bottom lip with her teeth.

"Is there a problem?" I asked and she stilled when she looked at me.

"Sorry? Oh no, I'm just planning and thinking of items I'll need. And where to source them." She stopped biting her lip, suddenly regaining her composure. "I can do this."

"We can get you anything you need; ask, and you'll have it." I looked at Bee, and she nodded. Nothing would be off-limits. "How soon can you get started?"

"Immediately, once I have the items I need. One may be a little tricky, though. I need some of the human's blood," Gabriela said, a hint of doubt creeping into her tone. It wasn't—I already had some. I'd expected that, which was why I'd taken a vial from the hospital.

"That's not a problem." I pulled the small container from the side pocket of my jacket and held it up to the light. The thick, crimson liquid coated the inside of the vial.

I saw both Bee and Gabriela study the blood, but it was the witch who spoke first. "I can make a start today. I will need a few other things as time progresses. I'll be in touch about that." She stood and made a move to the door.

Her brow was furrowed, and she was counting on her fingers as she reached the door. It appeared she'd already started work. "Bee will be your point of contact," I said, nodding my head to my number two. Gabriela didn't acknowledge my response, seemingly wrapped up in the task at hand. "Gabriela…"

She turned to face me. "Sí?"

"I want to be told as soon as you know anything. We need to establish a link, so you can keep me informed." Her eyes widened at the prospect of our minds connecting. I could psychically communicate with all demons and fallen, but

Gabriela didn't belong to Hell. As a witch, she was outside of my connection. Creating a link would change that.

She bowed her head low and nodded in agreement. Bee and I walked towards Gabriela. Bee pulled out an ornate dagger from her boot, and I held out my hand. I remained still as she sliced the flesh on my palm, which caused blood to immediately pool in my hand. She turned to Gabriela, who already had her hand out, palm upwards. I was impressed that not a single muscle in her entire body moved when Bee cut her. I held my hand out to her, and she took it. As the blood intertwined, I could feel the link form and strengthen and Gabriela gasped when it solidified. Her eyes shot to meet mine. Good, she could hear me.

Gabriela, if you need anything Bee is your first point of contact. But as soon as you have any information, you tell me directly. No one else, do you understand?

She nodded her head.

One more thing before you set to work. You speak of this to no one, and you tell no one of what you have been tasked to do. If I hear any whispers or rumours of your involvement, you will pay with your life.

She once again nodded, and I saw her swallow, hard.

"I think you'll need this, Ms. Morales," I said as I held out the vial to her. She tentatively moved towards my outstretched hand, and carefully took the container before she stepped back. "Would you give us a minute please," I said to Gabriela. She once more bowed her head and left the room, closing the door behind her.

"You like her?" Bee said immediately.

"I do. I'm not alone there, though, am I?" I couldn't help the smile that played on my lips.

"What do you want?" she asked, folding her arms across her chest like a scolded child.

"Keep a close eye on her. If anything seems off, I expect to hear about it from you."

"Of course. Do you intend to tell Tess what you're doing?" she asked.

Absolutely not. Things were tenuous enough, and I didn't need to add that shitstorm to the mix.

"No, though I don't like going behind her back. You know I normally love all this "cloak and dagger shit," but this… this just feels wrong. Like I'm deceiving her all over again." I held up a hand before she could preach to me about how it was a necessary evil. "I know this needs to be done, but I don't like it."

"If you want to protect her and keep her safe—"

"I know, I know. I don't have any other options," I said, dismissing her.

"Needs must," she echoed before strutting out of the room.

Things were now in motion. Hopefully, the mystery that was Tess would soon be solved. Maybe then I could begin to rebuild things.

9

TESS

Eurgh.

The familiar buzzing of my phone woke me, just as it had done every morning since I'd returned to my place.

I already knew it was Luke, but as usual I ignored it. He'd phone again later this evening. He was persistent, I'd give him that. I'd never once answered. I wasn't entirely sure what he wanted from me, but I wasn't ready to find out.

I rolled over and hit the cancel button. As usual, a text came through almost immediately. I tilted the phone towards me.

Morning, Red X

I set the phone down. Same thing every day. I'd initially replied to tell him that I needed space, time to figure things out. Now I'd stopped bothering. He'd told me he wanted to give me as much space as I needed. He didn't seem to understand that was the opposite of what he was doing. Yes, I hadn't seen him in person since the hospital, but he was far from leaving me alone.

As I lay in bed, contemplating what to do for the day, another text buzzed through. *Jesus, take a hint.* I carefully propped myself up in bed. My ribs were better than they had been, but they still made me wince a little. I slowly reached over and snatched up my phone again.

To my surprise, it wasn't Luke. The text was from Emma, asking if I was up for a trip to the bar. I was trying to get back to normal, but I hadn't yet felt up to going back to the bar, pretending things were fine when they weren't. Emma was persistent, though. I fired a text back, asking when she was working. If she was on in the next couple of days, I'd drag my ass there.

I had to get a grip. If I wanted things back to normal, I needed to make an effort. The bar had been a huge part of my life in the city, and it was about time I went back—plus it would be nice to see everyone. I'd missed them all.

I put my phone back on the bedside table—an exact replica of the table I'd smashed and then used to kill Daniel with. I'd expected things to be off when I'd returned home—like I wouldn't be able to settle—but the exact opposite was true.

Despite the horror that had happened here, I felt strangely at peace with it all. I'd thought that the guilt of killing Daniel might creep up on me, slither into my subconscious, and chip away at me. It hadn't, and I wasn't sure it would. When he'd been alive, Daniel was a ghost of my past that continued to haunt my new life. Now, I'd exorcised that demon… and traded him for another.

Luke wasn't a demon, though. I believed him when he said he wouldn't hurt me. But I wasn't convinced that he loved me. *Is the Devil even capable of that?*

I had been expecting to have flashbacks and feel uneasy in my place. But it remained the calm, soothing space I'd fallen in love with. I think it felt safer now. That might have had something to do with Conrath, who always appeared from the sidelines whenever I left the building. I liked him. He wasn't intrusive or pushy in any way, but I was always aware of his presence. He remained my shadow and would be until Lilith was apprehended… or killed.

I headed to the bathroom, in an attempt to wash the drowsiness away under the hot spray. Conrath hadn't really said much about Lilith. I'd asked, but he'd been cagey. I got the impression this wasn't his story to tell, and he'd been ordered not to divulge any secrets. In all honesty, that pissed me off.

I flinched as I raised my arms to wash my hair. *Stupid broken ribs*. I slowly lathered my locks as I thought. I had a right to know just exactly who was hunting and trying to kill me. I knew she was the queen of the vampires—and from what I'd understood, Luke's ex. But that was it. I had no clue what she even looked like. I could have already seen her. I could have talked to her.

Tipping my head under the spray, I allowed the water to wash over me, rinsing the shampoo off my hair and down my battered and bruised body. I admit that I looked like a fucking mess. That didn't mean that they all had to treat me as if I needed wrapping up in cotton wool. Apparently, I should be protected like a child. That *really* pissed me off.

I was the one who killed Daniel, not Luke. *I'd* gotten rid of that threat, not him. I was capable of looking after myself. I just needed to prove it. I combed some conditioner through my hair and gently washed myself, careful not to press too hard. I couldn't wait to be fully healed so I could get back to my routines. I'd missed my self-defence classes and my running, although I was in no state to do anything at the moment, which annoyed the shit out of me.

As I stood under the spray, I became more and more annoyed with the whole situation. I had worked myself up and was livid with everything that was going on. All of this was Luke's fault. *All of it.*

He'd brought Daniel back into my life. He was inadvertently the cause of my injuries—both physical and emotional. He was the reason I had to be protected. At this moment in time, I wanted to beat the shit out of him.

Although… I also wanted him to fuck me into oblivion like I knew he was wholly capable of doing. Make me orgasm so hard that I saw stars and forgot all of my troubles.

That was crazy, right?

I turned off the shower, then wrapped myself and my soaking wet hair in towels. Heading back to my bedroom, I checked my phone—still nothing from Emma. I pulled out some comfy clothes and quickly changed. Some leggings and an oversized tee would do for a quick walk around the park. I need to get out for some fresh air. I was going stir crazy being cooped up.

I towel dried my hair quickly. I couldn't lift the hairdryer for too long due to my injured ribs, so that was out of the question. As a result, my hairstyle options were, therefore, limited. I decided on a low ponytail—it would do.

The puncture marks Daniel had left on my throat were nearly gone. No one else could see them, but I knew. I'd always know they'd been there, and how I'd gotten them. I imagined I'd always be able to see the trace of them when I looked in the mirror. My neck felt bare without my necklace and pendant, but I couldn't bring myself to put it back on. Like the rest of my stuff, the necklace had been repaired and was waiting for me when I returned home. But instead of putting it back on, I'd hidden it away in a box. I wasn't sure why it bothered me. But it did.

My phoned buzzed again. Picking it up, I didn't recognise the number. As I read on, though, I immediately knew who it was from. Lilith.

Be seeing you soon, Tess. L.

Shit, this isn't good.

I made my way to my front door. As I unlocked the door, I poked my head out, looking around. It was empty. "Conrath?" I whispered. I jumped a mile when he appeared from the shadows. It was like he had literally just appeared before my very eyes. *That's fucking awesome.*

"Yes, Tess. Is everything okay?" he queried, concern evident on his scrunched-up face.

"Not really. I just got this." I held my phone out for him. He silently moved towards me and grabbed it. I saw his jaw clench as he read the message. Without saying a word, he handed me the phone. He looked deep in thought; his eyes had gone slightly glassy as he stood stock-still. I assumed he was contemplating in silence.

"What do you think it means?"

"I don't know, but Lucifer is on his way. He wants to speak with you."

Oh hell no. I'm not ready for this.

I pushed my phone back into Conrath's hand and stepped back inside my condo, as I said, "Show him the message, I'm not seeing him."

"But he—"

I closed the door before he could finish his sentence, then made sure to fasten all the locks. It was probably pointless, he was the Devil and if he wanted to get in, he probably could.

It didn't take long before I heard voices outside, near enough as soon as I'd stepped away from the door. I moved back so I could listen to what was being said. But I couldn't really make it out. Looking through the peephole, I understood why. They were standing at the other end of the corridor, Luke with his back to me. But I knew it was him.

I continued watching, and he became more and more animated as he spoke to Conrath. Part of me felt sorry for my shadow. None of this was his fault, yet he seemed to be getting grief regardless. Luke turned. As stupid as it sounded, it felt like he stared directly at me as I looked through the peephole. It was like his gaze had met mine, which was impossible because there was a door between us.

Does he know I'm here? Can he sense it?

Of course, he can he's the Devil. Who knows what he's fully capable of.

I backed away from the door, not wanting him to know I was curious, that deep down I wanted to see him. I didn't want him to know that I wanted to savour looking at his face and to re-familiarise myself with the angles of his jaw, memorise his dark, brooding eyes, and I wondered again just how soft his lips were.

A sharp bang on the door jolted me from my thoughts. "Open up, Red," Luke said from the other side of the door. I didn't reply. Instead, I leaned against the wall next to it and tried to breathe as quietly as possible in an attempt to calm my pounding heart. All of that just from the sound of his voice, it was crazy the reaction he elicited from me without even trying.

"Red," he chastised.

"Look, Luke, I'm not opening the door. I don't want to see you. Say what you need to say and leave." I heard a heavy sigh spill from his mouth.

"Conrath showed me the message. We're working hard on this, I promise. Are you okay?"

Well, I'm sorry if your promises mean shit to me.

"Peachy."

"Please let me see you, Tess." There was a need to his voice, though it wasn't the usual lust-filled need I was used to. This was softer. Gentler.

"No, Luke. You need to leave. Just let me know when this is over." I headed to the radio and turned on my favourite rock station.

"Red. Red…" He continued to call my name, so I did the only thing I could. I turned up the volume.

10

LUCIFER

I WAS PACING, and I couldn't stop. I was sure there would be a patch of carpet worn away, yet it was all I could do to stop myself from doing something stupid.

Tess still refused to see me. She'd dismissed me from her place without even a glimpse of her. Despite the text she'd gotten from Lilith, she was still choosing to block me out. She acted like I was nothing, nothing but an annoyance.

It felt like an eternity since I'd seen her in person. To someone who was immortal, that was saying something. I was pissed. The longer I went without seeing her, feeling her, kissing her, the worse my mood became. Both Bee and Levi had told me I was a fucking delight to be around at the minute.

I knew that I was being unreasonable to anyone that crossed my path, but I couldn't contain it. I was starting to forget the little things about her. Like how soft her skin was, or her intoxicating smell—like summer flowers, vanilla and a hint of spice. I barely remembered what she tasted like, but I'd never forget what it felt like to be buried deep inside her.

To me, that was Heaven. Like she'd been made to take me, I started getting hard just thinking about it.

But I couldn't be buried balls deep inside her when she wouldn't even see me. I yearned for her—all of me, not just my cock. My body ached to be with her; I was like an addict going through withdrawal. But it wasn't just physical—I'd never experienced these emotions before, and I didn't know how to process or handle them.

"What?" I snapped as I felt the presence enter the room. It had to be Levi or Bee. They were the only two who could enter without permission. I'd allowed them that privilege because I wanted any updates on Lilith immediately.

"Pleasure to see you too," I heard Levi say, a smile evident in his voice. "You need to hurry up and sort this shit out with Tess. You're being a dick," he said with a chuckle.

"Fuck off, Levi. Don't you think I'm trying? She won't see me."

"Since when has that ever stopped you? You need to force her hand, *make* her see you. It's not like you to hold back."

He was right. Whatever I wanted, I took, but that was before. Before Tess. If I went in guns blazing, it would push her further away. Ruin things for good. The whole thing had to be handled delicately, with kid gloves. That was why I was struggling so much, since that was the furthest from what I'd been doing for millennia.

"Everyone is ready for you," he said. "Except for the team with Tess." He remained standing, knowing that we wouldn't be hanging around.

I stopped pacing and stood straight, then flexed my neck from side to side, in an attempt to relieve the tension. I knew it wouldn't do anything, but I had to try. I shrugged off my jacket and laid it on the chair behind my desk. I saw Levi watching me. "What?" I queried.

"Have you decided what you're going to do with the witch?"

A wicked grin split across my face and I nodded. Then, I shifted forms; if this was to have the desired effect I'd have to pull out all of the stops. I needed to not only look the part but *be* the part. "Let's go," I said.

Once outside I took off but saw Levi unfurl his wings and follow after me. As we soared through the sky on our way to the circle of Envy, I noticed how quiet it was—not surprising, considering I'd summoned everyone to the meeting.

I swooped and soared giving my wings a workout. It had been a while since I'd used them. They tended to draw attention, but down here at this moment, they were exactly what I needed. Levi soared next to me, though he hung back slightly and allowed me to take the lead.

We quickly made time and I saw our destination—and the thousands of demons and fallen below me. From this height, they looked like tiny ants gathered together. All were awaiting my arrival. I flew lower, making my way across the crowds and to the clearing where the others were standing.

I landed smoothly and felt Levi touch down next to me. When I turned I saw him tuck his wings away, though I left mine out. I intended to make myself as big and menacing as possible, and the wings always helped with that. I made my way to Bee and Delphyne. Delphyne was the guardian of Envy, and as such was well aware of what was about to happen.

"Is everything ready?" I said quietly to the pair of them.

It was the saraph demon who answered, "Yes, Sir, everything is prepared." She was in her human form, but her serpent side was always visible to me. The pupils of her eyes were black slits, and as she spoke her forked tongue was visible when she slightly hissed her s's.

"Thank you, Delphyne, let's get this done." I turned around to face the crowd that had amassed on my orders. I allowed my power to radiate out, felt my skin crackle, and I stretched my wings as far as I possibly could. I stood, silently taking everything in before I spoke.

"It had been brought to my attention that there are many rumours circulating recently about me and my loyalties. It's been said that I'm no longer dedicated to the cause and that my priorities no longer rest with Hell. I'm here to assure you that is not the case. And if *anyone* questions me again, they will pay dearly. Hell and its prosperity have long been my priority. They always will be." I studied the crowd, trying to make out the faces of those who clearly weren't convinced. What would happen next would be partly for their benefit. But mostly, this was for me.

"To show you all just how much I don't appreciate disloyalty, or being doubted, I intend to show you all just what happens to those who can't follow orders. Bring her." I could hear a commotion behind me, but I didn't turn. I continued watching the crowd. There was a clear scuffle behind me, and then came the pleas. She begged for forgiveness, mercy, leniency, and pity. She would get none.

Delphyne dragged her along and threw her onto the floor in front of me. I still didn't look at her—I was determined to make this as cold and calculated as I possibly could. I flexed my wings, once more making myself a terrifying sight.

The cougar from the bar was before me; she'd been difficult for my people to track, but we always found them in the end. She'd sought refuge, but when you're wanted by the Devil, not many will grant you sanctuary. In her case, no one had.

"This witch meddled in my affairs. She and no one else has the right to question me or the way in which I conduct myself—"

As she clutched at my leg she said, "Please, Sir, I beg you, please. Everything was done for your benefit. I meant no disrespect, I…" She trailed off as I lowered my gaze on her. In my demonic form, I knew she would see the pure darkness of my eyes. The blackness would show her the pure anger that raged through them.

She let go of my leg immediately and, on her knees, got as low as she possibly could. She began to plead and beg, looking up at me with her bloodshot eyes.

I again turned my focus on the crowd. "A lot has been said recently. In particular that a human woman has made me weak, made me forget *what* and *who* I am. I'm here to assure you all that I know *exactly* who I am. You're all about to witness just what I'm capable of."

The witch started sobbing, and the crowd began to chatter loudly. "Silence," I bellowed. My words demanded everyone's full attention—I wanted there to be no questions after this was done.

"Stand up," I said to the witch. She didn't move, just continued to remain on her knees, arms stretched out, begging for mercy. "*Stand up!*" I cast a sidewards glance to Bee, who stalked towards the witch and dragged her to her feet. She pushed the witch in my direction, still remaining close behind her in case she tried to flee.

"Blair Albu, you have been brought to Hell to be punished for the crimes committed against me. You are—"

"Master, please. I beg for your infinite mercy." She was wasting her breath. Ignoring her, I carried on.

"I have decided that your punishment will not be death—"

"Thank you, Sir, thank—"

I looked down at her, now addressing her directly before I continued, "Your punishment will be much worse; in fact, you will probably beg for death." Her face paled and she fell silent. Tears stained her face. The amassed crowd remained silent, observing. What could be worse than death?

"You have committed the sin of Envy. You have coveted something that was not yours to possess. You have allowed your envy to consume you to the point where you have interfered in what was not your business. You saw a human woman with me, and you deemed her unworthy of being in my company. Instead of holding your treacherous tongue, you saw the attention I was giving her, and you wanted it for yourself. You did this to yourself, and you have *yourself* to blame for what will happen now."

She once more began to sob and made a move to fall to the floor. Bee scooped her up forcefully, abruptly strong-arming her to stand.

I turned my attention to my followers. I remained silent for a while, taking in their faces, building the anticipation.

"You are to be stripped of all of your powers, except for your immortality. You will be forced to renounce any claims you have to any covens or associations of a similar nature. Your assets are to be forfeited to Hell. As the sin you have committed is Envy, you will spend…" I trailed off, thinking of how long an appropriate punishment was. Whatever figure I deemed reasonable, I was about to make it twice as long. I had to make an example that disobedience would not be tolerated. "Six hundred years atoning for your insolence."

I heard the gasps of the crowd and I saw the witch crumple to the floor. I slightly turned my head to catch the attention of the saraph demon—a silent invitation—and she stepped forward to join me. "As you know, the guardians take their roles very seriously, and I have instructed Delphyne here to show no mercy. She has assured me that what she has devised will be severe." I turned to her and caught the wicked grin spread across her face. She slowly bowed her head in my direction, and then grabbed the witch by the back of her clothes. Delphyne dragged the witch to her feet and thrust her forward towards the crowd.

"This witch will pay the price for her actions. To those of you who work in my circle, you are expected to follow my lead when it comes to her treatment. She has disobeyed our master, and I will make her pay the price. Let us show her the true price of treachery!" Delphyne had been speaking to her troops, but everyone erupted into shouts of agreement.

Bee leaned in to me and whispered into my ear, "I think she's enjoying this a little too much. Do you have any idea what she has planned?" I shook my head. I didn't know, but I knew that Delphyne had a wicked streak and she really did enjoy coming up with inventive new punishments. Whatever she had planned, I knew it wouldn't be good. And it would be repeated every day for six hundred years.

Delphyne then pushed the witch farther into the depths of Envy and eventually disappeared out of sight. Once they were gone, the remaining guardians turned to the throng of people left in front of us.

"I hope this has shown you all exactly *how* I handle my affairs. For the majority of you, your undivided loyalty all of these years has been appreciated, and I hope you feel it was well placed. For those of you who have questioned me, this is my message to you: I will not tolerate discord in Hell. If you are found to be the cause of it, you will pay dearly for it. I have ruled Hell for millennia and do not intend to let it go to shit now. I am Lucifer, the first fallen and ruler of you all. *I am the Devil.*" The crowd erupted into cheers, screams, and shouts. The group had approved of my display and Hell seemed to be sated by my actions. "Now, get back to work."

Levi and Bee moved to my side, watching the crowd of people disperse. It was Levi who spoke first. "I think that seemed to do the trick. I doubt anyone will be challenging you any time soon."

"Yes, I believe you have once more exerted your control. I doubt there is anyone left who would consider disobeying you," Bee agreed.

Well, that isn't strictly true. I can think of one human who takes pleasure in doing just that.

11

TESS

I sang along to the music that blasted from my radio. I loved listening to music whenever I got ready to go out. Emma had sent a text to tell me she was working, so I'd decided that I wouldn't just sit around in my condo waiting for Lilith to be gone.

I would push on. Start to enjoy myself again and rebuild my life. Again. For the briefest moment, I'd honestly thought that Luke... Lucifer—I had to get used to calling him that—was my happily ever after. Boy, could I have been any more wrong?

I had to force myself to get over it, and getting back to normal was how I would do that. I'd showered and dressed—and let's not lie, danced around my bedroom while singing along to the radio. It wasn't my usual dancing though, it was much more gentle, since my ribs were still giving me trouble.

I'd picked out tight black jeans, a vest top, and a checked shirt. I'd chosen long sleeves to hide the bruises and marks that still covered my body. Emma knew about the severity of my injuries, but I didn't really feel like explaining myself to anyone else.

After applying some moisturiser and a little mascara, I looked at myself in the mirror. I still had some dark circles under my eyes, but I was starting to look like myself again. I was just about to remove my hair from the towel on top of my head when I heard someone at the front door.

Making my way out of the bedroom and through the condo, I wondered who it could be. I doubted it was anything to worry about, not with Conrath standing watch. In fact, that was probably him with an update or to check what time I was planning on heading out.

I arrived at the door and looked through the peephole, and then instinctively backed away. I tried to move as silently as I could. I genuinely don't know why. Lucifer knew I was inside—Conrath would have told him. Still, I continued retreating, though I half expected him to barge his way through.

"Red, I know you're there. Please let me in," he said through the door. I moved closer to the door again, looking through the peephole. He stood directly outside the door; he once more appeared to catch my gaze with his eyes, but I knew he couldn't see me. *Or could he?*

"I need to see you, Red."

"Look, Lucifer, I don't know how many times or how many different ways I can say this. Go away." I watched through the peephole as he turned on his heels and skulked off. I continued watching until he disappeared around the corner. I pressed my hands against the door and rested my head against it. After I took a few steadying breaths, I managed to compose myself.

Opening my eyes, I checked the peephole. The hallway was clear, and he'd gone. I turned and began to make my way to my bedroom to carry on getting ready, but I stopped dead in my tracks. *What the fuck?*

"How did you get in here?" I demanded. "You have no fucking right to—"

"I portaled in. What else am I supposed to do when you refuse to see me?" He looked utterly dejected, and it tugged at my insides. But then I remembered he'd just stomped all over my fucking privacy. He took a step toward me, arm outstretched, and I backed up. It was instinct—*who wouldn't back away from the Devil?*

"No, you don't get the right to do that. You're supposed to respect my wishes and not be a total dick. But when have you *ever* given a shit about what I want?" I shook my head, done with him thinking he had any rights to my business. I tugged the towel from my head and threw it into the hamper as I moved past him to my bedroom. I wasn't surprised when he followed me.

"Are you fucking kidding me?" he said, as I shot him the darkest look I could muster, but he carried on. "*Everything* I've done has been for you. *You're* the reason for all of it. I have to keep you safe, Tess. I can't lose you."

"You never had me. What we had was built on a lie. There is no *us*, Lucifer. Now leave." I turned my back on him. Instead of leaving, though, he continued.

"It wasn't a lie, Tess. I love you. I really do." I could hear the emotion in his voice, and instinctively turned to face him. I wanted to soothe him, calm him—my body was caving to him. I had to stay strong.

"I can't, Lucifer. I don't know who you are, not really—"

"So, let's start again," he said, taking a step towards me. I moved backward, but he continued to walk. I jumped when my back made contact with the wall, and then he was in front of me. His arms caged me in; I was trapped. But instead of feeling threatened, my body longed for his touch. I stood tall, determined not to cower away from him.

He leaned forward and buried his face into my neck, nuzzling the soft flesh and inhaling deeply. A heady moan escaped him, and it stoked my own fire, igniting a need inside of me. My eyes rolled, and my back arched towards him—longing to be close to him. *Fucking traitor*, I thought to myself.

"No, Lucifer, I can't do this." A gasp escaped me when he gently kissed my neck, trailing kisses down towards my collar bone. His lips were as soft as I'd remembered, his touch feather-light but hot and needy.

"I've missed you so much, Red. Please. Please, just let me have this," he asked in between his kisses. His hands moved from the wall and snaked up my back underneath my shirt. They smoothed up and down, and he was hot to the touch. But he was igniting a fire within me that needed attention. His hands pulled me towards him, so I was flush against his body.

I could feel his hard cock pressed up against me, straining to be set free. *Fucking hell*. He moved one of his hands from my back, around to my front and leisurely trailed it up my body to my face. He tipped my head up, and I opened my eyes when I felt him go still.

He was looking at me fiercely. It wasn't just the extreme unadulterated need that raged through him and flared behind his eyes. There was genuine affection. No, it was more than that—he was telling the truth. It was love. He loved me—despite me not wanting to believe him, I could see it written all over his face.

Before I could do anything, he closed the distance between us and his lips pressed against mine softly. It was gentle, yet it was filled with everything that he'd wanted to say but didn't know how to. I melted into him and kissed him back. That was all he needed. He took it as my acceptance for him to continue.

He knew what to do with my body, and it reacted to him

like it never had to anyone before. I felt my nipples harden against his firm, muscular chest. His hand moved down my back, and he grabbed my ass, squeezing and then lifting my thigh to wrap around his waist.

"Fuck, Red. You have no idea what you do to me," he mumbled against my lips as he continued kissing me.

Wait, what am I doing?

I snatched my body away from his grasp and pushed my hands against his chest. The shock made him stumble back slightly, but he was still in my personal space. "No, Lucifer. I can't do this. You're the Devil," I said breathily. I shook my head in an attempt to dislodge the sexual fog that had taken root. "Please, leave."

"But, but…" he trailed off. There was genuine hurt plastered across his handsome face. He looked dejected, almost broken.

My insides were once more in turmoil. I was fighting an internal battle, body and heart versus head. I wanted to close the distance and soothe the sting my words had just caused him, but I couldn't. That wasn't the sensible thing to do. Even though I knew I was hurting him, I had to protect myself.

His shoulders slumped as he took a step away from me. He didn't argue, just moved to the front door. I followed, though I wasn't sure why. Hand hovering over the doorknob, he spoke. "Tess, I may be the Devil, but I love you. I would never in all of my years do anything to hurt you or put you at risk. I will spend all eternity protecting you, whether you want me to or not. I would never forgive myself if anything happened to you." Still facing the door, he opened it and left, allowing it to fall closed behind him.

12

LUCIFER

I WATCHED and waited for Tess to emerge from her building. Conrath had told me she was heading to the bar, and tonight I need to be near her. If that meant waiting outside in the pouring rain, then that was what I'd do. I was tucked away in the shadows, but I was still subjected to the dreary New York night.

It had felt so good to feel her, kiss her, have her close to me. I wanted it so badly—no, I *needed* it. Her body did things to me that no one had ever done. Ever. My desire for her burned so intensely; it was white-hot. But this wasn't just lust. It was love. It had to be. I'd never experienced it before, and it was the only explanation for what was going on.

Tess had burrowed into me and become a part of my very soul. She was as necessary to me now as air or water. If I didn't have her, I was sure I would wither and die. If she didn't want me back, I was sure I'd be an empty shell, incapable of anything. Without her by my side, I'd be a void and empty vessel in which only despair remained.

I'd meant everything I said to her. I would protect her until the end of time until she or I no longer walked the

Earth. I'd lied to the crowd in Hell; *it* was no longer my priority. She was.

My words to her were the truth, and I did love her. If I was honest, the whole thing had taken me by surprise. When I'd made a deal with Daniel, the last thing I'd expected was to fall in love—especially with a human. I'd denied the feeling for a while, thinking it was simply lust. I'd tried convincing myself that when I had her, the feeling would disappear.

I'd been standing in the rain for an hour when I finally saw her appear. I was soaked to the bone, but the numbness I was feeling had nothing to do with the cold. She had her leather jacket on, with a wooly hat and thick scarf. When she reached the street, she put her umbrella up and made off towards the direction of the bar. I'd figured the bar would be the first place she'd go when she was feeling up to it.

Seconds after she set off, I noticed Conrath emerge from the shadows and begin tailing her. She must have sensed his presence, because I noticed she turned and gave him a genuinely warm smile. She'd quickly gotten used to him and his role, which I was relieved about. At least I didn't have to fight her on that—just everything else.

I moved in the shadows on the opposite side of the street, watching her shapely ass sway as she walked. *Fuck me. She's beautiful.* I found it hard to believe that I hadn't immediately seen just how beautiful she was. To me, she was perfect.

I followed with purpose as I stalked her silently. I saw Conrath turn to the shadows where I was, and he nodded his head. Then he continued to move behind Tess, and she seemed comforted by his presence.

She arrived at the bar and let down her umbrella. She left it inside, just near the door. I could see the reaction of her friends through the windows. She waved at those behind the bar and made her way to her usual seat. As she gently shrugged off her coat and hung it on the back of her chair,

Emma ran over to her and scooped her into a hug. I winced with her when I saw Emma squeeze a little too tightly. A swell of anger surged through me—Emma needed to be more careful. It was irrational, I knew it, but all sense went out of the window when it came to Tess.

Tess pushed Emma away, and I could tell that Emma was also pissed at herself for hurting her friend. *She should be.* Tess was still recovering. She sat down just as Harry placed a large tumbler of whiskey in front of her. He leaned across the bar and took her hand, squeezing it.

He needs to remove his fucking hand from her or I'll rip it off and smack the shit out of him with it. No one can touch, not if I have anything to do with it. My fists were clenched by my side, and my jaw was clamped shut. *Prick.*

Harry then went back to work, but Emma stayed to talk with Tess for a while, at least until her boss came to shoo her away and encourage her back to work. He paused and spoke to Tess, his face soft and full of concern. My fists once more balled up when he gently patted her on the shoulder before walking away out to the back of the bar. I knew Tess was fond of the bar owner, Jerry. But it didn't matter who it was. She was mine, and *no one* got to touch her.

After about five minutes, Emma returned, and I tuned into their conversation.

"What's wrong, Tess? You seem a little on edge," Emma said, taking a seat next to her friend and dismissing the look Harry gave her.

"Luke came over just before I left," Tess said with a sigh. She rubbed her temples with her fingertips and closed her eyes. I wasn't sure what she'd told Emma about me, but I very much doubted it was the truth.

"What happened between you two? I've never seen you so happy, Tess. Surely you can work this out?" Emma said, nudging the drink towards her friend.

Tess lifted the glass to her lips and took a huge gulp before placing it back on the bar. "I'm not saying it's over. But I don't know how I feel about him. For now, I just don't want to think about it. I want to drink. Drink and forget."

"But…" Emma trailed off when Tess held up a hand. She tried to catch Harry's eye for another drink, but he was busy.

"Em, I'm done talking about it. I wanna be numb, and whiskey can do that. Now, are you joining me?" Tess asked as she drained the tumbler in front of her. Emma simply nodded at her friend and moved behind the bar. She came back with a glass and a bottle of Jack Daniels.

Tess was hurting as much as me, which meant she still cared. Hell, she'd said it wasn't over. I had to grab onto that with both hands and clutch at the hope. Never let it go. If she'd decided she was done with me, Emma would have been the first to know. But no. There was still a chance for me to fix this.

Her refusal to see reason would have to change. I'd have to show her that I was no different than when she'd first met me. I had to make her see.

But tonight I'd be content in watching from the shadows. Ensuring she was safe, secure, and protected.

Tonight, she could be numb. Tonight, she wouldn't have to worry about anything.

13

TESS

I'd stopped counting after Emma poured my fourth whiskey; I had no clue what number we were on now. The alcohol definitely had the desired effect. It wasn't just my emotions that had begun to numb, my face had too.

I didn't care; I was drinking to forget. Emma was drinking whiskey too, which was always a bad idea. She didn't like it, yet she still thought she could handle it. She couldn't. But Emma carried on regardless.

"The problem with men," she slurred, "is that they think with their fucking dicks. Totally ruled by them. Take Sean, for example. I let him do whatever the hell he wanted to do, except for one thing. Because I wouldn't do that, he went elsewhere. All because his dick did the thinking. One teeny, tiny thing I wouldn't accommodate, and he went elsewhere." She turned to me and whispered, "I let him do *everything* else." She slowly nodded her head with her eyes closing involuntarily.

Emma had been "seeing" Sean for a couple of months, and he'd probably been the most serious of the guys in her life since I'd known her. She'd never gone into detail about what had gone on between them, but it must have been something strange for her not to go along with it. Emma was very much free-spirited and was confident sexually. She was always telling me about new things she'd tried and what "got her going." She was an over-sharer, despite me never asking.

"So, what happened between you two? What was it that you wouldn't do?" I mumbled, taking another sip of my drink.

She raised her hand with her glass still in it and stuck out her index finger. "It's too embarrassing, babe. I… I can't," she said, clumsily shaking her head.

"Jesus, Em, now I really wanna know what it is. Come on, spill. I won't judge."

She turned her head, looking around to see if anyone was in close proximity. She leaned in close to me and lowered her voice to a husky whisper. "Well, you know I'm pretty open about things." I did, she'd told me repeatedly. "You also know I like things a little… rough." She'd also told me that on several occasions. "Well, he liked to choke me a little. A little I'm fine with, that show of dominance I like. But he wanted to take it a little further. Who am I kidding, he wanted to take it a *lot* further. He wanted to suffocate me. Put a bag on my head while we were fucking until I passed out." She turned to face me. "You know I'm down for a lot of stuff, but that I really didn't feel comfortable with. I said no, but he just wouldn't let it go, kept on and on about it. When we were having sex, his choking got more intense, and I said he had to rein it in. You know the rest of the story."

The rest of the story was that he'd gone elsewhere, namely an escort agency. The kicker? He'd used *her* credit card to pay to get his weird fantasy fulfilled. I shook my head, a disgusted look on my face. "What an arsehole. You're better off without him. God knows what he would've done to you next." She nodded in agreement and then downed her drink.

She went to pour me another, but I held my hand over my glass to stop her. "I gotta go, Em. I've got stuff to do tomorrow, and if I leave now then it won't be a total write off." I'd suffer from the whiskey, but I'd still be able to function.

"She pursed her lips and gave me a disappointing glare. "You suck." Turning her attention to Harry, she said, "Has Jerry left yet?" He shook his head at her.

"He had some tax stuff to sort for his accountant," Harry replied.

It wasn't like Jerry to stay this late. He loved the bar, though he hated being out in the city too late—his wife hated it too. Emma attempted to stand but nearly fell off her stool. She steadied herself against the bar.

"I'll go check on him, Em." I turned to Harry. "Can you make sure she gets home safe?" I asked, tipping my chin towards Emma, who was now slumped over the bar. He nodded sympathetically at her.

I carefully stood and took a couple of steadying breaths. I could do this—I was fine. Barely even drunk. *Liar.*

Jerry's office was at the back of the building, and I'd be able to use the rear entrance to leave the bar and make my way home. I jostled through the crowded bar and punched in the code to get into the employee-only area. As soon as I closed the door behind me, the sounds and music became muffled. Back here it was quieter; Jerry needed the peace when he did the books. *"I have to concentrate"* he'd always tell us.

I made my way past the staff room, cleaning closet, and storeroom and arrived outside of Jerry's office. I called out his name as I pushed the door open.

It took my eyes a while to adjust to the dimly lit room. As they did my heart immediately sank and a nauseous feeling surged through me. Jerry was sat in his chair, slumped slightly back with his head lolled to one side. He was as white as a sheet. My immediate thought was that he'd had a heart attack. I sucked in a breath as I began to realise he might be dead.

I took a step forward and surveyed the scene before me. Then I went rigid. My body shivered as if someone had walked over my grave. I felt chilled to the bone as my eyes focused on the two puncture wounds on the side of Jerry's neck, blood oozing from them.

"Jerry," I said as I went to move to his side—only to be stopped dead in my tracks by the figure that emerged from the shadows in the corner of the room. I wasn't sure whether she'd just appeared from thin air or whether she'd always been there—lurking just out of sight.

"I wouldn't do that if I were you. Tess." She moved closer and stood firm next to Jerry's side.

How the fuck does she know my name?

I was immediately drawn to the elongated, pearly white fangs that protruded from her mouth. They dripped with Jerry's blood, blood that also trickled down her chin and neck.

"I don't think we've been properly introduced. I'm—"

"Lilith, yeah, I know. I also don't give two shiny shits. So how about you fuck off and leave me alone."

Her face hardened, and I saw her fists ball up. *Shit, Tess. Not smart.*

She stilled herself and continued, "You have something that belongs to me. I want it back. The longer you continue on this path, the more I will take from you." She ran her finger up Jerry's neck, catching some of the blood that trickled down. She brought the bloody finger to her lips and licked it clean, maintaining eye contact with me the whole time. *Creepy bitch.*

Anger surged through my body, and I felt it build inside of me. *This bitch is going to pay.* Before I had the chance to move, Jerry stirred slightly in his chair and let out a raspy moan. *He's still alive.*

"Jerry!" I cried. But before I could do anything, she'd hoisted his body from the seat in one fluid motion and held him in the air with a hand on his throat.

We stood there, staring at each other. I swayed due to the whiskey, and Lilith remained as still as a statue. She was holding a fully grown man with one hand. *Fuck, she's strong.* I suppose being a vampire had its perks.

"I swear to God if you hurt him—"

"You'll do what? You have no power. You are insignificant. I can't imagine why Louis wants anything at all to do with you, but he's always been unpredictable like that. Once he sees I've come for him though, that will change." It was clear she believed every deluded word. He'd been right; he *did* have crazy exes. But that didn't help me at this moment.

"What will it take for you to leave Jerry alone?" I'd do anything. He was a good guy, and he didn't deserve this. He had a wife, kids, grandkids. He was about to retire and spend more time with his loving family. He didn't deserve for his story to end like this.

"You misunderstand, Tess. He's as good as dead, just because I feel like it. I can do *anything* I want. I just wanted you to be aware of that. Now, regarding Louis: you'll tell him you don't want to see him anymore. Tell him it's—"

She didn't get the chance to finish her sentence before the door behind me crashed open and I was almost knocked over by the force of someone rushing into the room. I steadied myself, pulling myself together through the whiskey-induced haze that had settled itself deep in my head. It was the smell that hit me first, and I knew it was him.

"Put him down, Lilith. This won't end well for you if you

don't do as you're told, I promise you that." He spat his words in her direction and the menace intertwined in them made my skin prickle.

I glanced at him before once again focusing on Lilith. He was soaking wet from head to toe. His black hair stuck to his forehead and his suit was dripping wet. His white shirt was completely see-through. The water literally ran off all of his extremities. *What the fuck has he been doing?*

He never once took his furious gaze away from Lilith. Didn't even cast a glance in my direction. *She* was his focus, not me. For some reason, that pissed me off. It was irrational, and I knew it. But it was how I felt.

"Ahhhh, Louis. Nice of you to join us. You look *good*," she purred. There was no misunderstanding her tone, and she really was trying her luck.

"It's Lucifer, and you know that. No-one calls me Louis. It's not my fucking name. Now put him down and come with me," he ordered.

"I'm sorry, handsome, but that's not going to happen. We'll be together soon, I promise, but not before I tie up some loose ends." She shot me a smirk, her lips curving into a wicked smile.

After that, everything seemed to happen in slow motion. Lilith flicked her wrist, and Jerry's head twisted to an unnatural angle. I watched on in horror as she let go of his body. Watched as it crumpled to the floor with a heavy thud, like garbage being dropped into a dumpster and I instinctively knew he was dead.

The soaking wet figure next to me made a move to jump over the desk, as Lilith was plastered with a wicked smile across her face and then disappeared into thin air. She faded before my very eyes. One moment she was there, and then there were just the two of us and Jerry's corpse.

I stood, feet rooted to the spot. My ears began to ring, and my head buzzed. Lucifer, I realised, was standing in front of me. He gently placed his hands on either side of my face. He was talking to me, I knew he was, but I didn't hear him.

I'd come to the bar to make myself numb. And that was exactly how I felt. I just hadn't expected the night to end like this.

14

LILITH

Are you fucking kidding me?

He had come to her rescue. *My Louis* had come to her rescue and had treated me like what? Shit on his shoe. That little bitch had done something to him. She had to be controlling him in some way.

He would never treat me like that. *Ever.*

It was her fault. Tess must have some form of power over him, and I had to find out what it was. I needed to figure it out in order to break him free and liberate him so he could return to me after all these years.

No matter what anyone said about the two of us, we were meant to be—destined to be together eventually. It was just taking a little longer than I'd planned for us to make our way back to each other again.

It wasn't a case of fire and ice with Louis and me. No, it was fire and *Hellfire*. Both of us were strong-willed and independent, which was what had drawn us together in the first place.

One of my very first memories was of him. He had been there at the start. The start of everything. My beginning. I'd loved him instantly, which had obviously caused a few problems. But I was my own woman and couldn't be swayed from what I wanted.

And what I wanted was him; it always would be. I would kill everyone who stood in my way. I'd burn the world to the ground until it was just the two of us. My love was that fierce.

His had been too.

He always denied that was the case, but I knew it deep down. He was protecting his reputation. He was the Devil, and he couldn't allow himself to be weakened by succumbing to the love of just any woman. I thought after I changed to be something *more*, it would be different, but he still held me at arm's length.

Well, I was tired of waiting. He had shown this tramp the affection and devotion he should have lavished on me. She was taking my spot, and I wasn't about to sit back and watch. Tess was trying to live my life, steal my position, *and* fuck my man.

I'd get to the bottom of who was pulling her strings. She was a puppet and I'd kill her. It was her master I was more interested in. Who wanted her at Louis's side, and why?

I was looking forward to killing her. I'd given much thought to how I'd do it, yet I still wasn't sure. I needed to make it long and painful. It would be what she deserved; a quick death was too good for her.

I took a seat in the plush bedroom of my New York hideout. New York was where Tess and Louis were, so naturally, that's where I was. I couldn't exactly carry out my plan if I wasn't in the same city. I had brought a handful of my most trusted children with me. I knew they would do anything for me, and they'd gladly lay down their lives if I asked them to. It might come to that in the end. But I wouldn't lose any sleep over it.

Before I did anything else, though, I had to rest and regroup. It was vital I take some time to recover, but I was too wired. I needed something to take the edge off, something to make me forgot the torrent of emotions raging through my weary body.

Fading always sapped all of my strength. Louis could use portals at will, but fading was a one-off ride. Even though I'd tried to bolster the power, I'd never been able to manage more than one trip. Although my powers came from him, they weren't the same. I was powerful, yet I knew I wasn't his equal. No one was.

"Matthew," I shouted out. Within seconds he appeared in the room, dipping his head slightly and lowering his gaze. Before I could say anything, he spoke.

"Your Majesty, I sense that you need to feed. I'll bring someone immediately." He made a move to leave the room, but I stopped him before he got a chance.

"Get two, and one for yourself." He nodded and left.

I made my way to the bathroom attached to the room to clean up and rid myself of the old man's scent and blood. I preferred younger blood to feed on, but he had been a means to an end. By killing someone close to Tess, I knew it would draw attention to my presence in the city. That was the plan.

I wanted them to *know* I was nearby. I wanted them to feel uneasy. I wanted them to be watching their backs. The thought of them permanently on edge made me smile.

Once I was clean, I dried myself off with a towel and made my way back into the bedroom. I didn't bother putting any clothes on—they'd only become covered in blood when I fed. Also, vampires were highly sexualised creatures, especially when feeding. Any clothes I put on, would be coming straight back off, so why bother? I found Matthew seated on the comfortable chairs with three others. Humans.

Matthew's eyes remained on mine, but I knew the

humans were taking in my naked form. Two men and one woman watched me with curiosity. Their hearts were beating furiously in their chests. I could sense fear—that was understandable. But there was also a longing, a sexual need that vibrated through them.

Groupies, I thought.

Groupies were people who believed in all the things that went bump in the night, and who wanted to be part of our world. In particular, they wanted to be turned. They would willingly give themselves over so we could feed. In return, they'd expect us to change them; it was rare we ever kept up our end of the bargain. I'd taught my children to be particular about who they turned. Groupies would never make good, loyal vampires.

I made my way to the bed and sat on the edge. Then, I crossed my legs and leaned back on my hands, pushing my breasts out. "Care to join me?" I said to all of them, including Matthew. I watched as the three humans looked at each other, deciding on whether to be active participants. They would—after all, it was why they were here. Matthew moved first, and on his way over shed his clothes. We'd fucked too many times to mention over the years. He was an above-average lover, but no one compared to my Louis. Matthew was merely a substitute.

He sat behind me on the bed, leaning over to scrape his fangs over my shoulder. His hands moved to cup my breasts, and he tweaked my nipples. I never once let my attention drift from the humans.

They stood and began to strip. Once naked, all three made their way over to the bed and slowly climbed up. The woman immediately moved to Matthew, and both of them disappeared to the head of the bed. The men took up position on either side of me and began to kiss and caress me.

Matthew and the woman were out of sight, but I could

hear her pleasure-filled groans from behind me. The smacking of flesh on flesh told me Matthew had buried himself inside of her and was taking what he needed. I sensed the exact moment he climaxed—it was the same time the woman's heart stopped beating.

The two men had been attentive, eager to please royalty. I knew they were aware of who I was. Matthew would have told them. I was straddling one of the men, riding him hard, which caused throaty moans to rise from him—he was close to coming. The other man was pressed against my back, caressing and palming my breasts and nipples. I felt Matthew move behind the man who was attentively playing with my breasts, and the hands disappeared.

The man below me was mere moments away from climax when he suddenly sat upright. He grabbed my hips in an attempt to get deeper inside of me and he moaned deeply when he did. He was unaware of what was happening behind us, too focused on the rhythm of his thrusts and biting and sucking on my neglected breasts. He was too preoccupied to see Matthew grab the man behind me by the throat and force him to watch me ride his friend—he wouldn't till it was too late.

Picking up my pace, I gripped his jaw and forced him to look at me. "Are you ready?" He didn't answer, just thrust deeper. And then I felt it—at the moment he finished, I forced his face to the side and bit down hard on his neck. His climax would make his blood pump faster. It would also make his blood sweeter, full of serotonin and oxytocin. The chemicals would boost my recovery time, and I immediately began to feel stronger.

I heard him gasp. Now that his face wasn't buried in my breasts he was able to see his friend being forced into submission, no doubt a look of horror on his face. It could also be the feeling of his life draining from his body. He didn't fight—he couldn't. There wasn't much fight in a man just after he came, they were usually completely sated. And the speed I sucked his blood would only weaken him further. His eyes drifted closed, and his heartbeat slowed, slowed further, and then stopped.

The remaining human's heart was hammering in his chest. The beating was so hard I thought it might break through his ribs. The reaction wasn't pleasure, it was fear. Fear caused that response. I withdrew my fangs from the lifeless body and climbed off him, pushing the corpse off the bed, and it fell to the floor with a loud thud. Still naked and with blood on my chin, running down my throat, I turned to Matthew and the other man. Seeing my movement, Matthew shoved the man farther up the bed so I could trace my fingers down his chest and abs.

"No need to be scared, this will be over soon," I purred into the man's ear as I licked up his neck. I could feel his pulse hammer beneath my tongue.

"But… but they said you'd turn us," he said shakily.

Matthew still had his hand firmly wrapped around the man's throat and I leaned over him to take Matthew's mouth, nipping at his lip with my fangs, drawing blood and licking it up. He smiled and then tipped the man's head back, exposing his neck for me.

"My love, they lied." And with that I sliced the man's neck with my fangs, covering both me and Matthew in his blood. We both drank, bit, and lapped at the blood till no more flowed. With one hand, Matthew lifted the body and threw it to the floor.

The feeding had boosted my strength, and I was starting to feel powerful again, more like myself. I felt like I was able to take on the world, Louis included. But at that moment I had another man on my mind.

Matthew moved towards me on the bed. Before he had a

chance, I pushed him on his back, straddling him and lowering myself onto him. When he was inside of me, I took the reigns. I didn't need Matthew to do anything, just lay there so I could use him—this was about *my* pleasure. I rode him hard and fast until I made myself come. Louis made me come like no one else. He pushed my limits of pleasure and everything was more intense with him—and it would be again. And soon.

15

LUCIFER

Conrath followed Tess as she made her way to Jerry's office, but two surly vampires blocked his path. As soon as he saw them, he linked me, but I heard the commotion from my vantage point across the street and was soon by his side. We quickly took care of the vampires, and then I forced my way into the office.

Fear surged through my body at Tess being unprotected and in danger. It was a new sensation, and I didn't fucking like it.

Then I saw her, worry and concern etched on her face. She wasn't scared—that emotion was absent from her features. I looked her over, checking she was unharmed before I even considered scanning the rest of the room. I'd deal with whatever else was going on after I knew she was safe. Tess wasn't hurt, but her eyes were locked onto something across the room. I turned to where her eyes were fixed, and saw Lilith.

Fuck. She had Jerry by the throat, his feet dangling off the floor. Everything happened so quickly and she faded before I could reach her. Leaving me, Tess, and a very-much-dead Jerry alone in the office.

Tess's gasps rang through my ears as we both stood in place, taking in the sight of Jerry's dead body. I didn't think anyone would come into the office, but Conrath was standing guard outside just in case. She was frozen to the spot, not moving and unblinking. I walked to her, placing my hands either side of her pale, clammy face. I spoke to her, tried to snap her out of the trance-like state she'd slipped into—but nothing.

Still cupping her face with my hands, I stroked my thumbs across her cheeks and tried to bring her back to me. "Tess, sweetheart, can you hear me?" No response. "Red, we have to go now."

She blinked at my words, then flinched back from my touch. "I'm not leaving Jerry. He needs me." Tears had begun to stain her face.

"He's gone, Red. There isn't anything you can do about that. We need—"

"You go, I have to help him," she said, ignoring what she knew deep down.

I stepped towards her and made a move to hold her shoulders, but she shrugged me off. I was trying to comfort her, yet it had the opposite effect. Her chest began to heave, and tears now flowed from her eyes.

She made a move towards Jerry's body, but I blocked her path. She clenched her jaws, and her eyes narrowed. "Move," she growled.

"No, Red. We need to leave. Now."

She again tried to take a step forward, and I again blocked her path. She lashed out—punching and clawing at me, trying to get me to move aside. I heard the door open and knew it was Conrath entering. Tess didn't stop attacking me despite us no longer being alone.

I had to do something. I needed to get her away from here. If I had to, I'd take her kicking and screaming, but I'd rather avoid that if I could. I wrapped an arm around her and pulled her close to me, so her body was flush against mine. I had to try. I held my hand against her forehead, and she stilled and went limp against me. My powers worked. It might be because of the link we now had. Despite her attempts to shut it down, it was still faintly there. Or maybe it was just because she'd drank a shitload of whiskey. I wasn't even sure how she was still standing. I didn't know why my powers worked—I was just thankful they had.

"Sir, are you okay?" Conrath asked from behind me.

I held Tess tightly, not once taking my eyes from her unconscious face. "Yes, but we need to sort this mess out."

I linked Bee, asking her to join us immediately. She stepped through the door in an instant. When she arrived, she blew out a breath, taking in the sight before her. "What happened here?" she asked.

"Lilith. Lilith fucking happened," I said through gritted teeth. Bee's gaze shot to mine.

"She is one ballsy bitch, I'll give her that," Bee said, eyes widening as she came across the corpse behind the desk. "What do you need?"

"There can be *no* trace of Lilith being here. Make it look like a robbery. There can be no link to Tess."

"As soon as it's done I'll meet you at her condo," Bee said calmly.

"No. I'm taking her to Hell. It's the safest place."

"But..." She trailed off after I shot her a look that warned her not to test me. "Go, I've got this." She moved around the room, tipping over files and wrecking furniture.

I'd already begun to move towards the closest door, and then I portaled us to Hell. To my circle. To my fucking bedroom. Tess was in no fit state to do anything, and she needed rest and peace. As shady as it sounded, my bedroom was the best place for her to get that.

No one could disturb her here, and no one could harm her. Here, she was safe.

I gently laid her on the bed, removing her jacket and shoes with little trouble. She was out cold—would be for a while; she'd had quite the night, after all. As I looked at her, my stomach knotted. She was so *beautiful*. I marvelled at her for a while, simply taking in her beauty.

Moving to Tess's jacket, I removed her phone and sent a quick text to Emma, since I'd heard Emma tell Tess to text once she was home. If she thought Tess was home, she wouldn't worry about her when they found Jerry's body. She wouldn't believe that Tess was in danger, or that she'd had any involvement.

Tess's phone buzzed with Emma's reply.

Thanks for letting me know babe, speak to you soon XX

I turned back to where Tess was sleeping soundly on my bed. I perched on the edge next to her and watched the slow rise and fall of her chest, the slight flicker of her eyes, and the gentle twitching of her fingers. Every single movement made me feel at ease—they showed me she was okay.

Lilith had gotten too close tonight. She was toying with us, playing a game I wanted no part in. She could have ripped Tess's throat out in a blink of an eye, but she hadn't. Lilith wanted to torture her, drive her to madness. I wouldn't let that happen; I couldn't. The thought of anything happening to Tess twisted my insides and caused bile to creep up my throat.

Needing to be close to her, I shuffled up the bed and laid behind her. I pulled her to me, my chest against her back while I nuzzled her long auburn hair. I held her tightly, never wanting to let her go. I could smell the whiskey on her. *No wonder it hadn't taken much to subdue her.*

She'd feel the alcohol in the morning, as well as the aftereffects of my powers. It'd be like a really bad hangover, and it'd probably take a couple of days for it to fully clear.

I knew that when she finally roused from her unconscious state, she'd be pissed. I was well aware that I would bear the brunt of her rage, but I pushed those thoughts to the back of my mind. Instead, I focused on Tess curled up against my body. I held the woman I loved tightly, wishing we could stay like this forever, never wanting to let her go.

16

TESS

Shit.

My head hammered against my skull, and I could hear my blood pumping through my body. I took a few steadying breaths, but it was absolutely no good. I felt like death. I'd had much more whiskey than I'd intended to, and I knew I was paying the price.

I'd had bad hangovers before, but this was the worst I'd ever felt. Any slight movement and my head throbbed. Trying to calm my frayed nerves and settle my churning stomach, I took several more deep breaths. I didn't dare open my eyes—just the thought of trying to focus on anything made my head hurt.

I must have slept on one of my arms, because pins and needles started radiating through it and traveled to my fingertips. *Motherfucker that hurts.* Despite knowing it would make my head worse, I had to move; the tingling was extreme, and most definitely not in a good way. I shuffled slightly, attempting to move onto my back and free my trapped arm. Only, I couldn't.

I was being held. Fear crept up my body, and my skin

crawled at not knowing what, or who, held me. I had to open my eyes now, and as I did I realised I had no clue where I was. I certainly wasn't in my bedroom. This one was plush and decadent, and definitely not mine.

I looked down to see a strong arm draped across me, pinning me in place. It held me tightly to a strong body that I could now feel pushed up against my back. Lucifer. I'd recognise his strong, possessive touch anywhere.

But this wasn't his place. I'd spent time at his New York home, and this wasn't it. Now as I looked around—albeit slowly—his stamp was all over everything in the room, but I didn't recognise it.

I had to get up, get out of here. And most importantly, I needed to get away from Lucifer. I struggled against his grasp, trying to lift his muscular arm off my body. My skin felt clammy, and goosebumps covered my body, despite still being clothed—thank God.

"Easy, Red," he said soothingly into my ear as he tried to pull my body back towards him. I used the little strength I had to push his arm off me, then quickly shuffled to the side of the bed. I swung my legs out and with a massive effort stood. My stomach rolled, my head hammered, and my vision blurred. *Fuck*.

I heard him shift behind me, but I couldn't move—it was taking everything in me not to fall to the floor. *Come on, Tess, deep breaths—slow and steady.* It wasn't working. I was feeling worse.

From behind me, he stroked the tops of my arms. "Steady, sweetheart, you've had quite the night," he said softly. The goosebumps already on my skin intensified at his gentle caress, and I wanted to melt against him. But I couldn't; I wouldn't let myself get swept up in him.

I forced myself to take a couple of shaky steps forward and very slowly turned to face him. "Quite the night?" I echoed back to him. *What is he talking about?* Whatever it was, I knew immediately from his expression that it wasn't good. He looked worried, sad even. But why? I desperately searched my foggy brain for an explanation as to why he—

"*Jerry,*" I whispered as my gaze shot to his.

"Red, it's okay—" He didn't have time to finish his sentence before he had to move to catch me and keep me from hitting the floor. He steadied me, holding me while I regained my composure. I shoved him back and glared at him.

"I don't need your fucking help, Lucifer," I spat. My words were laced with the venom that I felt at that exact moment. He said nothing, just watched me and allowed me to unleash on him.

Jerry. Jerry is dead.

As the memories flooded my brain, my stomach rolled at the flashback of Jerry slumped in his chair with blood trickling down his neck. My skin prickled as I remembered Jerry being plucked by one hand from his chair like a rag doll. I began to sweat when I thought of Lilith's red eyes focusing on mine as she fucking smirked at me. Bile slowly crept up my throat when I thought of how she'd snapped Jerry's neck like it was a twig.

"Bathroom?" I demanded. He didn't speak, just pointed to a door on the other side of the room. I took off as quickly as I could, hands clasped over my mouth. Every step shook my throbbing head, and I knew I was going to be sick. Rushing through the door, I slammed it shut behind me and collapsed in front of the toilet.

Tears stung my cheeks—not from how violently I was sick, but from the loss of Jerry. The thought of never seeing his gentle, caring face again. The thought of never hearing his soft, fatherly voice. The thought that his wife, children, and grandchildren wouldn't see him again. My stomach rolled again and again.

My ribs burned with every heave, and I knew I was probably undoing the healing that was going on. But I couldn't stop.

I knew the sheer amount of alcohol I'd drunk the night before hadn't helped my stomach, but this was caused by raw emotion. I didn't know how long I was in there before I heard the gentle tapping on the door. "Red—"

"Don't," I warned.

"Please come out, Red. We need to talk," he said softly through the door.

"Give me a Goddamn minute, Lucifer," I said through gritted teeth. He didn't reply. I sat on the floor a little while longer; the tiles were cool and gave me relief from the sweat that had overtaken my body. I gently pushed off from the floor and made my way over to the basin, rinsing my face and mouth with water. I carefully re-did my hair, taking extra care not to aggravate my ribs further.

After I sucked in a few more deep breaths, I slowly made my way to the door. I did my best to compose myself, then I pushed it open. Lucifer was standing directly in front of me, and he moved to one side as I stepped out. I had to sit down. I knew I'd fall again if I remained standing. Scanning the room, I saw a couple of plush armchairs and made my way to one. As I gently lowered myself into it, I noticed he'd followed me and took a seat in the chair opposite.

"Water?" he asked tentatively. I nodded, and he poured me a drink from a jug on a table. I took the glass and took small sips of the water. It was ice cold and soothed my throat, which was still burning from the whiskey-filled vomit. My stomach churned again at the thought, and I took another small sip.

Neither of us said anything for a while. I could feel him

watching my every move. I focused instead on the water, playing with the condensation that had formed on the glass.

"Tess, I'm sorry about Jerry and what Lilith did to him, she'll pay I promise," he said, clenching his teeth and balling his hands into fists. Yeah, he was pissed, but his feelings didn't compare to the rage that coursed through my veins at that moment.

"Do you have her?"

"No, she faded before we got a chance to grab her," he replied, shaking his head and letting out a long sigh.

"Faded?"

"Can you remember last night?" I nodded. "When Lilith disappeared into thin air, that's what vampires refer to as fading. It's the ability to portal on the spot from one location to another. But it weakens them, so they can't use it often. Lilith will need time to recover and regroup, but she will come for you again." His brow furrowed and a glimmer of something I couldn't quite determine had taken root in his eyes as he looked at me. Concern? Fear, maybe? I didn't let myself dwell on it.

"I want to go home. I need a shower and a change of clothes, and I need to speak to Emma."

He shook his head.

Is he kidding? He has no right to stop me leaving.

"You should stay here, it's the safest place for you. Here Lilith can't touch you." He was deadly fucking serious.

"Where am I, Lucifer?" I asked cautiously, not sure if I wanted to know the answer.

"You're in the safest place I could think of." He was stalling, and I felt my body tense at his hesitation.

"Where am I, Lucifer?"

He took a deep breath before he spoke. "You're in Hell, Tess."

What the actual fuck?

17

LUCIFER

She shot up from the chair, but then immediately clutched on to the arm to steady herself. She was still feeling the effects of the booze and my powers. *Yeah, I wasn't going to mention that I'd used my powers on her any time soon—she's pissed enough at me.*

I stood to help her, but she held up a hand to stop me. "Don't you fucking dare, Lucifer," she warned. Remaining still, I waited for her next move, unsure how this would go.

"Red, I—"

"Don't "Red" me. I'm in Hell? What have you done?" She looked at me incredulously, like I was delusional.

How did she not see that Hell was the safest place for her? Here she was under my complete protection, and no one could touch her. For fuck's sake, Hell itself was unassailable, especially my inner circle. This had been the most logical course of action for me to take. I said I'd do whatever it took to keep her safe, and bringing her to Hell would do just that.

I shook my head, trying to understand why she couldn't see I was protecting her. "Tess, this is truly the safest place for you. No one other than me, Bee, and Levi can enter my inner circle. *No one* can get to you here. No one can hurt you," I said in earnest, hoping she'd see that my priority was her and that it always would be.

"But I'm in *Hell!* How is this safe? It's filled with the worst of the worst. Surely whatever is down here is even worse than Lilith." She continued to glare at me, and I could tell she was seriously pissed. "How can I be in Hell? This just looks like a house. I don't understand," she said, heading to the window. The heavy, lined curtains were closed. I watched as she grasped them and pulled them open.

I couldn't see her face, but I heard the sharp intake of breath. "What the fuck, Lucifer?"

She stood, arms folded across her chest. It was as if she was trying to comfort herself. I desperately wanted to move behind her, hold her close to me and be the one that offered her that comfort. But I knew she wouldn't let me, so instead I stood next to her as she looked out of the large window.

My presence next to her didn't distract her from the view; she knew I was there, but she couldn't tear her eyes away. I'd come to think of the view as beautiful. Eerie and foreboding, yes, but beautiful at the same time.

The sky was a bright crimson with dark, brooding grey-black clouds scattered throughout. Constant forks of lightning permeated the clouds and illuminated the red sky. It was no doubt ominous and terrifying to anyone gazing on it for the first time. It was meant to be. Hell couldn't be all sunshine and rainbows.

I turned to face her. She was still tightly hugging herself, and her eyes were wide. Her soft, gentle face was now etched with terror. It was there, clear as day. I moved and stroked my thumb along the side of her face. The contact shook her back to life, and she whirled to face me.

"How is this even possible? Am I dead? You said I'd come

here after what I did to Daniel, so is that it?" she asked, face still frozen with fear.

"No, Red. You're very much alive. I brought you with me so I could watch over you until this matter with Lilith is dealt with." I once again moved my hand to stroke her face, but she slapped my hand away.

"So I can leave? Now?"

"I think you should stay, Red. No one can touch you here," I said, keeping my tone as gentle as I could.

"Except you? If I stay here, you can do whatever you want. I told you I needed time, yet you're refusing to give it to me." She held a hand up, sensing I was about to interrupt her. "I get Lilith is a threat, but to be honest, I'm not sure that you aren't either."

It was like a sucker punch to my gut. Her words cut me deeply. *How can she even think that?*

"All I want is for you to be safe, Tess. I'll do my best to show you I'm not the monster that you think I am. Will you let me?" There was a plea in my tone, and I knew she'd heard it.

"I need to leave, Lucifer. Please." She reflected my own tone back at me.

I sighed heavily before responding to her. "Fine. But there will be more people with you now—"

"What about Conrath?"

"Conrath will remain, but he will have many others with him. He will remain your go-to, though. If you insist on leaving… can I ask something of you?"

"What?" she asked, eyeing me curiously.

"Unblock our link. With the link intact I'll be able to sense if you're in danger, and you'll be able to contact me if you need to. Please, Tess. Please." I was begging her, something I'd never done.

She watched me, weighing up her options. "I'll think

about it. It's not a no. I just need to figure out if I want you in my head."

At least she hadn't immediately shot the idea down; it was progress. Baby steps.

I heard Bee link me. *Is it safe to come in?* I could tell she was smirking.

What do you have?

It's taken care of. One of the bar staff found the body.

Come in. I'll be there in a second.

I once again focused on Tess, who was looking at me curiously. I heard the doors open, and knew Bee had arrived. Tess had heard it too, and her head moved to the sound before she asked, "Were you expecting someone?"

"It's Bee. She's waiting for us downstairs with an update."

"Who is she to you? Not your business advisor, I take it?" I heard it in her voice, the tiniest hint that she'd let slip through. I internally smirked. She was jealous of Bee, and it was the boost I needed.

"She is, in a fashion. Bee is fallen, just as I am. She's my number two here in Hell. She and Levi help me run things. They were cast out shortly after I was. It's been the three of us ever since." I deliberately didn't acknowledge the obvious and unsaid question. If she felt jealous of Bee, hopefully that might just work in my favour. I wasn't about to extinguish that possibility.

She moved to the door that led downstairs. "I need you to take me back now."

She'd been right, part of me did want her to stay so I could persuade her, seduce her, and fuck her until neither of us could take it anymore. But she wanted to leave and I wouldn't stop her.

18

TESS

I was leaving Hell. Now.

I pushed open the heavy wooden door, which I assumed was the exit from the bedroom. Thankfully it was, so I didn't look like an idiot by going into a fucking closet. I made my way out into a grand hallway, spotting a staircase at the end. I turned and walked towards it. I could hear the clicking of heels. *Bee,* I thought.

He hadn't said that their relationship was solely professional, and the thought of them together made me bristle. I wasn't the jealous type, never had been with Daniel. But with Lucifer, everything was different. I felt a possessiveness towards him, despite everything that had gone on between us.

It took me a while to get to the top of the grand staircase. The place was vast—far larger than his residence in New York. Despite its location, it seemed just like any other home. Had it not been for the horrific view from the windows, you'd never have guessed you were in Hell. I shuddered slightly as I caught another glimpse of the ominous—and let's not lie, creepy—sky. It gave me a real sense of foreboding. *He thinks I'm safe here? Is he fucking insane?*

Once I started to make my way down the large, ornate staircase, my eyes fell upon Bee. My stomach knotted, but this time not with the urge to be sick. There she was, in Lucifer's place. Like she belonged. She must have heard my footsteps as she turned to look up at me. She smiled while she called my name. At least she acknowledged my presence. I nodded back, then continued to make my way past her, towards the front door.

I had no clue how a person was supposed to leave Hell, but I thought trying the front door might be a good place to start. They were dark, rich, heavy wooden double doors. They had black wrought-iron handles, and the wood was intricately carved with swirls and patterns. They fit well with the rest of the decor and were quite beautiful.

I turned one of the handles and pulled the heavy door open—all the while very aware of Bee and Lucifer's presence behind me. The heat hit me first before anything else. It was stifling, as if I'd walked into a sauna. The smell was smoky, like burning, and suddenly Lucifer's heady scent made sense. It was etched into his very being.

The sky once again drew my attention as I stepped through the door and down some steps to the rocky ground below. Despite the constant lightning, there was no thunder. There was, however, a continuous crackle, like a burning fire with wood snapping and creaking.

As I looked around, I quickly realised there was nothing else here. No other buildings or people. Just the three of us and the house. *How the fuck am I supposed to leave? Do I hail a demon cab?* I whirled on the spot to face Lucifer and Bee. Both were standing at the top of the steps, waiting for me to do something.

"How do I leave?" I asked, not at all calmly. I caught Bee

look at me, clearly not up to date with what was going on. She looked at Lucifer, who cast her a sideways glance and shook his head.

"We'll use a portal to get you back. That is, if you still insist on leaving and won't consider staying?" It was another wasted attempt. I glared at him, and my silence answered for me.

"I need to go and find out what's happened with Jerry right the fuck now," I snapped, losing all my damn patience with the whole messed-up situation.

"It's all sorted," Bee said while looking at me coldly.

"What do you mean "it's sorted?" What have you all done?" Some unknown feeling had lodged itself in my stomach, at her words, but before I had time to dwell on it, she continued.

"After you two left, we made it look like a robbery. Messed the office up and took the money from the safe. One of the bar staff found him. Harry, I think it was. Shortly after, the police arrived and closed the bar. I have it on good authority they are convinced it was a robbery, so it's done." She didn't have a hint of emotion as she rattled off the story. Why would she? She didn't know Jerry, or how he had been planning to retire. That he was a veteran and that he'd loved his family dearly. I did, though.

The feeling that had taken root in my stomach grew, and I now recognised it. Anger. Before I could stop myself, I exploded at them. "So it's covered up? Brushed under the carpet? Does his death mean absolutely nothing in the grand scheme of things? Don't you fucking dare, Lucifer." He'd opened his mouth to speak but immediately shut it again. I was having my say, and the pair of them would listen. "Jerry was killed because of *you*, Lucifer. And me. This happened because some psycho has convinced herself that I matter to you and she doesn't like it. So, people *I* care about end up as collateral damage." I was practically screaming at him; my anger felt like a physical thing inside of me. It was a raging ball of fury nestled deep within me that seemed to be getting bigger the longer I stayed there.

"Tess, please," Lucifer said, his face falling.

"You don't get to ask anything of me anymore. Send me back. *Now!*" My fists clenched, and I was sure my knuckles had gone white. My teeth ached from the severity of how much I'd been gritting them, but I couldn't calm down. I wouldn't until I was out of Hell, away from them both.

"Bee, can you please send Tess home?" he said as his shoulders sagged and he took a step back away from the heavy front door.

I watched as Bee moved to the door and opened it. As I looked past her through the open door, I realised it no longer led back into the house. It was now a direct path into the living room of my condo. Trying to hide my amazement behind the veil of anger that still covered me, I stalked towards the door. At no point did I glance at Lucifer when I passed him; at this moment in time, I couldn't even look at him.

Then I was back in my place. The coolness of the air conditioner hit me, as did the familiar fresh scent. Home, it smelled like home. I took a deep breath, ridding my nostrils of the smokiness of Hell. The click-clack of heels told me that Bee had followed me in. I turned to face her, and then saw Lucifer. He was standing on the other side of the door, still in Hell and he looked utterly dejected. My eyes remained on him, trying my best to show no hint of the guilt I was experiencing. Bee had closed the door as she walked towards me, and he was gone.

We remained in silence for a while. I was unsure of why she'd followed me, but I wasn't prepared to acknowledge her presence. I headed to the kitchen; I needed water and some painkillers. After I swallowed the medication, I carried on taking small sips of the water. My stomach was still feeling delicate, and I didn't want to risk throwing up again.

I jumped slightly when there was a knock at the door. Bee made her way to it as if it was her place and not mine. She opened the door, and I saw a familiar sight enter. It was Conrath, and I must admit I was glad to see him.

"Tess, I'm sorry about your friend and that I wasn't there to protect you. I'll never let you out of my sight again. I promise," Conrath said, worry carved into his face.

I didn't have the chance to reply before Bee said, "Conrath will remain with you, despite his failure. In addition, there will now be a further team of people with you at all times." She held up a hand, preempting my protests before I even got to voice them. "No arguments, Tess. Lucifer's orders and I answer to him, not you."

Fucking bitch.

Leaving Conrath in my condo, she headed back to my door and opened it. Once again, it didn't open up into the corridor outside my place, but instead led her back to Hell. I glanced over, expecting to see Lucifer still standing there. But he'd gone.

Without looking back, Bee walked through the door to Hell and closed it behind her.

19

LUCIFER

I HEARD Bee before I saw her. I knew she was going to give me shit, and I *really* wasn't in the mood. Rounding the corner into the living room where I was sprawled on the large sofa, bottle in hand, she said, "I do like Tess. She's feisty." The amusement in her tone was very clear.

I shot her a look, my face stoic, and she simply raised an eyebrow in my direction. "Bit early for that, isn't it?"

I shrugged and took a long swig of the spirit. She was probably right, but at that moment I needed something to take the edge off. Who was I kidding? I was drinking to get wasted. I needed to forget everything for just a minute. I didn't want to think about how Tess had blamed me for everything, and just how furious she was with the whole situation, herself included.

"Lucifer, is this wise? Perhaps you should—"

"Don't fucking tell me to walk away, Bee. I couldn't do it even if I wanted to." I wasn't sure what had given her the impression I could. I'd told her repeatedly that Tess was all I wanted, all I needed. Clearly, Bee wasn't convinced.

"Look, I know you care about her. I like her, but you

have to consider the fact that she might not come around. She's pretty pissed at you right now. I think you need to prepare yourself for that possibility." She spoke soothingly, like she was a doctor delivering bad news. I knew her words came from a good place, but I didn't want to hear them. I wasn't ready for this to be over, nowhere near ready.

I took another long swig from the bottle of spirits and shuddered as I swallowed it down. This wasn't a human spirit—this was a demon liquor. It was made from ingredients found here in Hell. Liquida Mors—or liquid death, as it had been affectionately named—was a drink that had been enjoyed by countless demons over the years since it was first created. It was a red, shimmering liquid that looked very inviting and beautiful. This was a particularly strong batch, and therefore the colour and shimmer were intensified. Because of how strong it was, it tasted like actual fucking death. But it would do the job: send me to oblivion, even just for a short reprieve. I'd feel the effects for days, but the numbing sensation that had already begun to spread across my body would be worth it.

Bee looked on disapprovingly, but I didn't acknowledge her. She was clearly opposed to me torturing myself and trying to drink myself unconscious. "Tess is home safely. Conrath is with her, and the others are strategically placed around her building. There'll be a team of ten on her at all times. Are we sure Conrath is fit to be her main guard?" She questioned. She'd personally ripped Conrath a new one when she'd heard about what happened with Lilith.

In all honesty, if I didn't think he was up to the task, I'd have slit his throat, but he wasn't responsible for what happened. He had followed all the protocols and done everything he should have. Lilith was just a sneaky, manipulative little bitch. Conrath and Tess had a good relationship, and I didn't want to make things worse by removing him from her guard.

"He is. He's fond of her, which makes him more dedicated to keeping her safe. Plus, Lilith caught us *all* off guard. We didn't expect her to be so bold." I took another long swig, spilling some down my face. *Shit, this stuff really is strong, and it's working fast.* I hoped Bee hadn't witnessed it, but as I rubbed my chin, glancing in her direction, I saw her slowly shake her head. Changing the subject, I asked, "How did things go at the bar, really?"

"We completely ransacked the place. Stole all of the money, any other valuables we could find. We also bloodied Jerry up a bit more. Make sure no one would find the puncture marks."

"Was Emma still there when they found him?" I asked, curious how long it would take before Tess would have to deal with her reaction.

"No, one of the staff put her in a cab before he was found. They didn't come across him till closing time. Police got there pretty quickly after that. Detective Archer is dealing with it. We've already spoken, and he's up to date on how we want the case to go."

Detective Archer had been one of ours for a while. He'd made a deal about eight years ago when he was a rookie cop. Though he wasn't the most academic—or even capable officer—he was desperate to work his way up through the ranks. But it wasn't happening, so Archer had sought out my services. As a result, we used him whenever we needed to. He was also absolutely terrified of Bee and had a massive crush on her at the same time.

"Bet he was pleased to see you?" I asked with a smirk.

"Fuck off, Lucifer. Anyway, what was going on between you and Tess. Seemed cosy," she replied sarcastically.

I took another long drink from the bottle, the liquor was

definitely having the desired effect; my face was going numb. "Wasn't it obvious? She hates me," I slurred.

Bee let out a deep sigh. "Considering how long you've been alive, you really can be fucking clueless sometimes," she said, shaking her head in my direction. "She doesn't hate you, Lucifer."

"Are you serious? Did you not see what just happened? She doesn't want to be anywhere near me or hear anything that I have to say—especially how I feel about her. It's as clear as day that she hates me; I can't believe you'd think otherwise."

She looked at me for a while, like I had two heads, before she spoke again. "No, Lucifer. She doesn't hate you. Yes, she's pissed, I wouldn't expect her to be anything else. But she's lashing out because she's confused."

"Confused?" I echoed back to her.

"Yes. She not so long ago found out you're the Devil. In case you had any doubts, that's a pretty big deal and enough to confuse anyone. She cares for you a lot. But who you are makes her question things, makes her question *you*. Plus, how you met doesn't really leave her with a sense of confidence. I know that things changed as soon as you met her, but for her there is still doubt about how you feel—"

"But I've told her, tried to show her how I feel. She keeps shutting me out!" I said, my tone harsher than I'd intended.

"In normal circumstances, she'd need time to process things, work through all the crazy stuff that has been thrust upon her. But she hasn't been able to do that because she keeps being bombarded by even more shit. At this moment she's upset, yes, but it *will* pass; I have no doubt that she'll come round. She loves you, Lucifer. Anyone can see it."

I stilled at her words. The thought that Tess loved me—felt the same feelings that I felt, wanted the same things that I wanted—it gave me hope. Bee claimed she'd seen it, and she'd never once steered me wrong all these years, but the venom in Tess's tone and the look in her eyes made me think that on this occasion, Bee was wrong. I drained the remainder of the spirit from the bottle and let it fall to the floor. It landed with a loud thud as it bounced off the thick rug before rolling away.

I shook my head at her. "You're wrong about this one, Bee. I know it."

"Don't give up just yet. Trust me."

"What happens between Tess and me isn't the important thing here. Keeping her safe and away from Lilith, that's what matters. I will always protect Tess, regardless of what happens. Now she knows the truth, she'll never look at me the same way again and we both know that. Right now, all I can do is make sure she stays alive."

I'd resigned myself to my fate. I knew there was no coming back from this for Tess and me. My chest tightened, and my stomach knotted, but I knew neither was from the copious amounts of Liquida Mors I'd just quaffed. No, that would make me numb. The fact that I could still feel anything meant only one thing.

I pushed myself from the sofa and made a move to leave the room.

"Where are you going?" Bee questioned.

"To get another bottle, and then hopefully to slip into oblivion."

20

TESS

THE BUZZING of my phone woke me up. It was still dark in my bedroom, but the thick-lined curtains blocked out the light meaning it could literally be any time of day for all I knew.

When Bee had brought me back to my condo, I'd just wanted to be alone. Conrath apologised profusely for letting me come to harm, and it had taken me a while to convince him that I was fine and that what happened wasn't his fault. He'd finally come around and before he left, made sure I knew he'd be close if I needed anything at all.

After he left, I went straight to my bedroom and crawled under the sheets. I didn't shower or change, just collapsed on the bed. And then I cried—sobbed, actually. I couldn't remember stopping, so I must have cried myself to sleep.

Now, my phone buzzed, nearly as onerously as my head did. I regretted not changing or showering. The smell of Hell stuck to my clothes, skin, and hair. It reminded me of him, and that made my insides churn and my chest tighten. I was just so fucking messed up and lost with everything that was going on. I had no clue how to handle the torrent of emotions fighting for my attention. For now, I'd try to bury them deep and deal with the matter at hand: Jerry.

Before I looked at my phone, I knew that it would be Emma, knew it in my bones. The phone stopped buzzing, but my head, unfortunately, didn't. I was feeling like shit anyway, and a night full of tears had only made things worse. I'd slept, but not well, and as a result my body ached.

Dragging myself out of bed, I made my way to the kitchen for painkillers and water. I needed to take something before I spoke with Emma, had to pull myself around and try to seem like everything was normal—like I didn't know what she was inevitably going to tell me.

Sitting down on the couch, I went over everything that Bee had told me. All of the steps they'd taken and the lies they'd told to make it all look like an accident. Everything they'd done to cover up Lilith's involvement and the fact that I was there when it happened. I couldn't really explain to Emma how Luke was actually Lucifer—the Devil—and that his crazy ex-girlfriend—who was also the queen of the vampires—killed Jerry and was after me. She'd think I was a lunatic.

After Bee's debrief I now knew exactly what I couldn't and shouldn't say. I just had to figure exactly what I *would* say.

Just thinking about it all boiled my blood, and I was suddenly aware I was clenching my fists. I couldn't believe that Lilith would do this, for what? Someone who said he didn't even want her and hadn't for *years*. I wanted to know more about her and more about her relationship with Lucifer. *What exactly had happened between the two of them?*

Lilith wanted Lucifer, and she cared about nothing else. That was clear from what she'd already done. Turning Daniel and sending him after me, and killing Jerry to get to me. It was clear to me now that one of us wouldn't make it out of this alive, though I wasn't sure who that would be. In all honesty, I wasn't immortal, so I didn't fancy my chances, but I was damned if I was going to hide. I wouldn't make things easy for her. I'd fight till my last breath. I'd survived Daniel, and I could survive Lilith.

Lucifer, on the other hand, was a whole other dilemma. My feelings for him were jumbled, and I'd have to work through them before I could figure out what the best course of action was. I cared for him, and I couldn't deny it. But I was also unsure and pissed off. At the moment, though, the overwhelming emotion coursing through my body was guilt. It wasn't just Lilith that was to blame for Jerry's death—I was. I felt guilty that he'd gotten dragged into my mess. Without me in his life, Jerry would still be alive. And knowing that was eating me up. It was gnawing at my insides like a trapped rat.

Now, though, I had to ring Emma, so I steeled myself to make the call. I knew fine well I had to act oblivious and not let on that I was already aware of what she was going to tell me. Taking a few steadying breaths, I scrolled through my phone until I came across her number. *Here goes.*

It rang a couple of times before I heard her answer, and I immediately caught the pain in her voice. "Tess, where have you been?"

"Hey, Em, sorry. The whiskey hit me harder than I thought. Is everything okay? You sound off." I tried to seem at ease, to ignore the sense of foreboding that had settled within me.

"Tess, it's Jerry. He… he…" Her voice cracked as she spoke. "He's dead."

Silence filled the line. I allowed it to wash over me while I took in what she'd said. Somehow hearing it from Emma made it more real, despite having seen it happen.

"What do you mean, Em?" I replied eventually.

"There was a robbery at the bar last night, they broke in through the back door. Forced Jerry to empty the safe and then…" I heard her sob and my own stomach tensed.

My stomach rolled as the events from the night before flashed through my mind again.

"But… But…"

"Tess, he's dead, you must have been the last person to see him alive before you left. I was so worried about you this morning when Harry phoned, but then I looked through my phone and realised you'd texted to say you'd made it home, so I knew you were okay." I hadn't texted Emma. The last thing I remember was being in Jerry's office and then waking up. I'd passed out in Hell. With the fucking Devil curled up next to me. *Lucifer.* Of course, it had been Lucifer.

"I don't understand… I don't understand."

"Harry found the body when he was taking the cash to the safe when he was closing up. Phoned an ambulance and the police but he was already gone. The police have shut the bar, and there's a detective looking into things. He'll probably want to speak to you at some point, as you were the last person to see Jerry—" Alive, she was going to say alive, but another sob wracked her body.

"Em, is there anything we can do? What about his wife? His kids?" I wasn't sure why I'd asked. I couldn't face Jerry's family. The guilt rat in my stomach gnawed again at my insides.

"No, Sheila said the bar will be closed indefinitely. I spoke to her this morning, and she asked if Harry and I could help with arranging the wake at the bar. She said she'd be in touch, but for now, there isn't anything any of us can do." I immediately felt relief I'd have more time to ready myself before facing her. I wished I never had to, but I knew that wasn't the case—I'd have to face her at some point.

"How are you doing?" I asked Emma, softening my tone.

She'd known Jerry for years, thought of him as family. Their relationship had been up and down, but she loved him like a father. She had to be feeling his loss badly.

"I've done nothing but cry all morning. I don't know how I'm feeling. Heartbroken, angry, sick, and lost, to name a few." I could hear all of them in her voice. Emma had never been very good at hiding her emotions. We were very different in that sense—well in every sense, really.

"Do you want me to come over? Or do you want to come here?" As hard as it would be to lie to Emma's face, I had to be there for her. Considering everything, it was the least I could do.

"No, I want to go out. Drink, dance, maybe fuck someone. The last thing I want is to be stuck in an apartment wallowing. Life is too short, and Jerry wouldn't want us to mope." Her voice sounded different. She was compensating for her loss. I knew if we went out, she'd get wasted with the sole purpose of forgetting everything. To be honest, I think that was what I needed too. And not *just* to forget about what had happened with Jerry.

"You sure you want to do this, Em?"

"Yeah, I want to get absolutely wasted."

"I'll pick you up in a couple of hours."

21

LUCIFER

ARE YOU FUCKING KIDDING ME?

There was a long pause before I heard Conrath's voice again. *I thought you'd want to know immediately, Sir. I've requested extra demons, and they'll be with us before we leave. I won't let her out of my sight.*

Fine. Anything happens, let me know immediately. I massaged my temples with my index fingers. My face was still numb from the sheer amount of demon spirit I'd drunk.

Tess had to be trying to piss me off. She must know that this was a bad idea. She *had* to know it was a bad idea, yet she just didn't care. She was acting like a spoiled brat, selfish and stupid. Not only was she risking her own life but also Emma's, not to mention all of my people following her.

By going out into such a busy, crowded place, Tess was asking for trouble. I could only hope that Lilith hadn't yet recovered from the previous attack. Fading would severely weaken a vampire, even one as powerful as Lilith. Surely even *her Majesty* wouldn't have recuperated just yet.

She was showing me that I couldn't control her, couldn't bend her to my will. The thing is, I already knew that. I'd known that from the moment I met her; it was part of the reason I'd initially been drawn to her. At that moment, though, I detested the trait, because her strong-willed character would get her killed.

I knew she was probably doing exactly the same thing that I was trying to do: numb the pain. Bee had pretty much told me as much when she'd returned from Tess's place. Bee had assured me Tess was just upset, hurting and therefore lashing out. Bee said it was clear that Tess loved me, but I wasn't convinced. I saw anger in her, and it licked at her insides like a flame. I could see it behind her eyes. Maybe I'd done too much damage.

Tess knew that Conrath would tell me what she was up to; I could, therefore, only assume this little display *was* for my benefit. If she wanted my attention, she had it. Despite wanting to drink more Liquida Mors, I knew I couldn't let myself get buzzed again. Not while she was out in public. Not while she was exposed to so many dangers. No, tonight I'd have to feel the pain. If anything were to happen, I'd need to be sharp, and getting shit-faced definitely didn't leave me at the top of my game.

For a second, the thought of going to get Tess crossed my mind. I could portal to her condo and then drag her kicking and screaming back to Hell and lock her in a room until Lilith was finished. Having her locked up in Hell would make me feel a lot better about her safety. But Bee was right: if I smothered her, pushed too much, it would only make things worse. She'd likely back away even more and then I would have crushed any glimmer of hope.

So, I'd do nothing, even though the thought of it killed me. I wanted, no I *hoped* I could still turn this whole thing around, but I had no clue where to even start. This was all new to me. I wasn't used to this. I didn't chase or compromise. It sounded harsh but people came to me and I took what I wanted. I'd done that for millennia, but now, I would really have to work. *But where to begin?*

I heard the heavy door open and was surprised when both Bee and Levi entered the room. They both stopped in their tracks, eyeing me.

"Well, don't *you* look like shit," Levi laughed out.

"Screw you," was all I could muster in reply.

"He's right, Lucifer. You look like death. Actually, you look worse than death. He can be pretty hot when he makes an effort," she said with a smirk.

"I suppose you've heard?" I said, looking between the two of them.

They looked at each other, nodding, but it was Levi who answered. "We have, which is why we're here. We assumed you'd be pissed; I wasn't sure you'd want company though," he said, casting a sideways look at Bee. She shook her head.

"Regardless of *what* he wants, he needs to talk about what's going on. Lucifer, you aren't handling this well—"

"Really? You think?" I said, deadpan.

She glared at me before ignoring me and carrying on. "As I was saying, you aren't dealing with what's going on. We think it would do you some good to talk about this." The concern now etched into her tone.

She was right, I *did* need to talk about it, but where would I start? They knew most of it anyway. The only thing that was a mystery to them was how I was feeling. I wasn't entirely sure to how to articulate those feelings myself, never mind how to share them. So, I'd try and move the conversation on, at least for now. "Has anyone spoken to Gabriela?"

I heard Bee sigh deeply, but my focus remained on Levi, who smirked while shaking his head. "Well, I haven't. Have you, Bee?" he said, the corners of his mouth curling up into a wicked, knowing smile.

"Fuck you, Levi." Bee and Gabriela were evidently fucking. Bee enjoyed sex, always had, and as a result she was open to pretty much anything. Gabriela wasn't the first witch Bee had spent time with. "She's working on it, and she'll be in touch soon," Bee replied.

I cast a glance in her direction, and now it was my mouth that twitched into a similar smile to Levi's. "Is she in good health?" I quipped.

Before she had the chance to bite back, Levi replied, "Well I'm sure she is now that she's getting certain *benefits* from the guardian of Pride. After all, Bee is a perfectionist, and I'm confident she's making sure the witch is fully satisfied." Before he could react, he was hit by a crackle of electricity Bee threw his way. His reactions were a little on the slow side today and he should have known it was coming.

I laughed as Levi just chuckled and flipped Bee off. She still looked pissed. Despite our closeness, Bee was private. She didn't like everyone knowing her business, and I finally understood why.

"Don't change the subject, Lucifer. What's going on with you and Tess? What can we do to help?" Bee questioned. It was evident she saw how much this was all affecting me and wanted to help her oldest friend. Neither Bee nor Levi were used to seeing me like this, and I imagined it was off-putting for them, even unnerving.

"I need to make it right, but I don't know how to. You've both been in relationships before. You know more about all of this than I do." Bee smiled gently, but the look on Levi's face was pained. He'd had a wife, another fallen, but she'd died and it had nearly broken him. He had been a shell of a man for so long. At the time, I hadn't understood his reaction. Now though, it all made sense, and I felt a pang of guilt at how unsympathetic I'd been. I realised then that I'd been a shitty friend.

I hadn't understood how someone could work their way

into your heart and became an integral part of your life, or how you'd feel crushed at the thought of losing them. Tess was still alive, though, and therefore I had a chance. Levi's wife was dead, he had no hope at restoring that piece of himself, and I'd just dredged up all of his heartache by asking for relationship advice.

"Shit, Levi, I'm sorry."

He held up a hand. "It's fine, that was a long time ago. This is about you and Tess, not me and Jescha." I saw the briefest hint of pain flash across his face when he mentioned her name. But it was gone in an instant, and his resolve returned.

"Tell me how to fix this? Tell me how to get her back?" I said, rubbing my face with my hands. I looked between the two of them, waiting for a reply.

Bee smiled at me before she said, "We can do that."

22

TESS

It'd been over a week since Lilith had killed Jerry. A week since I'd seen or heard from Lucifer. I knew that was what I'd asked of him, but it left me feeling more confused than I'd thought it would.

At least when he was hounding me and invading my space, not giving me a minute's peace, I knew he wanted me. Knew that he was feeling what I was feeling. Now his absence in my life made me think he no longer cared and no longer wanted me, and I think that hurt more. I knew that was crazy, and it was the exact opposite of what I'd asked of him. But what can I say—my head was utterly fucked up.

I pushed Lucifer and everything else out of my head because I had to get ready for Jerry's funeral. I'd dreaded the day since Emma had told me and passed on all of the funeral details. I had to go, I had to, but it would mean facing Jerry's family—something I'd managed to avoid so far.

I was dressed in the only conservative black dress I owned, black heels, and my coat. Couldn't wear any of my other little black dresses, bit too revealing for a funeral. If I could have gotten out of going, I would have, but considering his death was my fault I *had* to go. I wasn't prepared for what the day would bring, nor if I'd be able to handle the gnawing guilt that hadn't let up in a week.

The last funeral I'd attended had been my mother's. The whole thing brought back so many memories. The one that overwhelmed me the most was the feeling of being utterly alone. When my mother had passed away, it was a shock, totally unexpected. She had suffered complications from a routine surgery, and it had completely broken me. When she left me, I was alone. No one was there for me. I think that was why I was so eager to make things work with Daniel, ignoring the signs that were so clearly there and forging on regardless. I could see that now.

I hadn't seen any signs with Lucifer though, and he'd made me feel wanted, adored, and in some crazy way… complete. His revelation had been a complete shock, one I was still reeling from.

My Uber pulled up outside of the church, and I thanked the driver before taking a deep breath and stepping out onto the sidewalk. I saw Harry and Emma waiting outside, and they waved me over. I slowly made my way over to them. "Thought we'd wait for you here so we can all go in together," Emma said as she rubbed my arm. "You look nice, classy."

"Thanks, Em. You too." She was dressed very demurely, especially compared to her normal everyday outfits. Black pants and a black top, still a little fitted to show off her curves but not at all her usual style. "Hi, Harry." He didn't reply, just nodded an acknowledgement. Emma had said that finding Jerry had hit him hard; he struggled knowing he had been there in the bar when Jerry was killed and that he didn't have a clue it was happening.

We waited inside the church, which was full, very full, and that made me smile. Then we heard the music, one of Jerry's favourites: an Irish folksong that he'd played on the jukebox in the bar a million times. Everyone stood, and then we saw them carrying in the casket, closely followed by Jerry's family. A lump settled in my throat that I couldn't seem to swallow away, no matter how much I tried.

It was a lovely service; people smiled and laughed at stories told by Jerry's oldest friends, and then Jerry's casket was carried back out for the trip to his final resting place. As his family passed by, Sheila saw me and gave a gentle smile. I knew at some point she'd want to speak with me, since I was the last person to see her husband alive.

Everyone filed out of the church onto the sidewalk, before getting into waiting cars and taxis that would take us to the graveyard. The one where several generations of Jerry's family were buried. Jerry would be buried on his family plot, just a lot sooner than everyone had planned.

The graveyard was beautiful and well-maintained. It was odd to call a place like that beautiful, but it was. Lush green grass, giant trees, there was a sense of stillness to the place which called to me. Although it was a place of death it—to me anyway—seemed peaceful. Calming, even.

We followed the stream of people to the graveside and watched on as the priest spoke a few more words. Then, I felt a prickle on the back of my neck, and my skin suddenly became covered in goosebumps, but I didn't feel scared. It was a familiar presence and not at all threatening. I looked around, studying the trees in the distance for him, and there he was.

Lucifer.

He was dressed all in black, and I could tell he was deliberately hanging back, away from all the other mourners. I doubted anyone else even knew he was there, but I did.

What are you doing here, Lucifer?

You opened the link? Why? He seemed surprised. I hadn't decided if it was a permanent re-establishing or not, but at that moment it seemed the easiest way to talk to him. As soon as I'd opened it, though, a torrent of emotions flooded me: *his* emotions. It knocked the composure out of me for a second, but I steadied myself.

Because I want to know why you're here, I replied as cooly as I could.

I wanted to pay my respects. From what I could tell he was a good man. He was good to you, and I respect that. Plus, I wanted to be here for support, in case you need anything. I could not believe him.

Lucifer, I don't need anything. This isn't about me, this is about Jerry. You should leave.

I know it's about Jerry, but you're hurting, I can tell. I can feel it now that you've opened the link. I want you to know that I'm here for you. Whatever you need. I could feel the strength of his conviction through our link.

I couldn't do this. I had to focus on the funeral and what was happening. I saw them begin to lower the casket into the ground. *I need you to leave.* Then once more, I closed the link, and my head fell silent. I looked up to see that he was still standing near the trees, a look of pain etched across his handsome face. But I couldn't concern myself with him. I had to focus on saying goodbye.

Once the casket had reached the bottom of the hole, Sheila stepped forward, picked up some dirt, and threw it into the hole and on top of Jerry's casket. She lingered there, seemingly unable to move. Unable to say her final goodbye to the man she'd been married to for forty-six years. The overwhelming sense of loss she must be feeling struck me like a ton of bricks. Then their son made his way to her, held her hand, and whispered something to her. She nodded, taking a deep breath, and then turned and walked away while gripping her son's hand tightly.

The other mourners followed suit by throwing dirt into

the grave as they said their own goodbyes. Then it was our turn. Emma and Harry lingered a little longer than most, and it was clear to see they were both distraught, feeling their own guilt about Jerry's death. Then I walked up, taking a handful of dirt in my hand and holding it out over the open grave. I stared down at Jerry's casket. *Jerry, this is all my fault. I know it doesn't mean shit, but I really am sorry. I'll make sure the bitch pays. I promise you that.* I dropped the dirt, and with my clean hand, wiped the tears from my face.

I moved to stand with Emma and Harry, and the three of us remained silent. Then everyone began filing back to the cars. I looked to where Lucifer had been, but he was gone. Probably vanished back into the shadows where he'd come from.

We made our way back to the bar for the wake. Harry and Emma had said they'd help out, so I took up my usual seat. As I sipped my drink, I studied Jerry's family and friends and then noticed Sheila approaching me. *Shit, shit, shit, I'm not ready for this.*

"Tess, dear. How are you? I haven't seen you in such a long time." She usually had such a soothing tone, but it was now laced with grief. Her voice was thick with it, despite trying to hide it. She had a gentle face, all warmth and love, though now it was also twinged with sadness.

"I think I should be asking you that," I said softly.

She reached over and cupped my face with her hand and it was then that I knew I had to do this for her, let her know how much he loved her and bury my feelings of guilt.

"Sheila, he loved you. More than I've known anyone love someone in my entire life. He told me he was finishing up, and then he was going home. Home to you. He hated being separated from you; you were always his priority. Always."

Silent tears fell down her face, but she didn't speak. She gave my cheek a gentle squeeze, and then walked away. I blew out a shaky breath and closed my eyes. I felt a presence behind me and an armed draped over my shoulder.

"That was a nice thing you just did, Red," Lucifer said as he tried to pull me to him. I desperately needed the comfort, but at the same time I was pissed that he'd once again ignored me.

"Do we speak the same language? The words that I'm speaking now, do you understand them?" I said, shrugging his arm off me and turning in the stool to face him. The smile that had been smoothed across his face disappeared when I found his gaze.

"Yes, I—"

"Then why are you here? I thought I asked you to leave," I said, my face stony and cold.

"I just thought that—"

"What. That I needed rescuing? That you could push your way back in when I was grieving? That what I want doesn't matter?" I stood and made my way to a corner of the bar, less prying eyes to watch the pair of us.

"Tess, I'd never do any of those things. I love you. I want to make sure you're okay," he said, but his tone was unsure like he was nervous.

"It's not enough. We're done," I said quietly, the words tearing at my heart and making the void that had taken root there that little bit bigger. I knew I didn't want this, but I didn't see any choice. His face stilled and hurt flashed across his eyes, along with fear. I wasn't sure exactly what he was scared of, but it was there.

"Don't say that, Red. We can work this out. We have to," he replied, swallowing hard.

"I don't have to do shit, Lucifer. This was over before it even began, you made sure of that." I made a move to walk away from him, but he blocked my path.

"No, it started the same way any other relationship would: a man meeting a woman. That's all."

"Tell me, do you believe your own bullshit or are you just expecting me to?" I said, once more trying to move back to the bar. He blocked me in again and went to take my hand, but I jerked it away.

"Tess, I knew straight away you were special, that I wanted to be with you. Everything I've done since I've met you has been to protect you." His eyes flashed, pleaded with me.

"So, you do believe it, then? Well, that makes one of us. Now if you'll excuse me." I tried to push past his solid frame, but he didn't budge. Instead, he snaked his hand round my waist and pulled me close, leaving his hand splayed on the small of my back. My body ignited again at his gentle touch, betraying me.

He leaned in and whispered into my ear, "It's not bullshit, Tess. I love you. I've never loved anyone before, but you woke me up, ignited something within me that I didn't even know was there. You're it for me, Tess. It's you or nothing." He nipped at my ear as he spoke, and my goddamn body wanted to melt into him. I had to fight it.

"Then I guess it's nothing," I whispered as I pushed him away and made my way back to my seat. He didn't follow me, but I was sure he lingered. I wouldn't look, I couldn't look. If I saw him there looking like a wounded puppy, I'd cave. Rush to his side and try and ease the pain that I'd caused him.

So instead, I forced myself to stare at my glass, compelled myself to keep my eyes front, and then I felt it.

He was gone, and I was alone.

23

LUCIFER

Is she blind? She has to be blind. How can she not see?

I'd laid everything bare for her, more than once, yet she still couldn't see. Or was it that she *wouldn't* see? Regardless of which it was, she didn't give a fuck.

I was livid that she had dismissed me twice. I'd gone to the graveyard to support her, be there if she needed me. There was no ulterior motive in my presence, I thought only of her. Okay, that wasn't strictly true—I'd wanted to see her, but that was it. I didn't want or expect anything from her.

I knew the wake at the bar would be hard, which was why I was there. I wanted her to know I'd always be there for her, to help her through dark times. But my gesture hadn't had the outcome I'd expected.

Yes, technically I'd gone against what Bee and Levi had advised me, but just a little. I listened to what they'd said and thought this was a sort of middle ground. Although, they'd probably be pissed that I'd ignored their advice after specifically asking for it.

But now, it was done. Tess had told me exactly that, and I felt like I'd died inside. That new part that had blossomed from knowing her, being with her, loving her, had been ripped out. The warm glow she'd cultivated had been dimmed, replaced with emptiness and anger that seemed rooted in my heart.

It was done, no going back. I opened my third bottle of spirit and began to drain it. My hands were tingling, and I knew the numbness would take over soon. But it wouldn't completely stop the pain.

I needed to get her out of my system, needed to *fuck* her out of my system. If I was balls deep inside someone else, I wouldn't be thinking about her, or just how perfectly I'd fit inside her, how she made me come so easily and so powerfully, how the pleasure had torn through us both when we were together.

What was the saying, "To get over someone you should get under someone else?" Well, that didn't sound like a bad idea to me. After all, I did like sex. I'd always found it a good distraction, and I definitely needed a distraction.

I portaled to one of the trendiest bars in New York, certain there would be an abundance of people there who could scratch my itch. Stumbling out of the toilets due to the couple of bottles of demon spirit I'd consumed, I made my way to the VIP area and sat at a table overlooking the dance floor. I ordered a bottle of whiskey and began the search. I scanned the dance floor for any potential conquests, then I saw them—a group of around ten women.

Bachelorette party.

I would have been able to tell even if the bride-to-be hadn't been wearing a fake, glittery tiara and a sash; in fact, they were all wearing sashes. Now, this would be interesting. I'd chosen my prey for the evening, and all of them would be mine.

I continued watching on as they danced and swayed to the music. They were all attractive in their own ways. Most were in their mid-to-late twenties, and they all appeared to be having a good time. Continuing to watch the group as they made their way to another of the VIP booths, I caught the waitress's attention and relayed my order.

The waitress and her colleague approached the party of women with five bottles of the most expensive champagne the bar sold. The women appeared confused at first, but then I saw the waitress explaining, and a couple smiled at me as I raised my glass in their direction. Then it started. I saw them chatting with each other, casting knowing glances towards me, trying to figure out which of them should approach. I already knew it would be the bride, but who would accompany her?

Sure enough, the bride-to-be sashayed her way over to my table, accompanied by one of her bridesmaids. I remained still, lounging in the chair and sipping on my whiskey as they approached. I knew how this would go, and I was ready for it. They would all be mine tonight, but I specifically wanted the bride. I wanted to ruin her in more ways than one. I would corrupt her and leave her wanting more, just like I wanted more from Tess. *No, stop it, she's gone.* I shook my head, dislodging the thought of her from my brain. I once more focused on the women, who were now standing directly in front of me.

"Hi there, we wanted to come on over and say thank you very much for your generosity. My name's Tamara and this is one of my bridesmaids, Mia. Would you care to join us?" She spoke with the confidence that only came when you'd had a few drinks. She was attractive—they both were. The pair were about the same height, I'd guess in my intoxicated state around five-foot-four. Both had slim builds, but the bride was much curvier than her bridesmaid. The women each had dyed blonde hair styled straight and long. They were stereotypically attractive, but I didn't care about any of that—they were just the distraction I needed right now.

"Thank you for the kind offer, ladies, but I'll leave you to enjoy your night. I just wanted to make sure you were given a proper send-off. Not every day a beautiful woman gets married." With that, I stood, took the bride's hand and brought it to my lips to gently kiss the back of it. "If you'll excuse me." And with that, I moved between them and began to walk away.

Five, four, three, two, one...

"Wait," I heard the bride-to-be say as she gently reached out to grab my hand. I turned to face her, smiling gently. "Please, come join us for a drink. It's only right that you have a glass of the champagne that you bought."

And just like that, I was in. I took my seat at their table, and the charm did the rest. It wasn't hard, and I'd had multiple millennia worth of practice in seducing women. I was good at it, *really* good at it.

We chatted for an hour or so before I suggested they all come back to my place to continue the party, and they all jumped at the chance. As I led the bride by the hand from the bar, I stopped in my tracks when I caught a glimpse of a curvy redhead, sitting at the bar. My heart pounded in my chest and a lump formed in my throat. I watched her waiting for her turn. It felt like an eternity before I saw her face, but when I did the feelings eased. It wasn't Tess and on closer inspection, she wasn't anything like her. Thoughts of Tess had buried themselves deep within me and I was starting to see her everywhere—except it never really was her. But I was here to dislodge her—that was what this was all about.

Once back at my place, I showed everyone in, opened multiple bottles of alcohol, and gave them the tour. As usual, they were impressed. It was hard not to be. My New York home was one of my favourites, but now it held many memories I wanted to forget. Moving the tour on, we finally ended up at the pool. I heard shocked gasps from the group of women, who all filtered in behind me; a couple of them muttered "holy shit" as they followed.

"Oh my God, this is totally amazing. I can't believe this place has a private pool. This is something else, Luke," said the tall, slender maid of honour whose name I had already forgotten. It didn't matter. I wouldn't be seeing any of them again after tonight.

"Thank you. Please, ladies, *do* make yourselves at home. The pool is heated, so feel free to take a dip."

There were a few laughs and whispers from some of the group, but I knew it wouldn't be long before they were all in the pool. "But we don't have anything to wear," one of the party said from the back of the group.

A smile quirked across my lips as I said, "Ladies, please, who needs costumes?"

There were once more laughs and giggles, but it was Tamara, the bride-to-be, who moved first. She slid her dress down her body, to reveal a lacy thong. She kicked off her shoes and jumped into the water, and it didn't take long for the others to follow. Watching the group, I made my way to one of the lounge chairs surrounding the pool and sunk into it, cupping my glass with one hand and allowing the scene to unfold. They laughed and joked, splashed each other, and continued drinking, all while I watched on.

"Luke, aren't you going to join us?" Mia said, swimming up to the side of the pool near to where I sat.

"Mia, sweetheart, I'm enjoying the view just fine from right here, I'll join you later." She gently splashed some water at me and then swam off back to the group.

Having finished my drink, I grabbed another bottle from the kitchen and returned to my seat to watch the frolicking continue. As I poured another large whiskey, I noticed

Tamara swim over to me, brace herself on the side of the pool, and elegantly push herself out, exposing her overly large breasts. From the way they were positioned on her slim frame I knew they were fake. She was tanned, and no white lines were visible on her body. That told me a lot about Tamara. She was clearly very confident with her body, not in the slightest bit shy. She was so unlike Tess.

No, get her out of your head. She doesn't want you.

I took a long swig of my drink as I focused on her walking towards me, swaying her hips as she moved. Tamara had set her sights on me and was like an animal stalking its prey. She ran her hands over her hair to smooth it away from her face; she never once took her eyes off me. She stood in front of me and leaned forward, grabbing the drink from my hand. She then stood upright and finished the drink in my glass. She deliberately let some of the liquid slip down the side of her mouth, then scooped it up with her finger. After that, she slipped her finger in her mouth and sucked the whiskey from it while looking me in the eyes. She knew *exactly* what she was doing, and it was hard to believe she was just about to be married the way she was carrying on, but I never judged anyone.

She set the glass on the floor and then sunk to her knees between my legs. As she placed her hands on my thighs, she looked up at me. And there it was, visible for everyone to see. Desire, want, need, and lust. The energy emanating from her was powerful, and it flowed freely from her and pricked my senses.

"How about being my last fling before I get married? There's something about you, Luke. Something that makes me want to be very, *very* bad," she whispered as she slid her hands up my thighs. Her hands edged closer and closer towards their desired destination.

Ordinarily, I'd be hard as a fucking rock, ready to go at a

moment's notice, but at that second there was nothing. Not even a slight fucking twitch. I'd had a lot to drink—namely three bottles of demon spirit. But deep down though, I knew that wasn't the reason for my little problem. *Come on, Lucifer, pull yourself together.*

I closed my eyes, taking a deep breath as I did so. Tamara slid her hands farther up my thighs, and up my chest to find the buttons of my shirt. She undid them slowly while making her way down; once she'd finished, she brushed her fingers across my chest, watching me for some response. I gave her nothing, because I was feeling nothing.

She leaned into me and whispered in my ear, "I want you in my mouth. I'm going to suck you dry."

Still nothing. She was throwing herself at me, and my cock wasn't at all interested. She moved her hands back down my chest to the waistband of my trousers and found my belt, which she made swift work of. Her fingers move to my zipper, and she looked up at me, biting her lip as she did. I hadn't noticed before, but her eyes were green. A dull green, though, like swamp water. Not like the brilliant, emerald-green eyes I loved staring into. Tess's eyes were striking, and I could get lost in them, especially when she had my dick in her mouth.

Tess. What am I doing?

I grabbed Tamara's wrist before she could go any further. "Don't," I said coldly. She pulled her hand free of my grasp and placed them back on my thighs, just above my knees.

"Sit back and relax, handsome. I've got this," she said, trying to sound seductive but just coming across as desperate. She once again moved her hands to my fly, and this time I snatched up both her wrists.

"Get your hands off me. Now. In fact, get out." Standing up from the chair, I bellowed, "Out. All of you out now!" Everyone turned to look at me, but no one made any attempts to leave. "Leave!" I screamed, using the slightest hint of my darkness. That certainly got their attention. Everyone scattered quickly, keen to get the hell out of there and away from me.

Ignoring them as they all made their way out of my place, I headed to the kitchen and pulled out another bottle of Liquida Mors. I drank half the bottle in one go, attempting to soothe the need for Tess that burned within me.

Fuck, why can't I forget her?

I had to see her, had to be with her. Just one more time. That's what I'd say to Tess, I'd tell her I couldn't get over her unless I had one more night with her. If I couldn't have her forever, I only wanted one more night. I'd beg her, grovel at her feet. I would do whatever she wanted, as long as I got one more night.

One more night to feel her pressed against me, kiss her full, luscious lips, run my fingers through her silky hair, trace every inch of her body with my mouth and tongue. I wanted one more night to worship her body and bury myself deep inside her.

I wanted it to be a proper goodbye. Then I'd leave her alone, despite knowing it would eat me up inside. I'd head to her place and lay everything out for her.

But first I needed another drink.

24

TESS

It was late, about 2 AM, and I was still at O'Malley's helping Harry and Emma clear up. Jerry's wake had been a lively affair with his friends and family *really* celebrating Jerry's life—it had been quite the sight. As a result, the stragglers had only just left.

I offered to help tidy up. Both Emma and Harry said they were coming in tomorrow to give the place a really good clean, so it was just a case of stacking all the glasses in the sink and getting rid of the leftover food.

I'd had a few drinks, but nowhere near enough to dull the pain that had taken root in my chest. Cutting Lucifer loose had torn me up inside, and I felt empty, but today hadn't been about me and my drama, so I put a lid on it, pushed it down, suppressed it. Emma had repeatedly asked what was wrong, but I managed to put her off; I couldn't deal with that conversation right now.

The three of us turned everything off and made our way out of the bar, locking the place up behind us. I hugged the pair and told them not to worry, that I'd be fine getting home alone. I knew I wasn't alone though, as I caught a glimpse of Conrath lurking in one of the doorways. There would be others, though I couldn't tell where they were.

"Okay, babe, take care. Text me when you get home. Promise?" Emma said, holding her pinky out to me.

"Promise," I echoed as I grabbed her finger with my own. "See you, Harry. Take care." He nodded at me, and then the pair headed off in the opposite direction.

As I began the short walk back to my condo, I felt Conrath's presence next to me.

"How are you doing?" he asked gently.

"It's been a really shitty day, and I just want to go home and curl up in bed," I said, hugging my coat around myself.

"I heard what happened," he said as he cast a sidewards glance at me. "Try to be patient. This is all very new to him. But it's clear he cares deeply for you. I've never seen him like this."

I stopped in my tracks and glared at him. "Should I excuse all of his bad behaviour just because he's "never done this before?" I don't think so."

"No, you absolutely shouldn't, and I agree he's not being fair. It's just he's trying with you. He really is. Just… try and remember that," he said as he once more set off towards my building. I sighed and quickly followed, catching up to walk alongside him.

Have I been too harsh on him? I didn't think so, but the thought of not being with him hurt more than everything that had happened between us. As much as it pained me to admit it, I cared for him, and deep down I wanted to be with him—whether he was the Devil or not.

I opened the door to my building, and we walked through, making our way to the elevator. I watched Conrath; his eyes were darting around, looking for any immediate threat. He always seemed ready to pounce. We took the elevator to my floor, and we stepped out together, then made our way down the corridor before we turned to where my front door was. I was digging around in my bag, looking for my keys, when I ran into the back of him.

"What's wrong…" But I could already see what was wrong. There was a body slumped against the door to my condo. It took me all of two seconds to realise it was Lucifer. *Oh fuck.* Without even thinking, I pushed past Conrath and ran towards him, thinking he was injured or worse.

"Lucifer, Lucifer," I said worriedly as I got closer to his motionless body. It was when I was pretty much on top of him that I saw the empty bottle cradled in his hand, and the smell of alcohol hit me like a freight train. He wasn't hurt, he was fucking drunk. "Are you shitting me?" I turned to see Conrath behind me, looking on, not sure what to do.

My attention shot back to Lucifer as I felt him grab my leg. "Red, Red, I've missed you so much," he slurred, just barely managing to get the words out.

Placing my keys in the lock, I opened the door, and Lucifer fell back into the condo. Stepping over him, I threw my keys and bag down on the little table. Lucifer turned onto his stomach and then crawled into my hall.

"Please let me in. I just need five minutes to talk to you. That's it," he said, once more slurring heavily. Ignoring him, I left the door and headed to the kitchen. I filled the coffee machine with water and turned it on. Out of the corner of my eye, I saw Conrath had come to Lucifer's aid and helped him up, ushering him into my living room and sitting him on the sofa.

Conrath turned and walked to stand next to me in the kitchen. "Just hear him out," he whispered before he made his way out of the door and closed it behind him. I quickly fired off a text to tell Emma I was home safe before turning my attention back to the coffee. I made myself a cup, then added sugar and milk; I poured another cup and left it black.

Composing myself, I picked up both drinks, headed to the living area, and handed the black coffee to Lucifer. He looked at me sheepishly and took the mug, cradling it in his hands and blowing the steam off the top. Without saying anything, I headed to the other end of the sofa and sat down.

"I'm sorry for turning up like this. I just needed to see you, clear this all up before you shut me out," he slurred, though it was quieter this time.

"Why?"

"You know why, Red. Because I love you." As he spoke the words, he looked at me, really looked at me, and I could see the pain in his eyes.

"Don't do that. You don't know the meaning of the word. You don't love me. I don't know what this is, but it's not love. I was just a way to piss off Daniel." I took a sip of my coffee, not meeting his gaze—which I knew was on me.

"You're right, that's how this started. And you're right, I didn't know what love was—b*efore you*—but now I do. You changed that, knowing you changed that. Loving you *changed* me, Tess."

Just because he loved me now, though, didn't change everything that had happened. "I think you should finish your coffee and leave." I couldn't look at him when I said it, since I didn't want to see that look on his face and know I was the cause of it.

We sat in silence for a while, both of us sipping our coffee and avoiding whatever was brewing between us. He let out a couple of sighs, I assumed in an attempt for me to ask him what the matter was. *Yeah, that's not going to happen.* Then as if

I had no control over my mouth, I said, "You shouldn't get so out of it when Lilith is still out there, you could have gotten hurt."

Still cupping his drink, he turned his body to face me, looking at me incredulously. "I could say exactly the same thing to you," he replied knowingly.

Shit.

I didn't look at him, just continued to drink my mug of steaming coffee, and he went back to doing the same. The silence once more settled between us, but I could feel him glaring at me. I could tell he was sobering up as his gaze grew more penetrating, and it started to make me feel things I'd fought hard not to.

I glanced at the clock and noticed about half an hour had passed yet he'd apparently completely sobered up. *Lucky bastard.* He stood, not at all unsteady, and made his way to the kitchen, where he put his empty mug in the sink before returning to me. But instead of retreating back to his seat at the end of the sofa, he sat directly next to me.

Before he had the chance to say anything, I spoke up. "You should be going now."

He leaned over and took my drink, setting it down on the floor, then he grasped my hands in his. I should have pulled away, but the slightest touch from him made me melt. "Tess, one more night. Please. If you truly want me out of your life for good and never want to see me again, then I'll go. But before I do, please, just one more night. That's all I ask. I promise, after that, I'm gone. It'll kill me, but I'll do it."

He idly stroked my hands with his thumbs, and then moved one of his hands up to cup my face, but I slapped it away before he could touch me. I knew once we started this, there would be no going back. If we did this, I wouldn't be able to let him go, and I wouldn't be able to say goodbye.

"One more night, Tess. I need this. *We* need this." His voice was husky and low, and it sent a tiny shiver down my spine. He once more brought his hand to cup my face, and I again moved to slap it away, but he grabbed my wrist before I could make contact. I tried to pull free of his grasp, but he tugged my arm towards his mouth, watching me the entire time.

He brushed his lips against the tender part of my inner wrist, and he peppered it with feather-light kisses while bringing my other wrist towards him. It was the slightest of touches, but fucking hell, it was hot. My body was betraying me, and it edged closer towards him, leaned into his touch.

I jerked my wrists free from his grasp and stood, putting a bit of distance between us. "Lucifer, I can't—"

"One more night, Tess, and you'll never see me again if you don't want to." There was a slight plea in his voice; it was subtle, but it was there. He took a step towards me, and I didn't retreat. He took another, and another, until he stood right in front of me, staring down at me. He searched my face for a cue, something, anything, but I remained still.

Then, before I had the chance, he slid his hands behind me and cupped my ass, pulling me flush against his body. His lean, muscular body that I'd missed so much. "One more night. Please." Before I could reply, he leaned forward, placing a gentle kiss on my cheek. I could feel his breath hitch when his lips brushed against my skin. I heard everything, because I'd forgotten to breathe. He shifted to the opposite cheek and pressed another tender kiss there. They were soft kisses, but they were by no means innocent. They conveyed passion and the need to possess me in every way. He retreated slightly, looking into my eyes.

Then he crushed his lips on my own, making me moan and arch into him. His teeth nipped my bottom lip, and his tongue darted out to soothe the sting. My arms instinctively laced around his neck, intertwining in his thick, luscious hair. I gripped it tightly, pulling him further into the kiss. He groaned at my new-found eagerness, and he pushed his tongue into my mouth, devouring everything that he could take.

He was intoxicating to me, and I yielded to his touch, my body stilling and reacting to every tantalising flick of his tongue, nip of his teeth, and squeeze of his hands.

Fuck I've missed his touch, but what am I doing?

Deep down, I knew this would only make things harder, more painful, but I was powerless to stop him. My body didn't want to stop him.

Wait, is he making me do this?

"Stop. Are you doing this? Are you making me react to you like this?" As soon as the words left my mouth, I regretted them. The look of sheer anguish on his face told me everything I needed to know. His mouth bobbed open repeatedly, but no words came out, he couldn't respond. He stilled for a moment, composing himself. Then he spoke.

"No, Tess, I would never." He took a step away from me, seemingly wounded. I'd hurt him, really hurt him. He stood still, unsure of what to do next.

I believed him when he said he hadn't used his powers; his reaction told me everything I needed to know. So, I took a page from Emma's book and committed myself to the moment.

I stepped towards him, once more snaking my hands around his neck and in his hair. I kissed him and swept my tongue against his. He seemed a little shocked and he just remained in place, allowing me to take the lead. I removed one of my hands from his neck, sliding it down his chest, lightly tracing his muscles with my fingers. I continued farther and farther down until I brushed my fingers against the colossal bulge in his trousers. He groaned and pulled his head back, looking hungrily into my eyes. Apparently, he saw whatever it was he needed to see.

He hoisted me up against him and, as always, my legs wrapped around his waist. He unzipped my dress as we moved to the bedroom, and then slid it off my shoulders before he gently placed me on the bed. He pulled my dress down my body, exposing my black bra and lacy thong. He moaned at the sight, before he said, "Fuck, Red, you're perfect."

He leaned over my body, placing a hand on either side of my head. He drank in the sight of me like it had been years since he'd seen my body, an eternity since he'd been able to touch me like this. He splayed one of his large hands across my stomach as he nuzzled his face into my neck. "If this is my last night with you, I'm going to make every second count. I'm going to worship every inch of your body, explore every bit of you, and make you come so hard that nothing will ever come close again," he whispered low into my ear before nibbling on it.

I had a sharp intake of breath at his words, and the bite to my ear that felt like he'd just directly nibbled my clit. *How did he do that?* He knew my body like no one ever had, knew what made me hot, knew what I wanted, and knew just how hard he could push me. I had a feeling that tonight he'd push me to my very limits.

He nipped and licked at my neck before making his way to my breasts. Then, he snaked his hand from my stomach to the clasp of my bra, making quick work of it before throwing it across the room. His fingers drew circles around my nipple while he moved to take the other in his mouth. My back arched into him, pushing my breasts further into his mouth and hand. I felt his lips curve into a smile. "Always so responsive, Red. I fucking love that." Then he grazed my nipple with his teeth, making it harden, making it so sensitive. His hand pulled and flicked my other nipple, making it just as hard.

Then, the grazes with his teeth became harder as he tugged and pulled, pushing the limits of pain and pleasure. He did the same with his hand, nudging the threshold. I gasped at the sensations that rippled through me. He then licked and soothed my nipples before starting all over again, and it began driving me so close to the edge. I needed him inside me now.

I slid my hands down his chest to the waist of his trousers, unsnapping the button and reaching for his fly. Before I had a chance to free him, he snatched my hands up and pinned them above my head. "No," he growled. "Do you trust me, Tess?" It was a question laced with so much emotion. But I didn't even hesitate, immediately nodding my head. His face broke into a huge smile, which quickly became mischievous as he moved off the bed and disappeared from view. "Stay there," he commanded.

I didn't move, and he quickly returned to the room, licking and kissing his way up my body as he moved up the bed, once more taking my hands. Then he watched me, waiting for me to object as he tied my hands together with one of my scarves before pushing them above my head and fastening the scarf to my bed frame. He pulled on the scarf roughly, ensuring I was trapped, that I couldn't go anywhere. Then he set back to work on my nipples, quickly getting me to the edge again before stopping and saying, "Look at me, Tess, I want to watch as you come for me." His voice was silky, and his eyes were full of lust. He began moving his hands, pulling and tweaking as my insides began to clench. He nipped and tugged harder when he sensed my orgasm was about to hit. Then I was wracked with pleasure, radiating outwards while my body shook—I had to bite my lip, hard, to stop myself from screaming. He wore a wicked smile as he continued to watch the after-effects of his handiwork.

"Good girl," he growled before leaning forward and kissing me deeply. His tongue stroked mine, probing and licking before he was gone again. I opened my eyes to see him removing his shirt and throwing it across the room. He was so handsome. Seeing his naked torso again made my heart beat faster, and my skin prickled with the anticipation of having him pressed against me. He leaned forward and kissed my stomach, slowly making his way to my thong. He traced the top of it with his tongue, taking the strap on one side between his teeth before letting it snap back against my skin. The sting made me gasp a little, and he quickly licked the spot, soothing the pain before he slid the thong down my legs.

I was vulnerable before him, totally naked with my wrists bound, but I didn't feel scared. All I felt was anticipation. His fingertips traced up the inside of my thigh, moving everywhere except where I wanted them. "Lucifer…"

"Shhhh, let me enjoy you, Tess." His voice was low and dripping with need. Then his hands moved, and he hooked my legs over his shoulders before gently swiping his tongue over my sensitive clit. I moaned loudly at the contact.

Shit. He knew just what to do and how to elicit my moans. He swirled his tongue over me and then sucked before humming slightly. The vibration of his deep, gravelly voice against me sent shivers all across my body and goosebumps erupted across my skin. Then he swept his tongue between my folds before pushing this tongue inside me. "Fuck," I gasped as he continued to move his tongue in and out. He moved once more to my clit, and then I felt his fingers gently push inside me. My legs dug into his shoulders, willing him to get closer, and for him to move quicker.

But he didn't, he kept his movements painfully slow and

rhythmic. His fingers plunged deeply in and out as he continued flicking his tongue against me. It was an exquisite type of torture, but I knew I was coming undone. My muscles clamped around his fingers, tighter and tighter, but he never let up. Then I felt his thumb push up against the bud of my ass. He applied a little pressure, but he didn't do any more. He worked all three movements together, and it was enough to send me crashing over the edge. I grabbed the scarf holding me in position and threw my head back; a scream left me as everything inside me ignited with my release. I panted when I felt him shift from between my legs, still keeping his fingers inside me, but I couldn't move.

I stilled, trying to catch my breath, and when I stopped seeing stars, I finally opened my eyes. Lucifer was watching me with a smile as big as his face—he was so handsome when he smiled. He looked happy. He withdrew his fingers and brought them to his mouth, licking them as he looked me in the eyes. I felt empty without him inside of me, lonely with the distance that was between us. I watched as he stepped off the bed and unzipped his fly. He pushed his trousers and boxers to the floor, and my eyes feasted upon him as he stood naked in front of me. I wanted him inside me, needed him inside of me. He must have seen the desire in my heated gaze while he stalked towards the bed. After crawling up my body, he stopped directly above me. He braced his hands on the bed as he took my mouth with his, kissing me hungrily like he craved it.

Then I felt him press against me, and he moved slightly, his cock just barely inside of me. "Fuck, Red," he bit out. Then, without warning, he pushed inside me and we both let out a lustful moan. My eyes snapped to his as he moved deeper, filling me, stretching me, completing me. He placed a gentle kiss on my lips as he withdrew again; then, watching me, he slammed back inside me.

Having him inside me felt so right, like I was where I was supposed to be. It sounded crazy, but he did things to me no one had ever come close to. He slowly thrust in and out, with deep and powerful strokes as he grabbed my hips, angling me just where he wanted me. I was desperate to touch him, scratch my nails down his back, grab his ass and pull him closer to me. But this was his show, and he was in control.

He started to increase his tempo and lifted my hips a little, getting an even deeper angle that hit my sweet spot just right. As he did, I uncontrollably clenched around him, which stopped him in his tracks as he groaned heavily against my neck. "I love you, Tess," he whispered into my ear as he once more began moving. He kissed and sucked on my neck and began to thrust deeper, more furiously—as if his own release was becoming too much to control.

I didn't think I could come again, didn't think it would happen, but then he sucked a nipple into his mouth and reached a hand between us, tracing circles on my clit, and I came undone. Everything in me clenched as the power of my orgasm took over my body. He thrust once more, and then I felt his own release consume him before he collapsed onto my body.

We laid there, still intertwined, breathing heavily for what felt like an eternity. We were both at peace, and I didn't want the night to end. I felt him shift his weight, and he moved up the bed to release my wrists. Once free, I rubbed them with my hands; they were marked where I'd been pulling against my restraints. Lucifer lay flat on his back and pulled me on top of him. Grabbing my wrists in his hands, he planted tender, soothing kisses on the marks.

"Did I hurt you?" he asked, a worried look on his face.

I reached up, stroking his cheek with one of my hands. "Not at all," I replied before placing a soothing kiss on his lips, letting it linger for a while.

A contented smile spread across his face, which now looked softer somehow, like the pain that had settled in him had been erased. I didn't know what would happen tomorrow, but tonight we had each other. He smoothed my hair with his hand and pulled me closer.

"Sleep," he whispered as he planted a gentle kiss on the top of my head. "I've got you."

25

LUCIFER

I STRETCHED OUT, grabbing the pillow and hugging it; I was sprawled on my stomach on a comfortable, albeit small, bed. I was still tired, but the thought of opening my eyes to find Tess lying next to me boosted my energy. I opened them—only to find she wasn't there; I was alone in her bed, and unease settled in the pit of my stomach.

I pushed myself up to see if I could see any sign of her in the bedroom, but I was alone. I glanced at the clock and noticed it was past midday. I wasn't surprised we'd slept so late. After our reacquaintance with each other's bodies, I'd woken twice more with an insatiable need to have her again. The first time I'd woken her by gently licking and sucking on her clit, she'd reacted so powerfully to my touch—like it ignited a fire within her that burned so intensely. Once she was awake, she'd straddled me, riding me as if our lives depended on it.

The second time she was curled up against me, my front against her back. I'd woken from her squirming in her sleep, grinding her oh-so-tempting ass against my cock. That was all it had taken, and I'd immediately become hard. I'd reached around, stroking and teasing before I pushed my fingers inside of her. She had moaned loudly, and once more rubbed her ass against me. I'd replaced my fingers with my cock and, taking her from behind, achieved a deepness that got us both to our release quickly.

After that, we'd settled back down, and I had slipped into a deep, restful slumber—one that had evaded me ever since Tess had learned the truth about who I really was. But there, with her wrapped in my arms, I'd found a sense of peace, even if it was only for one night. Just thinking about Tess had me hard, but now was not the time. We'd said one night, and unfortunately that night had passed.

I pushed myself out of bed, looking for my clothes. I slipped on my boxers and trousers, though I couldn't find my shirt. After making my way to Tess's bathroom, I looked in the mirror, raking my hands through my hair to calm it. I splashed some cold water on my face and used some mouthwash to freshen myself up.

This was it. Once I left the bathroom and found Tess, it'd be over. I lingered a little longer, not wanting to leave the safety of the bathroom. While I was in here, Tess and I were still a thing. It took me a good five minutes to build up the courage to leave.

I pushed open the door and made my way to the open-plan living space, and there she was. I quickly discovered why I couldn't find my shirt. Tess was wearing it. The bottom grazed the top of her thighs, and when she walked around the kitchen her movements allowed me a view of her curvy ass. I wanted to go up behind her, snake my arms around her waist, pull her close, and nuzzle my face into her neck. Instead, I let out a small cough.

She turned when she heard me. She smiled softly, and I could tell she was also apprehensive about how we should act, what we should do. Even now dressed in my shirt, with her hair tied in a messy bun on top of her head, and wearing no make-up, she was perfect. My chest swelled at the sight of her, but the feeling was quickly replaced with sorrow.

"Coffee?" she asked, her voice small and meek.

"Please. Milk, no sugar. Thanks," I said, matching her tone. I continued watching her, not sure what I should do while I waited. As if sensing my unease, she turned to me.

"Go sit, and I'll bring the coffee when it's ready." Nodding my head, I moved to sit on one of the sofas, the one with a view of the kitchen. If this was the last time I'd ever see her, I didn't want to let her out of my sight.

Without looking at me, she said, "Sorry about the shirt. I'll go change in a second."

"Don't. It looks good on you," I said truthfully. She turned to face me and gave a slight nod; the flush on her cheeks hadn't escaped my notice.

She made her way to where I sat and held out a steaming mug; I reached out to take it, and my fingers brushed against hers. Even the slightest touch from her caused sparks to spread across my skin. I looked up into her face, and I knew she felt it too—the look in her eyes gave her away. As did the goosebumps that had taken over her skin.

She moved to the other end of the sofa, tucking her legs underneath her and cradling her coffee as if she were freezing and it was the only source of heat. I knew she just wanted to occupy her hands; I knew because I was doing the same thing. If they were busy, they wouldn't try to reach for her.

I was about to speak when she said, "Maybe you should finish your coffee and go." My breath caught in my throat, and it felt like I'd been punched in the gut. I'd known this was coming, but the tiniest part of me thought that last night could have changed her mind. *Who am I kidding? It isn't a tiny part. It was every fibre of my being.*

"If that's really what you want, I will, but first please let me explain. It's important to me that you know the truth, and then I promise I'll leave."

"Lucifer, you don't need to explain. You don't owe me anything," she said quietly, avoiding my penetrating gaze.

"I do, Tess, I really do. I owe you everything. I was honest when I said I'd never lied to you." I held up my hands in surrender when she shot me a glare that could have turned me to stone. "I never lied, but you're right that I wasn't completely forthcoming with you. So, here goes. Ask me anything, anything at all. Whatever you want to know, I'll answer. I won't lie, and I won't hold back."

She shifted her body to face me. "How do I know you won't lie to me? How do I know it's the truth?" she asked sceptically.

"Open the link between us. Open it like you did at the graveyard. The link has changed, it's not just a method of communication now. I could feel what you were feeling. I could feel your pain, and your anger," I said, dropping my eyes from her gaze.

"I could feel yours too," she said quietly.

"So, open it, and then you'll be able to tell what I'm feeling or if I'm lying to you."

She nodded her head, and then the feelings flooded through me like a dam breaking. Anger, fear, pain, sorrow, confusion, and something else. I could tell the same feelings had hit her too, and my own emotions flowed through the link.

"I mean it, Tess, ask me anything," I urged.

I could see she was contemplating what to ask, where to start. It seemed like an eternity before she finally said, "Why does Lilith want me? Who is she to you?" Talk about going for the jugular. I blew about a breath, considering where I should even begin with that story.

"In order for me to tell you that I need to start at the beginning, the very beginning," I said, looking for the go-ahead.

"I have time," she answered.

"Okay. What do you know about Adam and Eve?" I asked.

"Are you fucking kidding? I thought you were serious about answering my questions," she retorted.

"This isn't a joke, Tess. Answer the question." As she studied my solemn features her face became sceptical, but she answered.

"God created Adam and Eve. They were the first people to walk the Earth, and they lived—"

"Wrong," I interrupted. "Adam was the first man, but Eve was not the first woman. Lilith was. God created Adam and Lilith from the very same clay, and they were created as equals, which is where the problems first began."

"Wait. What? Are you serious?" She stared at me open-mouthed.

"I am serious. Lilith was Adam's first wife and his equal. She was strong-willed, fiercely independent, and sharp. And all of those things made her incompatible to Adam. Both he and God wanted someone more... accommodating. Lilith questioned everything, wanted to know more, wanted more than what she was being offered, which is where I enter the story. At that time, I'd already been cast out, and I was determined to cause as many problems as I possibly could. So, I seduced her, told her there was more to life and that I'd show her if she came with me. For her, it wasn't even a choice. She had quickly become infatuated with me. I listened, offering her things she could only dream of. I became what she needed."

"So, she left with you and then what, she was replaced and written out of history?" Tess said, gobsmacked.

"Exactly. With Lilith gone, Adam was alone, and God

wasn't happy. He swore he wouldn't make the same mistake twice, so when he created Eve, he used a piece of Adam, his rib, ensuring that the matching wouldn't be one of equals. That meant that Eve was indebted to Adam for giving a part of himself to let her live. Even after that, she was tempted away just as Lilith had been, but that's a story for another time."

"So, what happened to Lilith?" Tess questioned, leaning closer towards me and crossing her legs to settle in for more.

A sense of guilt flooded over me, and I knew Tess would be feeling it. "She remained infatuated with me, and I'm not proud to say that I used her whenever the mood struck me. Looking back now, I regret my behaviour to Lilith. I liberated her, yes, but I was cruel after that. But then she did something I never expected her to do—it changed everything."

"Was that when she became a vampire?" Tess asked, and I nodded in agreement. "How did that happen?"

I massaged one of my temples with the fingers of my free hand. "Me," I finally answered. She sucked in a breath, seeming shocked at my answer. "It's not what you think, though. I didn't willingly turn her. It was out of my control." The memories began to surface as I thought back to that night.

"I… don't understand," Tess said. It had been millennia, and I still didn't fully understand how it all happened.

"Lilith had wanted to see me, so I invited her to my place. I knew she wanted sex. I'm not proud of it, but it didn't stop me from taking it from her; I took everything she could give and I never gave anything back. On this occasion, she decided to take matters into her own hands, and she took what *she* wanted. She drugged me, and I passed out. When I woke up, I was covered in blood, had a raging headache, and found Lilith cowering in a corner. I was furious that she'd tricked me and I demanded she tell me what had happened. It turned out she'd become friendly with a witch who had filled her head with nonsense, but she was desperate, so she believed it," I said. That was part of the reason I hated witches.

"What happened?" she asked as she leaned closer still, hanging on my every word.

"The witch told her that because I was fallen, my powers were in my blood. As an angel, I'd been born with powers, but when I was cast out and given my new role, it changed me. Made me something different. The witch told Lilith that my blood was the key and that if she wanted to be my equal, my partner, that she had to take it. Unfortunately for Lilith, it didn't work as she'd hoped. After she drugged me, she slit my wrist and drank my blood, believing it would give her the same powers I possessed. Although Lilith possesses many of the gifts I have, hers come at a much higher cost. My powers are unlimited and unwavering, whereas Lilith's require a sacrifice to maintain, and even then, they are limited."

"But I don't understand," she said, looking genuinely perplexed.

"Lilith drank my blood to obtain her powers, but as my blood was taken against my will, she became cursed. The creature she became was born from the darkness, and that is where she has to remain—in the darkness, unable to venture out in the daylight. Since she gained her power from my blood, she, in turn, has to feed on blood to maintain them. So, Lilith became the first vampire. All others were born from her, which is why she is queen. I created her, so all of this is my fault," I said, rubbing my hand down my face.

Tess leaned forward and took my hand, gently stroking the back of it with her fingers. "I'm not excusing how you were with Lilith, but I think you've come to terms with how shitty that was. The rest of it though... what she did. You can't blame yourself for that. You didn't turn her into what she is, she did that herself," she said, giving my hand a gentle squeeze.

I couldn't believe she was consoling me. I'd expected her to ask me to leave, call me out for creating a species of bloodthirsty killers. But no, she was showing compassion to me, and it made me love her even more.

"So obviously, she thinks you are hers. Even after all this time. Have you done anything to give her that impression?" she said, retreating back to the other side of the sofa.

"No, never. After I woke up and realised what Lilith had done, I told her she'd sealed her own fate. That I didn't love her, and that I never had. I told her I never wanted to see her again; she's tried over the years to get in touch, lure me back, but every time she gets nowhere. I thought she would eventually catch on, but she just keeps trying. She and Bee have had a few scuffles over the years, since Lilith was always jealous of Bee. Saw her as a threat when there was no reason to." She quirked her eyebrows. "What?" I asked.

"I can understand why she sees Bee as a threat. The two of you have apparently known each other forever and are extremely close—not to mention she's hot." I felt Tess's jealously flow through our link, and it made a glimmer of hope grow in my chest.

"Bee is my oldest friend and has always been there to support me. Nothing romantic has *ever* happened between the two of us. We're more like siblings than anything else. There is no need for anyone to be jealous of Bee." I allowed the truthfulness of my words to flow, hoping she'd pick up on them.

"So now Lilith wants *me*? Why?"

"Because Tess, you're special. In so many ways, but most importantly, you're special to me. All I've done since I met you is bring danger to your door, and for that I am truly sorry, but I wouldn't change it. I know that's selfish, but meeting you has been the highlight of my many, many years walking the Earth. And Lilith knows it. She knows that you're different from the others. Special. I think she knows I love you. Therefore, you're a threat to her." I kept my words soft and gentle, trying to convey the many muddled emotions that coursed through my body, ones I knew she'd be feeling through our link.

"But what makes me so special? I'm just a girl from England," she said, bemused.

"Honestly, Tess, I don't know what makes you special. But there's something else I need to tell you."

26

TESS

Despite all of the crazy shit he'd just told me, it felt like the most important part was yet to come. His face had grown solemn, and I could fear his anxiety through our link.

"What is it?" I asked, searching his face for any sort of tell.

"Tess, I want you to know everything. No more secrets," he said earnestly as he gazed at me. I nodded for him to go on.

Well, I've come this far, might as well lay everything out and see what other revelations he has for me.

"As the Devil, I've been making deals with people who want something for centuries. It's part of the role. Daniel came to me, and we made a deal." I shuddered at the mention of my ex's name. It seemed like an eternity ago since I'd killed him. The guilt still hadn't found me, though, and I wasn't sure it ever would.

"As you are well aware, he was a prick, and I immediately disliked him. He wanted you more than anything in the world. So, as obnoxious as this sounds, I planned to take you for myself before I handed you over." He held up placating hands when he saw the look on my face, and it was clear he could feel my rage following through our link. "I know, I know, but this is what I do, I'm the Devil. So, I learned about you before our first engagement. But when we did meet, it was odd. I felt… nothing," he said, raising his eyebrows.

"Wow, thanks for that!" I said a little hurt that I hadn't actually affected him, especially considering the considerable impression he'd left on me.

"No, you don't understand. I read people, it's part of my powers. I can tell how a person is feeling, what they desire, what they are scared of. I know the sins people have committed and, if I want to, I can influence them into doing whatever I want. But not you. You are a blank page to me, and I can't read you or influence you in any way. With you, nearly all of my powers are useless."

"Nearly all" his powers, I hadn't missed that but I could feel the truthfulness vibrating through the link. "So, you've never made me do anything? Everything that we've done, you didn't make me do any of that?" I needed to check.

"I couldn't make you do anything even if I wanted to. But, Tess, I *never* wanted to. I wanted you to want me, but not through compulsion, but because *you* wanted to. I'm drawn to you in a way I've never experienced before. Everything with you is new and fresh, and I have to put the effort in, something that I don't think I've ever had to do."

"So, this was all just about the chase? Because you couldn't get me, it made you want me more?" I felt cheap at the thought of being another notch on his bedpost. I hated the idea that that was all I was to him.

"I won't lie, Tess, that's how it began. Getting one up on Daniel, and then possessing something that I had to work at, but now… now you're so much more. You are one-hundred-percent yourself, straight-talking, sassy, and so fucking beautiful. The more I've gotten to know you, the more I've grown to want you for just being you. I quickly called off my agreement with Daniel, and my team and I were looking for him when Lilith became involved. I swear that's the truth."

I believed him, I could feel it. But I still had so many questions. "What makes me immune? There must be some reason that you can't read or influence me. Is it a common thing?" Could it be that one in ten people were immune to the Devil? One in hundred, or even one in thousand. I didn't know, but I wanted an answer. And by the look he was giving me, I already knew.

"It's far from common, though there have been a handful," he answered.

"A handful this year, the last ten years, what?"

"A handful since the beginning, Tess. You are unique, and it's important we figure out why." His words were laced with purpose. I was an enigma to be figured out, but once he solved me, what then? Would he leave? Would I become disposable? As if sensing my unease, he continued, "We need to find out why, so we can protect you. I won't lose you, Tess. I can't."

"So where do we start?" I questioned. Obviously, this was all on him. I had no clue about any of this, so if answers were needed, I'd have to rely on him to help me.

"With your father. He has to have the answers that we need," he said, his now-serious gaze fixed directly on me.

What is he talking about? I had no idea who my father was, so how could that help. "My father? But I—"

"I know you don't know who he is. We haven't been able to find anything about him either, which makes me even more convinced that this all comes from him." His brows furrowed, and he looked like he was concentrating hard.

"You looked into my father?" I was shocked at the level of detail he'd gleaned about my past. Jesus Christ, did he know about that one time in university when I'd sucked off my lecturer on a night out? I blushed at the thought and quickly tried to suppress the memory from my brain.

"We looked into *every* part of your life, Tess," he said with a smirk. Yeah, he probably knew about that—and everything else, by the sound of it. I was at a complete disadvantage with him. "By now Lilith will have figured out that you're different; she'll know that there is more to you and she'll have everyone she can looking into it. We need to do the same."

"But you said you'd done that and, yet, found nothing. Where do we go from here?" There was no one for me to ask about my father. I never knew anything about him. All of my family was dead—it was just me, and I was useless in this pursuit.

He turned to face me, a worried look spread across his face, and he picked at his nails. He was nervous; I'd never seen him like this before. He was usually so calm and self-assured, but he was worried about telling me something, which in turn made my stomach clench with dread.

"What is it? Why do I get the impression I'm not going to like what you're about to say?"

"Search the link, and you'll realise all my actions are born from a good place." I could feel his honesty flowing through, but it was laced with something else. Trepidation.

"Go on," I urged.

"I've sourced a witch—a very loyal witch, who is going to help us with this matter. Your father is the key, and the witch will help us find answers. I hope she can give us, and you, some clarity." Even after that, I could tell he was still holding something back.

"What aren't you telling me?" I probed, furrowing my brow as I searched his face for answers. He looked away from me before he continued.

"For Gabriela to work her magic, she needed your blood

to use in her spells. That was the only way she could get us answers…"

"Wait, she *needed?* As in, she did need it, but now she has it?" I leaned forward towards him, forcing him to look at me.

"I took your blood from the hospital. I knew that you wouldn't give it to me, and I didn't want you to know anything about this. If I'd waited, we'd be so much worse off now. As it stands, Gabriela is making progress, and we should have answers soon." He looked at me, abashed. Although I was pissed with him, I could tell his intentions were good, and he'd done it because he cared. That melted some of the anger away.

"Okay, so my father is the key?" He looked up at me, clearly taken aback that I was still calm.

"Wait. What?"

"I'm angry, but I get why you did what you did. Hopefully, answers will come soon. You're sure…" I trailed off as I saw his concentration lapse; he was still sitting in front of me, but he was no longer with me. He was concentrating on something, but whatever it was it wasn't in my place. "Lucifer, what is it?"

"That was Bee. She needs to see me in Hell. Something has come up." He tensed, and I felt uncertainty flow through him. He stood from the sofa, and I mirrored his actions.

"Go," I said quietly, not knowing what would happen next.

"I don't want to. We said one more night, and if I leave now, I might never see you again. I don't want to step out of this building knowing this it. Knowing that I'll never get a chance to be with the only person I've ever truly loved." His face was etched with sadness, and his normally bright features looked strained.

"Lucifer, I believe what you've told me, I do. But I need

more time to process all of this. I have to figure this out, figure out what I want. I hope you can understand that?"

His shoulders slumped, and a dejected look settled on his face. "Of course, Tess. I'll only be in touch if I hear anything from Gabriela about your father. Please, though, should you need me, just let me know. If you agree to it, I'd like you to leave the link open. It's the quickest way of contact. I promise I won't use it unless you do first."

I nodded. Allowing the link to remain open was the sensible thing to do. Now knowing what I did about Lilith, it would be foolish to refuse it. Plus, the connection between us made me feel safe—protected, somehow. I couldn't explain it.

I watched as, still shirtless, he headed to my front door. I followed him and said, "Wait. Do you want me to go change?"

He turned back to face me as I caught up, standing in front of him. His heated gazed raked over me, desire once more flashing in his eyes. I felt his lust through our link.

"I told you, it looks better on you." He leaned forward, cupping my face with his large, warm hand. I closed my eyes at his touch, aware he would now be able to feel my own desire. He bent forward and whispered in my ear, "I love you, Tess, that's the truth. Whatever happens, I need you to know that." He placed a gentle kiss on my cheek before he moved back. Still cupping my face, he reached up with his thumb and wiped away a tear I hadn't realised I'd shed.

Then he turned and opened the door, not once looking back as he walked out. I felt pain and anguish, and I wasn't sure whose it was. I watched him as he began to disappear from view. I saw Conrath emerge from the shadows in the hall but didn't pay him much attention. Lucifer was my main focus. As he finally faded from view an uneasy feeling settled inside me, one I was sure would be there every time he wasn't by my side.

27

LUCIFER

I RETURNED to Hell to find Bee waiting for me, her face hard and her mouth set into a thin line. She was pissed off, and I wasn't sure I'd like the reason why.

"Where's your shirt?" she asked as she watched me move towards her.

"With Tess. What's this about? You said it was urgent, has Gabriela found something?" I knew the pair had been spending a lot of time with each other. No, Gabriela was to contact me directly, so this had to have been something else, and I had a feeling I wasn't going to like it.

"No, Gabriela has been waiting on some supplies for the next stage in her spell, so she has no answers for us yet," Bee answered.

"Eye of newt hard to come by, is it?" Sarcasm laced my voice. In fairness, Gabriela had done nothing for me to dislike her. It was just the fact that she was a witch that got my hackles up. In this matter, though, she was doing me a favour, so I couldn't be *too* much of a prick.

Bee rolled her eyes at me, but pushed forward without commenting on it. "No, we have a visitor at the gates. Wants to speak directly with you, says it's urgent." Her tone was stern, and I immediately knew I wasn't going to like this.

"Who?"

"He summoned you, so who do you think it is? Levi and I met with him, and he said he wouldn't speak to the monkeys, he wanted the organ grinder. If I wasn't sure it would cause a war, I'd have slit his throat where he stood." The hatred she held for him was evident in her tone. She clenched her fists by her side, and I could see droplets of blood from where her nails had pierced her flesh.

Only a few could elicit such a strong reaction from Bee; one, in particular, sprang to mind. *But what is he doing here?* It had been a long time since I'd seen him, and that was fine with me. Coming here was a bold move on his part. Most conversations between the two sides usually took place on neutral ground, somewhere like Summerland. Summerland was another realm, neutral to both sides, where business was conducted and—if they wanted to—where both sides could mix freely. Mixing wasn't uncommon, and Summerland was the place to do it. There were bars, casinos, restaurants, hotels, stores, and everything else in between. It was a one-stop shop and had everything you could possibly need.

Coming here was *very* bold.

"Is he alone?" I asked Bee as I made my way upstairs to change first.

"No, he's brought a couple of goons with him. His soldiers probably. Can't be friends, since he doesn't have any," I heard her say, as she followed behind me up the stairs and into my room. "Levi is on his way."

After making my way to the closet, I pulled on a new suit, sharp, expensive. I knew he'd have done the same. To him, appearance was everything, despite the impression he tried to portray. Stepping back out, I saw Levi had joined us.

"Ready?" he asked with anticipation.

"Let's go." Both of them followed, and when we stepped outside I outstretched my wings, freeing them from their confinement. "I think we should make an entrance. You know he'll hate it," I said with a huge grin plastered across my face. Bee and Levi both released their wings, and we took off.

We quickly made our way to the gates of Hell, swooping and soaring in the sky. And there he was, waiting for our arrival. He looked pissed, and I couldn't have been happier that he'd had to wait. We landed behind the gates, then we approached the guests.

Abaddon was waiting for us, ready to fight if we needed him to; he was, after all, the first defender of Hell. Taking my time, I approached one of the hellhounds, then stroked under her chin. The hound leaned into my touch, relishing the praise from her master. I moved to the front of the gates, wings still stretched out with Bee and Levi taking position behind me. I gave Abaddon a nod to prepare himself and his people. They weren't visible, but I knew they were there.

Here we go.

The inferno parted as we stepped through the flaming gates. I walked with purpose, flanked by my two most trusted guardians, and friends. I left my wings out behind my back, and I walked until there was a small distance between us. I did not miss the look of disdain on his face, and that made me smile. He hated being here—he'd see it as beneath him—but he was here regardless. Never one to refuse an order, like a good, loyal soldier.

"What can we do for you, Michael?" I said, keeping my voice as collected as I could despite the hatred bubbling in my chest.

"That's Archangel Michael to you, *Lucifer*," he said, nearly spitting my name. Yeah, he was pissed and keeping him waiting had made things worse.

Mission accomplished, I thought to myself.

I shook out my wings allowing the updraft to whip dirt and smoke in his direction. It was a sign of dominance—this was, after all, my domain. I asked, "What do you want?"

"He should have taken your wings—none of you deserve them. I told Him I'd relieve you of them, hack them from your backs with my sword. But in His infinite wisdom, He allowed you to keep them." I felt both Bee and Levi tense at my side at the thought of him taking their wings. By following me, both of them had sacrificed so much—taking their wings was further insult.

Michael stretched his own wings out behind him, as did the two soldiers he'd brought with him. Angel wings were varying shades of white and cream: bright, like the feathers of a dove. Mine had once been white, the most brilliant white of all the angels; Michael hated me for it—amongst other things. Now, though, mine were as black as night, with a red lustre. Bee and Levi also possessed black wings. Each had a different shimmer or appearance, though, making them all unique.

When an angel was cast out from Heaven, they were seen as tainted. As a result, their wings were no longer the angelic shades and instead became darkened by whatever sins they had "committed" to get them cast out. It was an easy way for people to tell who was an angel and who was fallen. I'd never really minded the black, even at the beginning.

"I'll ask again," I said, eyeing the tall, muscular archangel in front of me. "What do you want?"

I studied the figure before me; I was right about him dressing for the occasion, but instead of a suit, he was in his battle gear. Yeah, he was *definitely* trying to send a message. He was exactly as I remembered, taller than me around six-foot-five and slightly more muscular, though not to the same extent as Levi. His armour was strapped to his body, and his sword was tucked away in a scabbard, ready to be unsheathed at a moment's notice. He looked older than me, despite being created at the same time. I'd always hated his floppy, sandy blonde hair that he was continually running his hand through. I would forever take pleasure in reminding him that vanity was a sin, just so I could see him grind his teeth. As we stared each other down, I noticed his bright blue eyes were filled with utter contempt, and that was fine with me—I knew my own looked the same.

After everything that had happened, there was no love lost between the two of us; we'd never liked each other, even from the start. Everyone here knew it, which was why the atmosphere was so tense.

"Come, Brother, no time for pleasantries?" he said, a wicked smile curling his lips.

"We aren't brothers. We never were, not even brothers-in-arms. It must still sting though, to know that I was his favourite, despite everything. He favoured me over you, regardless of how hard you tried." His jaw clenched and he moved his hand slightly to the hilt of his sword. I held up my hand as Bee and Levi took a step towards me. "Come now, Michael, what about the *pleasantries*?" I was enjoying fucking with him far too much.

"I'm here to deliver a message," he spat, seething with so much anger that it rolled off him. "From the Almighty."

"Must be important if he's sent the commander of the Celestial Army to deliver it in person?" I said mockingly, then turned to smirk at both Bee and Levi. They returned my glances with small smiles of their own.

"He knows about your little conquest. Tess, isn't it?" Now it was his turn to be smug.

Motherfucker.

I desperately tried to keep my body calm and my reaction to his words steady, but it was too late. Just hearing him speak Tess's name made my heart beat faster and my muscles flex, ready to attack.

"What of her?" I said, trying to keep my voice free of the rippling anger that flowed through me.

"She must be someone special if you were willing to renege on an agreement? Maybe I'll have to visit her, see what the fuss is all about," he said. He knew exactly what he was fucking doing.

The thought of him even talking to Tess had me struggling to maintain my human form; my dark side pushed to the surface, wanting me to unleash Hellfire against the smug prick who was grinning wickedly in front of me. I knew my eyes had gone dark—they were always the first to turn—but I managed to subdue the rest. Barely.

"Do it, go on. Let him out. It'd be the perfect opportunity for me to take you down." He was goading me, and he was enjoying it.

Lucifer, gather yourself, I heard Bee say through our link. Tearing my eyes away from Michael, I took a few deep breaths to compose myself.

"What's the fucking message?" I growled in his direction.

His wicked smile spread even further across his face as he said, "I'm here to remind you that you have a job to do, and God expects you to fulfil it. If not, there will be trouble."

"Trouble?" I parroted back to him.

"Yes, Brother. In fact, one could say all Hell might break loose."

28

TESS

AFTER LUCIFER HAD LEFT me in my condo, I'd felt a range of emotions surge through the link. I don't think he'd done it on purpose; it was more likely they were too strong for him to contain. And they were bad, very bad.

Trepidation, rage, anxiety, and then back to rage again. Yeah, whatever had happened, the news wasn't good. It worried me, but he hadn't been in touch, so I knew it didn't involve me. In fact, it had been a week since he'd left me wearing his shirt. A week, yet I hadn't heard from him.

He'd kept his word, staying away from me and my place. Not texting or calling, and other than the slight glimmer of emotion that crept through it, he hadn't used our link. He was doing as I'd asked.

So why do I feel so shitty? Like he's abandoned me?

I knew it was irrational; he was doing what I asked. But it hadn't taken me long to realise I didn't like the distance between us, didn't like him not being there. I still had reservations about the whole situation, but my resolve was breaking.

Conrath was still with me, of course, and he never

seemed to leave. I often wondered if he ever slept, as he was always "on duty." I'd have to ask him if his family missed him when he was on missions. *Wait, do demons have families?* Another question I'd have to ask. I'd become accustomed to having him there, a reassuring constant in the craziness that had become my life.

I moved to sit on the bed, pulling on my running shoes and getting my music ready. I needed to clear my head. Again. So, I was heading for a run. Running had always helped me focus, and I'd been doing it a lot. As I still wasn't cleared to head back to my self-defence classes or swimming, running had become my go-to.

Whenever I ran, I tried to work through the jumble of emotions that seemed to have taken root in my chest. My indecisiveness was weighing heavily on me, and everything just seemed to be eating me up inside. I wasn't eating properly and continually feeling sick, all because I didn't know the best course of action. I was worried about every little thing.

I'd just finished tying my shoes when I heard a knock at the door. Making my way out of the bedroom to answer it, I knew it couldn't be any threat—Conrath would have dispatched of that quickly. Maybe it was Lucifer—my heart skipped a beat at the thought, and a surge of excitement gripped my body, causing my cheeks to flush.

I smiled to myself as I looked through the peephole, and the feeling disappeared. It was Bee. *What is she doing here?* Maybe Lucifer had sent her to give me an update, considering I'd asked him to stay away. *One way to find out, I suppose.*

I opened the door, and before I could even speak, she said, "Can I come in?" I looked beyond her to see Conrath in the shadows, watching on in amusement. I didn't answer, but stepped aside, allowing her into my place. She walked past me as I closed the door, moving and taking a seat on the sofa.

"Drink?" I offered, unsure of the appropriate etiquette in this situation.

"No thanks, I won't take up too much of your time," she said calmly. She held a confidence that I'd never seen before—sure of herself and everything she did. I imagined she never second-guessed herself, that she threw herself into everything with conviction.

"Why are you here? Does Lucifer have an update for me?" I tried to keep my voice as calm as I could, but I knew it cracked slightly when I said his name. Something I was aware she caught.

"No, no update as yet. To be honest, Lucifer doesn't know I'm here," she said quietly, as if he could potentially be listening in. She seemed almost at war with herself, the façade of confidence slipping slightly. She steeled herself and carried on. "I want to talk to you about him. Lucifer, that is."

Well, this just became real fucking awkward.

I squirmed where I sat on the couch, not really feeling all that comfortable talking to Bee about my love life with her best friend. "I don't think that's any of your business, Bee." I said it calmly, but I wasn't going to be pushed around by her. No matter who, or what, she was.

Her lips twitched into the finest of smiles that I nearly missed—it disappeared so fast. "It *is* my business. He's my liege, and more importantly, he's my friend." I could hear the fondness for him in her voice. As he'd said though, it didn't strike me as romantic now that I paid closer attention.

"How do you two know each other?" I asked without thinking. The words fell out of my mouth before I could stop them. My curiosity had gotten the better of me.

She sighed heavily as if the memory was still painful. "I followed him, since I'm fallen like he is," she said somberly.

"Fallen?"

"Yes, we were angels once, but then we were stripped of our status and sent to the other side. We became fallen. Lucifer… was the first." Her voice was laced with melancholy. It was clear time had not healed this particular wound. Something in me doubted it ever would.

"What happened? What made them cast you out?" I knew I should stop asking questions, since it was none of my business. But I wanted to know. If I knew Bee's story, then I'd know Lucifer's story.

She looked up at me, and I wondered if she was trying to get the measure of me. "We questioned how things were being undertaken—questioned the fairness of certain decisions that were being made. We refused to toe the line when such atrocities were… Regardless, we started an uprising. Fought against those who followed blindly, but we lost. We were cast out as punishment. I won't tell you Lucifer's story; that is his to share," she said firmly.

I nodded in agreement before asking, "So you were cast out together?"

"No, we were expelled after Lucifer had already gone. But Levi and I followed not too shortly after. More and more angels were shunned. Hell was our punishment, *his* punishment. But we've made it home, made it work for us. You've seen it, it's not too shabby," she said proudly. "Hell is his home, Tess, but it's not who he is. It doesn't define him."

I scoffed, louder than I'd intended, but I didn't understand how she could say that.

"I've known him from the very beginning when he was an angel. His intentions were always good. He lost his way a little when he first fell, became bitter with the cards he'd been dealt, but he's not all bad. Lucifer's not evil, as some would have you believe. He was punished with a role and responsibilities in Hell that he never wanted, but he stepped up and takes those things seriously. Hell isn't what people think it is. It's about punishing those who deserve it, those who have truly sinned."

I didn't miss the sideways glance she gave me, and a shiver ran up my spine. *I* was one of those people. *I* had truly sinned when I'd taken Daniel's life. Trying to cover my unease, I asked, "What does any of this have to do with me?"

Her face softened ever so slightly, and she leaned towards me, bracing her elbows on her knees. "Since Lucifer met you he's been different, more focused and somewhat calmer. Protecting you, *loving you* has changed him. It's made him better, and for that I have to thank you." She looked genuine when she voiced her appreciation.

"Bee, I'm sorry. I can't talk about this with you. I know you know Lucifer, but you don't know me." I felt suddenly awkward in my own skin as I thought back to the information Lucifer had gathered on me. Bee had likely read it and therefore would know me. I wondered how many others had seen my information, *would all of them know everything about me?*

"You're right, I don't know you. But as I said, I know him. And he needs you. I'm not sure what'll happen to him if you leave…"

The thought caused a pang of pain in my chest, but I had to be strong in front of her. "As much as I don't want anything to happen to him, I have to do what's best for me, Bee. You have to understand that."

She nodded her head slowly. "I get it, and that's the right thing to do. But I just wanted you to know a little about him before you made any decisions. I want you to know that none of it was a lie; everything the two of you did and felt was real. I've never seen him as happy as when he talks about you. What you do with all this information is up to you," she said, then rose and quickly headed to the door. "I just thought you should know."

After stepping out of the door, she turned and gave me a small nod before disappearing, leaving me with more questions than answers and even more emotions running through me.

I definitely need that run now.

29

LUCIFER

PAUSING my pacing up and down Levi's office, I turned to see he was sprawled out on one of the antique wingback chairs. His frame dwarfed it, and I was unsure why he'd chosen to sit there when he surely would have been more comfortable on the sofa or behind his desk.

"Are we all prepared? Is everyone ready?" I asked. It was imperative that things progressed quickly, including having the forces amassed and battle ready. A sense of uneasiness had settled low in my stomach, waiting for Lilith's imminent move. It was a feeling I'd never really experienced before a battle, mainly because I'd never really had anything to lose.

I was always hyped up, excited to flex my powers and show the true reach of Hell, but this was different. Now I did have something to lose. Now there was Tess. She was what I was fighting for, and if I lost she would be gone forever. To me, that was unacceptable. A fate worse than death.

Levi smirked as his eyes followed me. "Everything is in place. Will you please *sit* down? Just watching you is making me tired," he laughed.

I let out a deep sigh before sinking into the plush sofa, raking my hand down my face to feel the five-day-old stubble that had overtaken me. I needed to clean up and look sharp—couldn't have everyone knowing how much this was affecting me.

"She's done a real number on you, hasn't she?" Levi's lip quirked into a small smile as he stared me down.

"Fuck off, Levi. It's none of your business," I hissed back at him, a little too harshly. But I wasn't in any mood to joke. The tension inside me had me wound too tightly, and part of me wanted Lilith to strike soon to alleviate it. But I knew that was foolish; that would mean Tess would be in danger, and that was the last thing I'd ever want.

Levi held his hands up in surrender before he said, "Hey, I'm not judging. I know exactly what it's like, don't forget." I saw sadness in his eyes as he thought about her.

Jescha had been his everything. They'd been together for as long as I could remember, and when he chose to follow me, she had followed him. He was cast out first, but it wasn't long before she'd followed him, unable to stay in a place that wouldn't accept her husband. So, despite the pain it cost them both, they remained together in Hell. Until a rogue soul killed her, and broke him in the process. For a long time, Levi was a shell of a man and at one point we thought he'd never recover. Eventually he did, but he was never quite the same Levi again.

"Do you still miss her?" I asked, not wanting to intrude but needing to know how he did it.

"Every second of every day," he said softly, his face becoming sadder. "I thought I'd die when she did, but I carried on, mainly for you and Bee. But… a huge part of me died with her that day, and it's left a gaping void inside me that I know will never truly heal. But I carry on, focus on the good things I have, and push forward."

Levi was right, and we'd all seen how her death had changed him. Ever since then, he wore a mask, one that would cover the deep loss. It was a mask I'd come to wear myself. I understood the feelings he'd expressed, but mine were different.

Jescha was gone forever. We'd looked at possibilities to bring her back, but it turned out to be impossible. Levi would no longer be able to gaze into his wife's face, never be able to touch her skin, kiss her lips, or make love to her. He couldn't, because she'd been ripped from his grasp.

Tess was still here. I don't know if that made it worse. I knew that she was still here, but that she didn't want me. If I wanted to see her, I'd have to watch from afar. I could no longer touch her, kiss her full lips, or feel her curves pressed against my body. No, if Tess didn't want me, I'd have to watch her eventually fall in love with someone else, watch her marry someone else, and watch her start a family with someone else. The thought tore at my insides like a predator ripping into its prey.

What a pair we were: the love of his life stolen from his grasp forever, mine refusing to have anything to do with me, despite my best efforts.

"How do you do it? Push forward without her?" I had to ask. I needed to know how to go on with life without Tess. It was looking more likely that that was what the future held for me.

"You take each day at a time. It's the only way to do it. If you try not to focus on the future too much, every day is a tiny little victory. That's the only way I can do it. Don't give up on her yet though, Lucifer. I think she'll come around. You can be quite the charming bastard when you want to be." He snorted as he threw his head back.

Unable to join his laughter, I decided to be honest with him. "I don't think I can lose her, Levi. She's part of me now, and I need her like I've never needed anything before in my life. If anything were to happen to her…" Just the thought of her bright emerald eyes being extinguished tightened my chest further.

"Hey, nothing is going to happen to her. We've got this. *You've* got this. I've been telling you for years, though, that we need to take care of Lilith, and I hope now you realise there's only one way this ends." He shot me a knowing glance but didn't lord it over me—at least not too much.

"As soon as we find her, she'll be taken care of. Lilith isn't my concern, however. Michael is. You know the smug prick won't let this lie. If he had any inclination as to how special Tess was, he'd have pushed for action." *I hate him, the self-righteous bastard.*

"He can't make a move without permission, and I very much doubt he'll get it. God doesn't want a war, Lucifer, no matter how much Michael tries to convince him otherwise." He rose from the too-small chair and stretched his back. "What the fuck was the battle gear for by the way? A bit over the top, don't you think?"

"Oh he was definitely trying to send a message; shame no one was listening," I said with a laugh, and he joined in shaking his head in amusement. "He looked like an idiot. I think his little show of dominance completely backfired."

"Regardless, there is no need for anyone to be worried about Hell. Things are running smoothly. We've had no major issues for years—we're a well-oiled machine, which makes things worse for Michael. To know we're succeeding in our "punishment"—thriving, in fact—when he wanted us to suffer. That will just anger him all the more." A gleam of smugness flashed across his features as he thought back to the look of rage on Michael's face. I had to admit, I'd felt the same. "In all seriousness though, if you need time to sort anything out, Bee and I can deal with things here. It's important you take time, Lucifer."

I nodded my thanks in his direction.

Time I have plenty of. But time with Tess, that I don't have.

30

LILITH

Finally, everything was falling into place. My time laying low was nearly over. I was fully recovered and feeling strong. Matthew had been fetching me the best that New York had to offer, and I was taking everything they had to give.

Now at full strength, I was almost ready to bring things to a close. In particular, that little bitch's life. Louis's new piece of ass had been a thorn in my side for far too long and I was done playing nice. Once she was gone, Louis would be mine again. We could rule together, now that he was clearly ready to commit.

I was still annoyed that he'd come to her rescue and treated me so despicably. Although, if he wanted to keep her I suppose he'd have to keep up appearances, even if it was just for her benefit. She seemed different, though, and I couldn't get a read on her. Her blood smelled different—there was a slight sweetness to it that had me thinking she wasn't completely human. Maybe that was what Louis wanted with her. Perhaps he needed her for something and wanted to stay on her good side.

I was curious about her, but not enough to let her live.

Anyway, I'd soon take the matter out of his hands, and I'd enjoy every single second of it. Things were already in motion. The plan was progressing as I'd hoped it would.

Matthew had done an outstanding job preparing Tess's temporary prison, and had sourced a witch with a personal grudge against my Louis, and the tramp. The witch had pledged her fealty to me and assured us our location would be sufficiently warded; Louis wouldn't be able to find either her or us. Once she was here, I was free to do as I pleased, without repercussions.

The witch had told us she was keen to stick around and help us in anything we needed, particularly if we wanted to make our new little friend suffer. Serena was ruthless, and I liked her.

Louis had people looking for me, but Serena's ward kept us safe. He had eyes all over the world, and so did I. Naturally, that meant we both also had people watching Tess, and anyone she was close to. I'd already managed to snuff out someone close to her, made her watch. A wicked smile curved my lips as I thought back to the genuine look of terror on her face—poor baby.

I stalked through the building, checking in on the state of the prison—it was filthy, cold, and damp, which meant it was perfect. Looking at the cell that would hold our guest, I pulled out my phone and dialed the number. "How long?"

"I'll be with you in ten minutes, my Queen," Matthew said down the line.

I quickly hung up and made my way to wait for our new arrival. Pacing up and down, I quirked a brow as I thought of the look on everyone's faces when I took my place next to Louis. Bee would be pissed. She'd always hated me because of Louis's feelings for me. I knew she wanted him for herself, but she was no match for such a man. Neither she, nor his little British tramp, were worthy. I was though—my power matched his own, and he *chose* me all those years ago.

The witch was waiting in the cell, and everyone else was in place. It was showtime.

I knew our guest wouldn't be conscious when she arrived, but I still wanted to be there and give her a proper welcome. It was, after all, only polite to welcome someone into your home, even if you were eventually going to rip their throat out.

I watched as the car drove up with Matthew at the wheel. He pulled to a stop in front of me, and then climbed out of the car smoothly. I hadn't wanted him to fade. I'd need him at full strength when I visited Louis. So, he'd used the car he'd stolen to blend in. We both made our way to the boot, and he popped it open.

And there she was.

I cupped his face, pulling him in for a firm kiss. "You've done well. You will be rewarded greatly," I whispered into his ear. His eyes flashed blood red with the thought of more sex. I could tell from our kiss that he'd fed on her—I could taste her blood on his lips. I didn't really care what happened to her. She was a means to an end.

Matthew dipped his head. "Anything for you, my Queen." He meant it; Matthew would do anything for me. He'd proven himself a thousand times over. That was why I kept him so close, and I enjoyed everything he had to give me. At least, I would until Louis returned, then I'd probably have to kill him.

"Bring her," I commanded.

He slipped his arms under the lifeless body and threw her over his shoulder. Carrying the dead weight behind him like a ragdoll, he followed me through the plush living space and down the cold concrete stairs until we arrived in the basement. Pushing our way through the door, we found Serena waiting for us.

She rushed over to the motionless body dangling behind Matthew, giving her the once over.

"Make sure she doesn't wake yet," I said, eyeing her as she began an incantation while focusing all her energy on the woman. I pushed open one of the cells for Matthew to enter. He flopped her onto the hard slab, raised slightly off the floor. Serena continued her spell. Once done, we all stepped back, looking down at the pathetic human in front of us.

They were so fragile, expendable, useless. They were simply food. They held no other purpose.

Removing my phone once again, I snapped a shot of the lifeless body, careful to capture the puncture wounds in her neck. It wasn't the best picture, but it got the message across. I quickly typed out the message before clicking send. I knew my phone would immediately start to ring. It was inevitable.

Sure enough, the phone vibrated in my hand.

"Who's this?" I said casually.

"You know fine fucking well who this is. What do you want?" the voice spat.

"I hardly think there is any need for that tone. You know exactly what I want, and you're going to give it to me. Aren't you, Tess?"

I knew she would try and save her little blonde friend. After her reaction to seeing the old man die, I knew that her friends would be the way to get to her. Looking down at Emma's pale, motionless body, I couldn't think why Tess would want to save her. But I didn't care. She would try, and then she'd be mine.

"What do you want me to do?" she said in a defeated voice.

"Thatta girl, Tess. Nice to know you can follow orders from someone more superior. Shame, it won't save you."

"Just tell me what you want, you crazy bitch," she replied, her voice laced with absolute hatred.

It fed my own hatred, but I wouldn't let her know that, not until she was in front of me. "Now, now, where are your manners? Keep your phone close. We'll be in touch shortly." And with that—still able to hear her protests—I hung up.

Stepping to grab the unconscious woman by the cheeks, I turned her face to the side and studied it. *Pretty enough, I suppose, in an obvious kind of way.* After this was all done, I'd let Matthew have her. Whether he killed her or not, I didn't really care. He might have some fun with her first, fuck her, compel her, and make her kill herself. She'd served her purpose, and now Tess would come.

Soon.

31

TESS

It had been over twenty-four hours since Lilith had contacted me and told me she had Emma in some dingy cell. My blood had boiled when I got the photo. She was a sneaky little fucker, but it wouldn't help her in the end. I'd kill her for hurting the people that mattered to me. I had a new sense of purpose, and that was to wipe that grin right off her old-as-fuck face.

I hadn't told anyone about Emma, or the call. I knew I couldn't, so I'd stayed inside, avoiding Conrath and anyone else who could pick up on my agitation and rage. I knew Lucifer could feel it, but keeping to his word he hadn't contacted me.

I wondered how they'd gotten to Emma, but once I journeyed down that rabbit hole it wasn't hard to figure out. Emma had been having a tough time since Jerry's death. She'd struggled with her emotions and had been finding solace in tequila and one-night stands.

I felt guilty that I hadn't been more available for her—don't get me wrong I was there, just not really present. I had my own shit that I was wading through and hadn't given her everything she needed. And now she was gone, bait in what I knew was a fucking trap. But what else could I do? I had no choice but to sit and wait for Lilith to call. I'd lost Jerry—there was absolutely no way I was losing Emma too.

It was late, and I sat curled up on the sofa, sipping coffee in a bid to keep the exhaustion at bay. I'd hardly slept. I was too worried and too scared that I would sleep through Lilith's call and seal Emma's fate. Time seemed to pass so slowly as all of the terrible things that could be happening to Emma floated through my head. She could be dead already, and I would have no clue.

When my phone buzzed to life next to me I jumped, spilling the coffee on the sofa. It was an unknown number, so I immediately knew this was it. On closer inspection, I saw it was a video call. An unease crawled over my skin, causing the hairs on my arms and back of my neck to stand on end. Taking a deep breath in a bid to compose myself, I answered.

Lilith's grinning face filled the screen and made me immediately want to punch it. She looked smug, and a wide smile was fixed on her pale but beautiful face. "Ahh, Tess," she cooed. "So nice to see you again."

"What the fuck do you want, Lilith?" I spat my words with venom.

"Now, now. I have your friend here, so surely you should be nicer to me. Remember, I could kill her in seconds." I didn't think it was possible for her smile to widen, but it did, and she was now grinning like a Cheshire cat.

"For all I know, you've already killed her."

"I assure you, your friend is still very much alive… for now." She spun the camera without hesitation, focusing on an unconscious figure sprawled out on a large concrete slab. I couldn't make out Emma's face, but the camera jostled as it moved closer to the figure, and her face was roughly turned, showing sunken eyes and a pale complexion. I could see the puncture wounds on Emma's neck and the trickles of dried blood where they had fed on her. My blood once more boiled, the rage rolling off me in waves.

The phone was turned back around, and Lilith's face once more filled the screen. "I'm going to send you an address. Go there now, and wait for further instructions," she said matter-of-factly.

"But, I have surveillance, and they'll know if something is off." I reasoned.

"Tell them you are heading to a club to meet your little blonde friend there, and wear something appropriate. We'll deal with the rest." Her voice was filled with arrogance. She was positive her people would have the upper hand against the team protecting me.

"Don't hurt any of them or I swear to God I'll—"

"You swear you'll what? Tell me, child, what do you plan on doing against a full nest of vampires?" She was enjoying this far too much, but I wouldn't give her the satisfaction of a response. "You are in no place to make any demands. Come to the address *now*. If you aren't there in an hour, your friend will be passed around my children. I suggest you hurry." Before I even had the chance to reply, the bitch hung up on me.

Fuck. Fuck. I moved quicker than I ever had, changing into some skin-tight jeans and a sexy camisole top. I had to look the part, but I still wanted to be able to move if I needed to fight; a dress wouldn't really give me the range of movement I'd need to, hopefully, kick some ass. I pulled my hair into a messy bun and quickly put some make-up on. After grabbing my boots and jacket, I headed to the front door.

I took a steadying breath. I had to sound confident in what I was saying, or I knew Conrath would see right through me. When I stepped out, I saw him immediately emerge from the shadows. "Heading out, Tess?" His voice seemed a little surprised that I was venturing out this late; after all, this wasn't a regular occurrence.

Come on. You can sell this. "Yeah, Em just called. She's out and sounds a bit, how do I put this nicely… incapacitated." I raised my eyebrows in a knowing look, and he smiled as he quickly caught on.

"As soon as she's safe I'll bring her back here, let her sleep it off. But I need to go get her, she's not been herself since Jerry…" I lowered my gaze as I continued walking, but I saw him nod in understanding.

We made our way across the city. All the while my heart beat hard in my chest—the anticipation of what was to come wracked my body, setting my nerves on edge. Pulling up outside the busy and very seedy-looking nightclub, Conrath turned to me, quirking an eyebrow. "She's in there?"

I nodded as I stepped out onto the sidewalk, assessing the shithole in front of me. Lilith had picked a lovely spot for it. Shady and dark, perfect for a fight between dark forces. My phone rang in my hand, and I quickly answered it.

"Make your way through the club to the staff-only area. Go now." It wasn't Lilith, but I knew I should follow the instructions. I motioned to Conrath, who immediately began to follow me.

"It's Em, she's out back. She's friends with one of the bar staff who said she could sit out back where it's quiet." As I walked, Conrath followed me. I knew he wouldn't stay put, so I had to make this convincing. Keeping the phone close to my ear, I listened for further instructions while we moved towards the staff-area door. Once there, I turned to Conrath.

"I've got this. You can stay here, grab a drink." I motioned towards the bar, hoping he would heed my advice; I didn't want anything to happen to him, and I thought this was a possible way to avoid it.

He shook his head like I knew he would. "Wherever you go, I go."

I turned away as I forced my eyes shut, inwardly apologising to him for whatever was about to happen. I pushed through the door to an empty corridor with several doors branching off. There was no one here, though—we seemed to be alone.

"Head down the corridor to the back of the club. There's a loading area outside. We'll be waiting for you there." And then the phone went dead. I shoved the phone into my clutch and turned to Conrath.

"Apparently Em's outside getting some fresh air." He seemed tense like he wasn't buying the bullshit I was selling, but he didn't question me. We carried on, looking through empty doorways as we walked. Then we emerged out into the loading area to find it completely empty. Not a soul was there.

"Tess, get behind me *now!*" I could hear the panic erupt in his words as he tried to take a step towards me. He was abruptly stopped by an unknown, invisible force that made his eyes bulge and breath seemingly get caught in his lungs.

A scream tore from me as I watched him collapse to the floor in a heap. I made a move towards him but was stopped by a familiar-looking woman. I didn't know her, and I knew I'd never met her, but I got the impression she knew me—there was something about her that I just couldn't put my finger on.

"I wouldn't do that if I were you," she warned. I suddenly became aware that I was surrounded and as I turned to study my whereabouts found I was indeed encircled by a group of red-eyed, fanged creatures. Vampires. As I looked around, I noticed Lilith was very much absent. I should have known that she wouldn't come herself. Of course, she wouldn't.

"Is he dead?" I asked the familiar woman.

"Not yet. Whether he lives or dies depends on how cooperative you intend to be," she replied, her voice calm and collected.

"If you let him live, I'll do whatever you want."

A tall, broad-shouldered vampire stepped forward from the circle, moving towards me with purpose, and I did my best not to flinch or react. Despite my best efforts, I knew my heart was beating so hard that he could probably fucking hear it. "Ms. Adams, if you'd take my hand." He reached out his inordinately bony and slender hand. It was almost skeletal.

I thought about all the possible options, but there was only one. To save Emma, and now Conrath, I had to go with them. There was nothing else I could do.

I jumped when several demons burst through the door and more filtered in through the loading area. The vampires broke off from the circle, and the two sides clashed. I knew that Conrath was never alone in watching me—Lucifer had told me as much—but I hadn't realised the sheer number of other demons that shadowed me.

Bodies clashed, screams echoed, and blood spurted. But before I could see too much the vampire in front of moved closer, stretching out his hand.

Before I reached out, I focused all my energy and I said through the link, *I'm so sorry, don't blame Conrath.*

Before he had a chance to reply, I took hold of the hand that had remained outstretched in front of me.

32

LUCIFER

Tess? Tess? Can you hear me? Answer me, Tess!

I tried and tried to desperately reach her through the link, but it was pointless. I knew it. The link was gone—not closed, but muffled. I knew she was alive, but that was the extent of it.

My liege, she's gone, Conrath said though his own link. I'd known before he told me. I could feel her ripped from my grasp, and Lilith had her.

Using my powers, I honed in on Conrath's location and portaled there immediately. It was a seedy-looking night club, and I wondered just what Tess had been doing there. I scoured the loading area and found him, seemingly paralysed on the floor, whilst other demons and fallen tended to each other.

Conrath, what happened? Why are you here? I leaned over him, studying his face as he looked up at me.

She told me Emma was here. Got a phone call and said Emma needed picking up. Tess told me it was Emma, but it turned out to be Lilith's people. Something is wrong, Sir. His eyes flickered, and his fingers twitched. Whatever had been done to him, it was wearing off, and he was starting to regain his faculties.

Levi, Bee, does anyone have eyes on Emma? Find out immediately. They both acknowledged the request, but it was Levi who answered first.

Emma's gone, and her apartment is empty. It looks like they grabbed Emma from here, there are signs of a struggle. What's going on?

Lilith has Tess. Get to my location now. Both of you.

It was mere seconds before they both stalked into the loading bay to find our injured people littered amongst the space, Conrath now sitting up and leaning against some concrete steps, with me pacing furiously.

"What the fuck happened?" Bee spat at Conrath. I shared her anger, but deep down I knew it wasn't his fault. Tess had told me as much before she was ripped away.

"This isn't on him, Bee. Tess lied to him, and before he could react, he was surrounded," I said, trying my best not to let my emotions seep into my words. "We all know Tess can be stubborn when she wants to be. My guess is that they took Emma as a means of getting to Tess. You all know how loyal she is. She's fiercely protective of those she cares for." It was admirable—stupid in this instance, but admirable.

"Conrath, tell us everything that happened. *Everything.*" I needed to know every minute detail so I could figure just what to do next. How the fuck was I supposed to find her? I knew Lilith would have Tess well protected, and that she would draw out Tess's death in a bid to punish us both.

The three of us listened intently to everything Conrath had to say, filling us in on the call, the ambush, and the ones that had taken her. "Sir, there's something else you should know," Conrath said uneasily.

"Go on," I prompted.

"It was a witch who incapacitated me. Serena Albu. She's working with Lilith. She has to be." Conrath's gaze flittered between the three of us, but it had settled on Levi when he finally spoke.

"Why would she ally herself with Lilith? Why would she be that stupid?" Levi said, genuinely amused. A slight familiarity struck me, but I couldn't quite place it. It was Bee who provided clarity.

"Because Lucifer fucked with her older sister. Serena is Blair Albu's sister," Bee said, shaking her head. I recognised the name, but I was at a total loss as to what exactly I'd done.

Have I literally fucked her? Offended her in some way, sided with someone else? I'm at a loss.

"You two are useless," Bee said glaring at the two of us in utter dismay. "Blair Albu is the witch that interfered with you and Tess. You made an example of her, sentenced her to six hundred years in Envy, "for her insolence," if I remember correctly."

Fuck.

"Serena will suffer a worse fate than six hundred years. Her betrayal will result in her death. It will be long, painful, and I might make Blair watch. Maybe I'll make one of them kill the other. Who knows." I had already been livid, and now I was ready to shift and struggled to contain my inner dark side.

"Conrath, how did they leave? Did they take her in a car? How?" Levi asked the demon, who had now risen to his feet, though he still looked shaky.

He shook his head. "Those we didn't kill just disappeared into the darkness, but whoever had Tess faded her out. She was gone in an instant. Sir, I understand you need to punish me. I deserve that, I know, but I care for Tess. I'll accept anything you deem appropriate, but please let me help bring her back. Bring her home," he said. His tone was adamant and resolute. It was a plea; he wanted to ensure she was safe, and I was grateful for that. I nodded my head in his direction.

"I want everyone on this, *everyone* we can spare looking for her. I expect everything to be fully investigated, even the whispers. I will not sit and wait for her body to turn up."

"It won't come to that, Lucifer. We'll get to her." Bee gave my arm a reassuring squeeze, and she was sure we would find Tess. I no longer shared her certainty on the matter. Now Lilith had Tess she wouldn't hesitate to kill her. A sick feeling had settled into my stomach. It was the gnawing pain that I might have already lost her, that I may never see her again. The thought broke me a little, and I had to steady myself.

"Do we have any allies with the vampires? Anyone who can get us any information? We could make it lucrative for them to betray their queen. After all, the hierarchy of the vampires will be changing as soon as I get my hands on Lilith."

"I'll look into it, see what I can find out," Bee said. "Levi has to go get the army ready to attack. I'll head to the vampires and express our… displeasure. I know a lot of them don't agree with going against you, even if it was ordered by their queen."

I nodded a silent thanks in her direction, one that didn't need to be uttered. She knew how much Tess meant to me—they both did. As a result, they would do whatever they could to ensure she was returned safely. I was doubtful that would happen, and it felt like a small part of me had already started to grieve. But I wouldn't let it consume me. I wouldn't let the grief overcome me until I saw her body, though I hoped that would never become a reality.

"I want regular updates and to know about any developments immediately."

I made my way to the closest door and opened a portal to Hell. "Let's go. We have an army to prepare."

33

TESS

I was dead. I had to be. The pain rooted in my very bones was so intense it could only have been caused by death, I was sure of it. If I opened my eyes I'd be in Hell, and Lucifer would be watching over me. At least there was that saving grace, knowing I would see him.

So, I readied myself, pushed my fears as deep down as possible, and focused the little energy I had. I forced my eyes open, taking a few seconds to blink and take in my surroundings. It was dark and dreary. *Yeah, I'm in Hell.* But Lucifer wasn't here—maybe he didn't know yet. Slowly pushing myself up from the concrete slab I was lying on, I cautiously looked out in front of me at my surroundings. Yeah, it was fucking bleak, and it was a cell. All grey concrete with a bucket in the corner. Metal bars kept me separate from the rest of the dark, damp space.

Hang on, it's damp. Hell wasn't damp, it was arid and red hot. This wasn't Hell, it couldn't be. I tentatively got to my feet, and then moved towards the metal bars to see if I could make out anything beyond them. I tried my hardest to focus, but the pain was too much.

Lucifer, can you hear me? Please hear me.

There was something, but I couldn't make it out. It was like someone was talking underwater: gargled noises that I couldn't understand, like my ears were stuffed with wool and someone was talking to me. I'd keep trying, but wherever I was, I was alone.

I reached my hands out to the bars, though as soon as they got close a crackle erupted from the metal; I snatched my hand back to avoid getting struck by whatever the hell it was. Yeah, this place was definitely fucking creepy.

Turning to head back to the concrete slab, I noticed there was another cell attached to my own. A lifeless figure lay curled up, facing away from where I stood. I ran over to the slab, instinctively pushing my hands towards the bar and the comatose person on the other side. My hands slid through the bars with no shock or sparks. Clearly their only concern was keeping us in and they didn't care about us interacting with each other.

I pulled the person's shoulder, turning them so they were flat on their back. *Emma.* She looked like she was an inch from death. Her normally bright blonde hair looked dull and matted, her bangs were stuck to her forehead, and her cheeks were pale and void of any colour. She looked grey, and her skin was waxy. She couldn't have been here for long, but they'd already caused her significant harm.

I stroked her face as best I could through the bars, but her skin felt like ice. I needed to check her pulse to ensure she was still alive; she certainly didn't look it. I moved my hand to her neck, trying to tilt it to get a good angle to find her pulse—that was when I saw the puncture wounds.

I moved my hand father across Emma's neck and down her collarbone to her chest, and I saw that she was *covered* in puncture wounds, not just the one set I'd seen before. When

Lilith had sent me the photo of Emma, passed out on the slab, she'd been careful to ensure the two perfectly round holes nestled in Emma's tanned skin were visible.

When I saw the picture of Emma, it had made a sense of rage spread through my body. But now, now I wanted to burn Lilith, and all those responsible to the ground. They'd been using her like a fucking buffet. Dried blood had stained Emma's clothes where it had spread from the fuckers feeding on her.

My hands shook as I traced back up her neck in an attempt to find a pulse. I was no longer sure that I'd find one. Especially seeing the state of her skin. I held my breath as I searched for the spot on her neck where her pulse should be. I searched and searched, and then suddenly there it was, the smallest, weakest pulse I'd ever felt.

I let out a sob. *Thank fuck*. She was still alive, but for how much longer I had no idea. It was then I heard the scraping metal of a heavy door and footsteps approaching my cell; I held on to Emma's hand protectively.

"Ah, I see you've found your little friend," Lilith said, amusement clearly lacing her words. The bitch was enjoying every single second of this.

"When I get out of this cell I'm going to kill you. Send you back to whatever fucking hole you crawled out of, you delusional bitch."

She laughed, which only enraged me more. "Now, now. Try not to get too worked up. I think—had we met in different circumstances—we could have been friends. You're feisty, and I like that." The look on her face told me she was deadly serious.

"Lucifer likes it too—that's why he enjoys the sex so much." I did my best to keep my voice relaxed and calm. I knew it wasn't smart to provoke her, but in all honesty, at that moment I didn't fucking care. I wanted to hurt her, push her, fucking kill her. So, I carried on, "He particularly likes it when—"

"You're a plaything to him, nothing more." Yeah, Lilith was pissed, and I knew I was on the right track. Maybe if I pushed her far enough, she'd make a mistake.

"Can't you see? He doesn't *want* you. He's moved on. Maybe you should too, because at the minute you're coming off as a pathetic old hag. I'm pretty sure he doesn't find that attractive." I stood, crossing my arms, then moved to stand directly opposite her. I wouldn't be intimidated by her, despite knowing what she was.

"When I kill you, I'll bring him your head as a sign of my devotion. He's not here to save you this time." She walked closer to where I stood, and steely determination was etched across her face.

"I don't need anyone to fucking save me, Lilith. I took care of the last threat you sent to get rid of me just fine." I stared her down, not letting myself cower away.

"What?" she said, uncertainty clear in her voice.

"Daniel. I took care of Daniel."

"You expect me to believe *you* killed him? We both know Lucifer did." She seemed surprised, and I was sure she didn't believe me. At that moment, one of the vampires that flanked her spoke.

"Your Majesty, if this is indeed the case we can't just kill her," he said meekly, and without looking her in the eyes.

"What?" she spat in his direction. "Why?" She rounded on the vampire, hands now on her hips.

"If she did kill her ex, as she claims, then she has sinned." Lilith still looked perplexed, like she hadn't understood what that meant. It was lost on me too. "If she has sinned like that, when we kill her she'll go straight to Hell… straight to Lucifer."

She tensed, and I instinctively started to worry. It was inevitable that I'd die, but now I didn't know what would happen. She sighed and whispered something to the vampire, who hurriedly left the room. Then, she spun to face me again, clearly more pissed off with my revelation than she had been before.

"Tess, it turns out you are quite the pain in my ass. Not only have you managed to seduce my Louis, but you continue to be a thorn in my side. Not to worry, though, we'll find a way." Before I could bite back, the male vampire returned with the familiar-looking woman from earlier.

"Serena, it seems we have a problem. Tess here has committed the ultimate sin. Therefore, if we kill her, she'll go straight to Hell, which is obviously not what any of us want. Do you have any suggestions? Is there a spell we can use to bind her soul? Or can we just—I don't know—push her through a black hole?" She fixed a sickly smile on me, clearly enjoying the thought.

The woman, Serena, looked me up and down with a sense of disgust. "There are many things we could do, but unfortunately they all take time—which we do not have. If you want her gone completely, the easiest way would be to turn her and then kill her. After all, when a vampire dies, their soul is gone. That would be my suggestion. Turning her would be the quickest option." She appeared different from Lilith's followers, and she didn't fawn over the queen as the others did. She was here for her own reasons, closely aligned to Lilith's no doubt, but not as clear cut.

"Thank you, Serena, an excellent idea. Louis won't appreciate me turning her before she dies, but he's not here so…"

Lucifer, if you can hear me, now would be a pretty good time to make an appearance. There was still no response. The muffled sounds continued through the link, but I couldn't push past that barrier.

Just you, Tess, I thought to myself.

"It won't take long for me to drain you. I wonder, do you taste as sweet as you smell?" she purred.

"I don't know, why don't you ask Lucifer next time you see him?" Quirking my lip into a wicked smile, I watched as the anger pulsed through her. She moved in a blur and pushed up against the bars, her touch causing them to crackle and spark.

"Serena, release the wards. *Now!*" The witch moved to Lilith's side and began babbling words that I didn't recognise. Tiny strands of silver light slithered from her fingertips and began to weave themselves around the bars, breaking down whatever invisible force had been in place. Then it was done. Lilith barged forward, slamming the cell door open with a clunk of metal on metal.

I should have backed up, shied away from the dominant force closing in on me, but that was what she wanted, and I wouldn't give her the satisfaction. So, I stood firm as she snaked her hand around my throat, gripped tightly, and lifted me from the floor. The pressure crushed my airway, making it nearly impossible to breathe. I clawed at her hand, desperately trying to get some purchase, break her grip, something, *anything* to relieve the pressure.

"Your Majesty, we can't kill her." I heard someone say. I was unsure who it was, since my blurring vision was fixed on Lilith. As if regaining her composure and snapping out of the rage that had consumed her, she slackened her grip and allowed my feet to touch the floor. She forced my head to one side, exposing my neck, and I knew what was about to happen.

"This is going to be very painful—I'm going to make sure of it," she whispered. I watched her features harden. Her eyes were a bright crimson, and as she opened her mouth I watched her fangs elongate. They looked razor-sharp, like they would tear into my neck with little effort. I tried to control the erratically fast pounding in my chest and show defiance, but I knew I was failing because I was terrified.

She smiled, clearly picking up on the feelings that surged through me. She leaned forward slowly and licked over my neck. "Ready?" she asked. I didn't answer, I *couldn't* answer.

Then there was searing pain. I felt her fangs rip into my flesh. She didn't puncture my skin with her fangs, she tore through it. She was right, it fucking hurt and my body tensed, silently screaming at the assault. I knew the pain was vibrating through my link to Lucifer and I couldn't help but wonder if he could feel it. After the damage was done I felt her mouth latch onto the wound and draw my blood into her mouth. It was a strange sensation—almost intimate, if it wasn't for the pain still coursing through me.

"What the fuck?" Lilith pulled away from me and, still holding my throat, thrust me out in front of her so she could study me. My blood covered her mouth and chin, but I was distracted by the absolute look of shock that was plastered across her face. "Does he know? Does he know what you *are?*" she questioned, panic in her voice.

I couldn't reply because the pain had rendered me unable. I worked hard to get a grip on it, but before I could answer, she screamed, "Does he know?" She watched me as I tried to muster the strength to speak, ask her exactly what she was talking about. "*You* don't know do you? You have no idea what you are? Oh, this is too perfect."

She let out a cackle before she once more pulled me close, tilting my neck to one side. "That explains why your blood smells so good—and why it tastes even better," she said as she licked the blood from my neck. She once more latched on and began to draw my blood through the wound, letting out little moans with every surge of blood that filled her mouth.

My eyes became heavy, my limbs began to feel like lead,

and I sagged against her. I felt her smile against my skin while she drained the life from my veins. This couldn't be it. I couldn't die like this. I *refused* to die like this.

I concentrated on what little energy I had left, focused it within me and tried to rally it into action. I had to fight. I was a stubborn bitch, and I'd told Lilith she wouldn't kill me. I *couldn't* let her win.

I thought of Lucifer and that I'd never see him again. That I'd never be able to tell him how I felt and what I *really* wanted. The energy inside me swelled at the thought of him, it became fortified with a desire to see him again. I felt myself surge—I wasn't sure what it was, but it felt powerful. Unsure if it was coming from me or from Lilith, I just tried to latch onto it, bolster it to become something tangible that I could use.

Lucifer, I need you. I need you now. Come to me.

I forced the words down the link, over and over as the power continued to pulse through me. When it felt like I couldn't contain it anymore, like it would tear me apart from the inside, I released it.

I suddenly hit the hard concrete floor, no longer in Lilith's grasp. In fact, she wasn't even in the cell with me. The force of whatever had happened had knocked her on her ass, and she was slumped on the floor outside, surrounded by the other vampires, who had apparently rushed to her aid. Those who weren't assisting Lilith had their eyes focused on me. What was that: fear, awe, both? The looks on their faces had me questioning just exactly what had happened, but before I could dwell on it too much, I heard him.

"Tess? Tess, where are you?" he said frantically.

Lucifer. He was here. But how?

He was in the room, flanked by Bee, Conrath, someone who looked like an actual giant, and so many others. His eyes darted around the room before they landed on me.

It was at that moment I realised he was about to unleash the true power of Hell. *Oh, Lilith, you're fucked.*

34

LUCIFER

I heard her. Tess.

Whatever had been blocking the link came crashing down, and her voice was like a scream through the link. Along with her voice was a sense of bone-deep pain.

Fuck. I have to get to her.

Hovering my hand on the door handle, I focused all my energy, every thought, every fibre of my being solely on Tess. Her silky auburn hair, her emerald-green eyes, the luscious fullness of her lips, the curves of her body, her infectious laugh, the way she made me feel alive, and the magnitude of the love I felt for her. Concentrating on all of that, I pushed the door open and emerged into a dreary, dark room; it appeared to be a basement of some kind.

Without hesitation, I ran in, followed by what felt like most of Hell. I skidded to a halt when I saw a flash, and then Lilith fly across the floor before landing with a dull thud. Her people immediately surrounded her, but my eyes continued to search the room, desperately seeking Tess out. It felt like an eternity, but then our eyes met.

Thank fuck she's still alive. I studied her. She was slumped on the floor in a cell. Caged like a fucking animal. My fists clenched uncontrollably as I struggled to contain my dark side. I'd let it out soon enough, but first I needed to check her, make sure she was safe. She looked pale; then I noticed the blood that coated her neck. Her hair was slick with it, and it was sticking to the gaping wound on her neck. She was seated in a pool of her own blood, and my heart clenched at the sight.

I took a step towards the cell, wanting to get her and make sure she was safe. I needed her out of that fucking cage and away from the threats in the room. But I was stopped by an all-too-familiar voice. My path to Tess was suddenly blocked by a group of vampires with Lilith at the front, looking a little shaken but trying her best to hide it.

"How did you find us? This place is warded," Lilith spat in my direction, casting a quick glance to a woman who stood at the edge of the room.

In all honesty, I had absolutely no clue *how* we'd gotten there. The only explanation I could think of was that it had something to do with my link to Tess. But I had no intention of relaying that information to Lilith. So, I said, "Turns out your allies aren't as capable as you think they are, Lilith." I glared at the woman I assumed was the witch. "You best hope you die here today, Serena. It will be easier than the things I have planned for you." Her face paled, and her mouth bobbed open and shut repeatedly. "Save it," I said coldly.

"Tess, are you okay?" I called over to her, ignoring everyone else in the room and focusing solely on her. She slowly raised her eyes to me, and she was about to speak before she was cut off.

"She is no longer your concern, Louis. She'll be dead soon enough, and then we can be together again, now that you're ready to commit." Her voice was full of longing, and I could see it in her gaze, which raked over my body with desire.

"Lilith, I don't know how many times I can say this: we will never be together. I don't want you. I never have." Keeping my tone firm, I stared her down, no hint of anything other than contempt.

"Come now, Louis, she's nearly dead anyway. You don't have to keep up the pretence anymore. Tell her you love me, tell her that it's *always* been me—that's why you seduced me away all those years ago. Because you wanted an equal, someone who you knew could be just as dark as you. You know I do whatever it takes. You saw it back then and you see it now." She was actually fucking delusional—she believed every single word that she spouted.

Bee leaned closer to me and muttered, "Good pick with that one. Really stable." I could hear the disdain in her voice. She hated Lilith, always had.

"Something to share, Bee?" Lilith spat, her own hatred clear.

"I just said it's nice to see that you're still batshit crazy. Let's get this over with, shall we? I have more important things to do than deal with deranged leeches." Bee remained stoic by my side, arms crossed across her chest, looking all too disinterested in anything Lilith had to say. She knew exactly the effect her words would have on Lilith. To Bee, this was a sport, and she thoroughly enjoyed it.

"Louis, are you going to let her talk to me like that?" Her face was full of rage as she glanced between Bee and me.

"Yes," I answered coldly, my voice devoid of any emotion. I couldn't give her anything, she'd read into the slightest emotion and twist it. She huffed deeply, standing tall in defiance.

Turning my focus again on Tess, I watched as she stood shakily while applying pressure to the wound on her neck that still oozed blood. I wanted desperately to get to her, but I knew I needed to deal with Lilith first. Once that was done

I could go to her, scoop her up into my arms, and take away the pain.

Lilith clearly saw where my gaze lingered, sensing that I wanted to go to her. She blocked my path. "You look good, Louis. I really have missed you. I look forward to catching up properly once this business is all tied up." Her desire-filled gaze once more raked my body from head to toe, and I saw her fangs bite her lip.

The thought of being with Lilith again made my stomach roll—the idea of being with *anyone* other Tess made me feel empty inside. But I had to deal with Lilith before I even thought about burying myself inside of Tess.

Meeting Lilith's eyes, I spoke, "My name is Lucifer, and it always has been. *You* are the only person who calls me Louis and I hate it. I apologise for what I did all those years ago, ripping you from the only home you'd ever known and turning your world upside down. But let me be perfectly clear here, Lilith: I don't want you. I never have."

"B—but you love me." Lilith slumped a little, like the air had been sucked from her lungs.

"No, Lilith, I don't. I never did. You were a pawn in a game that has spanned millennia. I took you, seduced you away to piss off God. That was all you were to me, a challenge." I knew my words were harsh, that they would cut her deeply, but she needed to know the truth. I'd repeatedly told her I didn't want her over the years, but not in such a direct manner as this.

Lilith's eyes blazed—the lust had been replaced with anger. It rolled off her in waves. Yeah, she was pissed. "But you love her?" she hissed, pointing an accusing finger at Tess. "You're choosing this little bitch over me?"

"Yes, Lilith, I am."

"Do you even know what makes her special? Do you have *any* idea why you are drawn to her? I do, I've tasted the blood that runs through her veins. I know *exactly* why you want her." Her face broke into a wicked grin.

Does she know? Does she know what makes Tess special?

I stiffened as Lilith focused her attentions on Tess, turning on the spot to face her. "I'll kill her before I let you have her, *Louis*. If I can't have you, I'm fucking sure that you can't have her. This way *neither* of us gets our "happy ever after." Tell me, did you really think she'd want to be with you once she found out all of your deep dark secrets? Let's find out before I kill her?" She looked over her shoulder at me smugly.

Fuck.

35

TESS

"Tell me, Tess. Do you know who I am? Who I was?" she cooed at me as I stood shakily in the cell, clutching onto my neck, which I think had finally stopped bleeding.

I knew it wasn't smart, but I couldn't help it. "Some really, really old, crazy chick who couldn't take no for an answer?" I said, trying to gather as much energy as I could to stop myself from falling once again to the floor.

I heard a snort of laughter from beyond the group of vampires and heard Bee say, "I like this one. She's sassy." But it was Lilith's penetrating glare that caused goosebumps to break out on my pale, clammy skin.

"You ought to watch that smart mouth. After all, that's what got you into this mess. Plus, you aren't really in a position to be so smug. I could kill you in heartbeat. So, you might want to listen carefully. I'll tell you just what sort of man you're involved with." She was looking at me, and a broad grin spread across her smug face.

It was clear she thought she was about to spill Lucifer's darkest secrets, that she was going to drop a bomb that would make me run away from this man that had wormed his way into my life and turned it on its head. My life had been forever changed by Lucifer, and it was in that moment that I knew.

The sound of her shrill voice shattered my inner revelation. "I am the first: the first woman to walk the Earth, Adam's wife, his *equal*. Before Eve, there was me. I was—"

"Yeah, yeah, Lucifer seduced you over to Hell, promised you all sorts of things, blah, blah, blah. He told me all of this already. I agree, it was shitty of him, but it was *so damn long* ago now that you really should have gotten over it." I watched as shock flashed in her eyes and her mouth bobbed open in surprise.

"He told you?" she asked, startled.

"Yeah he told me. He's told me *everything*, Lilith," I goaded her. "In all honesty, after finding out the man I've been sleeping with is the Devil, there isn't an awful lot that shocks me."

She looked smug again; clearly, another "revelation" was coming. "Really? Everything? He's told you everything, has he?" She turned her back on me, once more rounding on Lucifer, who was apparently biding his time. I could sense through our link that he was poised, ready to pounce like an animal.

"Tell me, Lucifer, does precious little Tess here know that you're looking into her family? In particular, her *father*?" I could hear the smugness in her voice, like she'd just delivered another bombshell. I couldn't see Lucifer's face, but I heard him let out a sigh.

"Yes, Lilith, she knows. Tess knows that I have someone searching for answers. She knows everything, so whatever you're hoping to achieve it won't work." He kept his response cool, but I could feel his anger for Lilith pulsing through the link.

She spun to face me, her gaze hard, her penetrating stare

attempting to bore a hole straight through me. "Impossible. You wouldn't tell her that."

I shrugged my shoulders at her. "What can I say, Lilith. He wanted me to know everything. No lies." I let a small smug smile play across my face.

"You bitch."

"Lilith, all you're doing is delaying the inevitable," Lucifer spoke from across the room.

"The inevitable? Pray tell me, Lucifer. What is inevitable?" I could feel her rage. Everything was slipping through her fingers, her plan was shot to shit, and she was losing the only man she'd ever wanted; as fucked up as their relationship was, she saw him as hers. If anything, I felt she was more dangerous than she'd ever been.

"Your death, Lilith. I hope you have your affairs in order. I have enough to manage without the extra work of dealing with your vampires." He was deadly serious. It was a statement, nothing more.

"But I know what she is. Surely you want to know that? If you let me live, I can tell you." There was a slight plea to her voice, but I knew it was pointless.

"It doesn't matter, Lilith. We'll have answers on that soon enough. Besides, I wouldn't believe a single word that you say about Tess. You cannot be trusted—you've proved that on so many occasions. This ends here and now." I felt his energy change through the link, and he let his dark side seep through.

I had to tell him—if I was going to die here I needed to tell him the truth before it was too late. It wasn't the ideal situation in a room full of vampires, demons, and fallen, but sometimes you just have to roll with the punches.

"Lucifer, listen to me. Since we met, people have been trying to drive us apart, and they nearly succeeded, but I have to tell you. I know exactly who you are, and I don't care.

I love you, Lucifer." I poured everything I had left into my words and through our link, hoping he could feel my honesty.

"I know this isn't exactly the best time to tell you this, but if I'm going to die here, you deserve to know. I've been fighting my feelings, trying to bury them, convince myself this would never work. I can't do it, and I have to admit it to myself as well as you. I know you aren't evil, I see that—I've always seen that. You live in the darkness, yes, but that's not who you are inside. I see you, Lucifer, and I love you." Once I started, the words just poured out of me, and I couldn't stop. I laid everything on the line for him, bared my soul for him to see. If I died now, at least he would know.

Before he could reply, a loud scream pierced the room, and my attention once again snapped to Lilith. "I will burn this world to the fucking ground before I let you have her, Louis." Lilith bared her fangs, and her eyes bled to crimson.

Yeah, maybe that wasn't the best timing for a declaration of love.

36

LUCIFER

What? She loves me? Tess loves me?

The feeling of euphoria swept over my body and settled deep within me. This was perfect, and not even the fact that we were in a dingy room with my ex, a group of vampires, and half of Hell could ruin this moment.

I tried to find Tess through the horde of vampires in front of me. I needed to look into her eyes, show her I was coming. The motherfuckers were blocking my view, refusing to let me see her. I had to get to her and get her out of Lilith's evil clutches, keep her safe.

I love you too, Red. I'm coming for you. Things might get messy, so stay in the cell and don't do anything rash.

Then Lilith began screeching again. Her voice was like nails down a chalkboard. "She's fucking dead, Lucifer. *Dead!*"

I tried to keep my tone as cool and calm as I could, despite the anger for Lilith that coursed through my veins. Lilith had let her vampire side show, and now I was ready to let my darkness out. "Lilith, we can make this easy. Let Tess go and I'll allow your children to live and I might even make your death swift." I would let her children live, though I wasn't sure if I could make her death swift, not after what she had done.

Lilith glanced at me over her shoulder, as she took steps towards the cell where Tess was—I had my answer and it was "fuck you." My wings sprang from my back, and my eyes bled to the dark black pools. My voice dropped a few octaves, and I growled, "Keep this up, Lilith, and I will make you watch while I rip your heart from your chest." She faltered slightly in her steps, and her crimson eyes grew wide with fear.

"I can't do that, Louis. She's the only thing stopping us from being together. When she's gone, you'll see that it was always supposed to be us. She has to die—but not before I turn her first." She was deranged, and she seemed to believe every delusional word she spouted.

"Lilith, fucking stop. *Now.*" It was a bellow that had even my own demons flinching. There was absolutely no way I was letting her get to Tess. I would kill anyone that stood in my way, regardless of who they were. Tess was mine, and *no one* would take her from me.

In a flash, more vampires appeared in the room to defend their queen. They were loyal to her—she had created them. But *I* had created her. None of their powers rivalled my own. It was foolish of her to call more, especially since the fading had sapped their strength; she had more bodies, but they were useless to her. They were lambs to the slaughter and she knew it.

The two sides faced off against each other; Lilith and her vampires stared down me, my lieutenants, and the variety of demons who had joined us. Despite Lilith now having more numbers, the two sides were far from equally matched.

All inhabitants of Hell were required to train daily, those in the legion more so—as a result, they were a force to be reckoned with. I felt sorry for Lilith's followers. They were pawns in her game, and they would pay for their loyalty with their lives.

As the vampires fanned out I managed to catch the slightest glimpse of Tess and Emma in the cells. Tess had crawled to her friend and was holding her through the metal bars that separated the cells. She watched on in horror at the sight unfolding in front of her eyes.

Don't worry, Red. I'm coming for you.
Be careful, Lucifer. Please.

Bee and Levi stepped up beside me, and Conrath remained slightly set back—I could tell he was eager to prove himself, but he wouldn't break protocol and join the three of us.

I saw Levi stretch out his neck from side to side and Bee roll her shoulders. The anticipation crackled in the air, tension setting Lilith and her followers on edge. They seemed jittery and uneasy. It wasn't surprising—many of them were going to die. Eyes flittered from side to side, watching, waiting, and scanning me and those behind me. Lilith's vampires would move first, probably out of sheer panic. My people stood statue-still, and I knew they wouldn't move unless they were ordered to.

All the vampires in front of me were powerful, no doubt. But my legion was stronger. Not all, but most. Each vampire had different powers—they all had the same key abilities, but some were blessed with more. Some could fade, some had the power to persuade and compel, and others could shapeshift, though it was rare.

The most powerful and dangerous of them all was Lilith. She possessed all of the abilities because those abilities had come from me. She had absorbed them when she drank my blood. That had, in fact, cursed her. Deep down she knew it, but she'd never admit it.

She possessed some of my abilities, but not all. Even

though she had them, she couldn't use them infinitely like I could. They drained her, essentially weakening her to the point where she could not carry on unless she fed. There were only two people she could feed off of in the room, and the thought of her touching them again made me ball my fists and clench my jaw. She'd already caused them enough pain, and I wouldn't let her cause anymore. I was worried that she would get to Tess before I did. She was already closer to her.

So, we stood in silence waiting, feeling the crackle of tension build and build until suddenly one of the vampires darted forward. None of my people moved, but the other vampires—who had all been tightly coiled like springs—erupted and into motion, launching themselves in our direction.

We held firm, unmoving against the torrent of fangs and crimson eyes that descended on us. They were practically on top of us before I bellowed, "Now!"

And then it began.

37

TESS

I WAS TUCKED AWAY in the cell, clutching Emma's hand tightly and trying to shield her unconscious body. I knew there wasn't much I could do in the state I was in, but I'd be damned if I wouldn't try.

I knew the cell was probably the safest place, but I still felt like a caged animal. I wanted to help, do something, anything. But in a room full of fallen angels, demons, and vampires, I was pretty sure a photographer from England could do shit.

The two sides clashed, and it was brutal. Screams and shouts filled the void, as did the sound of ripping flesh and breaking bones. My senses were assaulted from every angle: the horrific noises, the gruesome sights, and the smell of iron and smoke. Both sides were giving it everything they had, and it was hard to make out what was going on in the frenzy of violence playing out in front of me.

Bodies mashed together, the two sides moving so quickly with their supernatural speed that my eyes struggled to focus. I could make out certain things through the blurred activity in front of me, though I'd lost sight of Lilith and

Lucifer, unsure of where they were in the fray. Wherever Lilith was, Lucifer would follow. He'd promised to end this, end her, and I knew he would.

Trying and failing to focus on the battle in front of me, I turned my attention to Emma. I studied her for any change, and watched her intently.

She was still unconscious—which at that moment I was thankful for. She didn't have to witness the brutality unfolding mere meters away from us. If she woke up now, she'd probably die of terror at the bloody sight unfolding in front of us.

I pushed my other hand through the bars to check her pulse once more. It took a while, but I finally found it, barely there and weak. She was fighting to cling on, but she was fading fast. I didn't know what to do, or how to help her. I felt helpless—I couldn't help Emma inside the cell just as I knew I couldn't help Lucifer outside of them. My friend was dying, and I just had to sit and watch, hoping that she'd hang on long enough.

The wounds on her neck seemed to have stop oozing blood, though they were still gaping open. She remained pale and clammy, appearing to grow more and more grey as I watched. Whoever had fed on her had taken too much and she was dying of blood loss right in front of my eyes.

"Come on, Em. You can get through this. I *need* you to get through this," I whispered my plea quietly. Not that anyone could hear over the sound of the clash.

Still clutching on to one of her hands, I moved my other to her head, stroking her hair away from her face as gently as I could. Not willing to let her go, in every sense of the word. I begged her to be okay, begged her not to die. I concentrated everything I had on Emma; at that moment she was all that mattered. I could be with her till the end, make sure she wasn't alone. So I poured everything I had into willing her to pull through. I may have been doomed for an afterlife in Hell, but maybe I could get a miracle to help my friend.

I closed my eyes, trying to block everything out, focusing only on Emma. Then I felt it. A heat radiated from my palm, which had come to rest on Emma's forehead. My eyes flew open and I pulled my hand away from Emma as I saw an apparent glow fade from her face.

What the actual fuck?

Maybe I'd lost too much blood and I was hallucinating. Perhaps we were both dying and this was all in my head?

I studied Emma's face to see if whatever I'd done had hurt her even more. Maybe she'd died, and that was her soul or something. I was completely clueless at that moment. She was definitely still alive; if anything, she looked better—less grey. A slight flush of colour had spread across her face.

Unsure of what to do, I placed my hand back onto Emma's forehead. This time I kept my eyes firmly open and focused everything I had on her, and then felt the heat radiating from my palm. Pulsing energy repeatedly surged through my body, coming to rest each time on my palm that was pressed firmly against Emma's head. Studying the area where our bodies touched, I noticed a visible glow—whatever it was it was flowing through my hand into Emma's head. She was absorbing it like a sponge soaking up water.

I watched, transfixed, as the colour appeared back in her cheeks. Her breaths became more visible, and the wounds on her neck knitted together. I let my hand remain, scared to take it away in case whatever happened was reversed. I had to pull my hand away, though, when a surge of nausea overtook my body, and I dry heaved.

Taking some steadying breaths in an attempt to ease my rolling stomach, I managed to find my composure. Once again, I scanned Emma's body, and noticed she looked like she was sleeping. There were no signs of what she had gone through. When I looked at her now, she didn't appear at all like she'd been knocking on death's door five minutes ago.

I didn't understand what had happened, and I gazed between Emma and my palm, which now was no longer glowing. There was no trace of what had just happened anywhere, other than Emma looking absolutely fine, just apparently asleep.

Did I do that?

My thoughts were snapped out of the moment as I heard Conrath shout—I'd recognise his voice anywhere. I scanned the bodies in front of me, searching for him in the tangle of individual fights scattered throughout the room. I tried not to linger too much on the extreme violence on display, focusing on finding him alone.

Then I found him, and my heart clenched in my chest. Three vampires were overpowering him, and one had just torn a claw through his throat, causing a torrent of blood to gush from the wound. He was dead. He had to be. No one could survive that. I watched in open-mouthed horror, expecting him to crumple to the floor and bleed out in front of me. Instead, he pulled one of the vampires closer and head-butted her with such force that she fell to the floor with a distinct thud.

Just as the other two vampires were about to finish him off, the hulking man who had been standing next to Lucifer was by Conrath's side. He grabbed one of the vampires, turning them on the spot and hugging them tightly to his massive frame. The vampire became still in his grasp, and he then forced a blade through the vampire's chest. I'd assumed it had pierced the vampire's heart, as the vampire's skin immediately began to decay and decompose. The man dropped the dying vampire to the floor.

He nodded in Conrath's direction as Conrath took out the last remaining vampire that had been attacking him. The smaller demon nodded back, wiping the wound on his neck. It was then I noticed it had stopped bleeding and appeared to be healing before my eyes. His gaze met mine, and he winked at me. He was treating it like he'd gotten a fucking paper cut and not that his throat had nearly been ripped out. I stared blankly back, unsure of what the appropriate response was in that situation.

My eyes flicked to the rest of the room, and I noticed that everyone had become still. It had fallen quiet, and the numbers had definitely thinned. The majority of those that remained appeared to be fallen or demons, with the odd vampire smattered throughout. But at that moment, everything stopped. Everyone's attention had landed on a standoff.

Everyone's focus was on Lucifer and Lilith, who both stood in the middle of the room. Lilith's ivory suit was now stained with blood—some of which was my own. Her crimson eyes had settled solely on Lucifer, and she licked her pearly-white fangs as she gazed on him.

With his black wings exposed behind him and his eyes completely dark, he looked every bit the ruler of Hell. His power shrouded him, filling the room and forcing everything into submission.

Everything except Lilith. She struggled against it, and she stood her ground, unwilling to back down from him.

They faced off, staring each other down. There was a slight snarl on Lilith's lip, whereas Lucifer looked the picture of composure. I could feel through our link that was definitely not the case, but you couldn't tell by looking at him.

Now it was about the two of them. Everyone else just had to watch on.

38

LUCIFER

Lilith had exerted a lot of energy attempting to get to Tess, but thankfully she hadn't succeeded. Even with Lilith's best efforts, Tess remained safely inside the cell.

Despite her exertions, I knew Lilith still had plenty to give. The adrenaline and rage masked any injuries or fatigue and had steeled her focus. I could tell though that she thought she was walking away from this; she was not prepared for death.

I'd partially shifted. I could fully shift, but I didn't want to give her the satisfaction, since I wielded the same power whichever form I chose. Lilith had shifted as well, her vampiric traits on full display. We maintained eye contact as we circled each other. Like animals, we stalked, all in a bid to prove dominance. It was foolish on her part to challenge me and start all of this in the first place. But it was about to end, and then I could be with Tess.

I could tell her I loved her back, take care of her, make her mine in every sense of the word.

My focus snapped to Lilith when she began to talk. "Tell me, why did you do it? If you didn't want me, didn't love me, then why would you take me?" she hissed at me. Her voice was angry, there was no hiding that, but I wondered if anyone else could pick up the pain intertwined in it.

She already knew my answer, but she'd never believed me. Lilith had refused to accept her life was ripped apart for something so petty. But that's exactly what it was. "Lilith, you know why. Seducing you away from Adam was simply a sick, twisted "fuck you" to God. He wanted to create something good and pure, and I wanted to show him I could destroy anything he did. It was never about you, Lilith—or Eve—"

"Don't mention her fucking name," she spat. There was a lot of residual hatred between the two women. Eve and I were cool, there was never the same animosity or possessiveness that Lilith had. Eve was just glad to be free.

"It was never about the two of you. It was about him. It was always about him." I'd long gotten over my grudge against God, no longer caring what he thought and no longer worried about his opinion, or what he did—unless it interfered with Hell. Hell was my only concern. Hell, and now Tess.

It was only a matter of time, though, before God interfered again. I expected to hear from him soon; he'd probably send Michael again just to piss me off.

"But you love me." It wasn't quite a question or a statement. Her face softened a bit, waiting for my response. I had to be brutal, rip the bandaid off.

"Lilith, I used you for my own selfish reasons. You were a pawn in a much bigger game, and for that I'm sorry. I know that my apology has been a long time coming and that it probably won't mean shit to you, but I am sorry all the same." I was being sincere, and I hoped that came across. I was genuinely sorry.

She hissed in my direction, like a snake and bared her elongated, sharp fangs. "I'll make you suffer as I have.

Knowing that you can't have the one that you want, the one that you love." Her words dripped with venom, and then she moved in a blur.

She ripped the cell door off its hinges before hurling it across the room. In that second I saw her lunge at Tess who was still curled up, clutching Emma's hand through the metal bars. Lilith grabbed Tess by the throat and dragged her across the floor, Tess's feet barely making contact with the concrete. Once in front of the empty space where the door had been, she pulled Tess upright and held her tight against her body—Lilith's front to Tess's back.

I stood watching, my eyes bulging wide at sight before me. "Put her down. *Now!*" My voice had gone full Devil, and it shook the very foundations of the building. Dust fell from the ceiling as the tremors eased. Lilith said nothing, just quirked her lips into an eerie smile, and I knew we were in trouble.

Tess was clawing and scratching at Lilith's hand, trying to free herself from the vampire's grip on her throat. Lilith never flinched, as if she wasn't even aware of Tess. Her eyes remain fixed on me.

Lucifer, what do I do? What do I do? Tess's voice was stricken with panic, and I could feel the fear flowing through our link. I sensed the utter desperation she felt and her hope paled.

Don't give up Tess, just keep fighting. This is my battle, not yours. I tried to send my strength and reassurance through to her, pushed as hard as I could, but I wasn't sure it was having any effect.

I love you. Her words echoed through our link as I saw Tess still her hands and stop the scratching and clawing. Instead, she held them against Lilith's hand wrapped around her throat. She seemed calm and her actions were deliberate and methodical. I was about to speak but felt a power surge through the room; I had no idea where it had come from, but it was there, pulsing, causing everyone to take note.

I quickly studied the room to see if someone, something had joined us, but nothing had. When my gaze landed back on Tess and Lilith, though, my eyes widened, and my mouth fell open. *What the fuck?* Tess's hands were glowing, pulsing with some sort of energy against Lilith's skin—suddenly the vampire let out a blood-curdling scream of pain. She let go of Tess, who fell to the floor and quickly scrabbled out of the cell towards me.

Conrath stepped up to grab Tess and pull her to one side and to safety. He'd know full well that I wanted nothing more than to go to her, comfort and soothe her, but first I had to deal with Lilith. Knowing that, he stepped in and the slightest feeling of relaxation washed over me. She was away from Lilith, safe with Conrath, and now there was a barrier between them. Me.

I moved in the blink of an eye and appeared in the cell, grabbing Lilith by the throat and lifting her in front of me. Her eyes shot to mine and bulged slightly with the pressure that was placed on her throat. Her main focus, though, remained her hand, which she was clutching like a newborn.

Her hand was blistered and charred, and black scorched flesh had replaced her tanned skin. Up close, I could smell the burnt flesh. *What the hell did Tess do? And how the fuck did she do it?* I'd deal with that later—right now, I had a vermin problem to deal with.

I'd let her get away with far too much, for far too long. I could no longer let her have any influence on my life. I knew I held some responsibility for what she had become, but she had taken a much darker path than I ever thought she would. She'd become bitter, twisted, and lost herself in everything that had happened. I had turned her from the light, but I did not turn her into the monster that she'd become, that she was now. She did that to herself.

Squeezing her throat, I pulled her from the ground, so we were now eye-to-eye. Her feet dangled, and I could hear toes desperately scraping against the ground. It was pointless, there was no fight once I had her in my grasp. And although she knew it, she carried on struggling.

I brought her face closer to mine, and then I stared into her crimson eyes, which were filled with so many emotions. Fear. Anger. Desperation. And love, still there was love there. I whispered into her ear, low enough only for the two of us to hear, "I am sorry for this, Lilith, but you leave me with no choice." Pushing her slightly back away from me, so her body was exposed, I studied her.

Then I plunged my fist into her chest. The sounds of flesh tearing and bones cracking echoed through the now very silent room. Lilith's mouth fell open as she let out a silent scream, pain etched in her eyes, which had bled back to their normal hazel colour. She convulsed under my grip, and I could feel her heart in my hand. I could also feel the wetness of her blood against my fingers, the smoothness of her muscle under the palm of my hand, and I squeezed. She released a startled breath, and her eyes bulged.

As I looked her in the eye, I spoke loud enough for everyone in the room to hear. "You did this to yourself, your Majesty." Then, I pulled my hand back in a fraction of a second, her heart still clutched within it. I held it between us in the last seconds before she faded away to nothingness. An audible gasp filled the room from the vampires that still remained, those loyal to their queen.

I caught Lilith's eyes flit between mine and her heart in my hand before she fell to the floor with a dull thud. Her body instantly began to wither away. As if knowing they had no chance, the remaining loyal vampires fled. We knew who they were, and we would round them up later.

I wanted nothing more than to run to Tess, snatch her up in my arms, and hold her close. But I needed to ensure Lilith was gone, really gone. So, I remained in place over Lilith's slowly decaying corpse. Her skin dehydrated, shrinking back to nothing and exposing her bones, which disintegrated in front of me. Her heart—that still remained clutched in my hand—was the last thing to fade away to ash. I continued to study the view before me, eager to see an end to the years of torture that we'd put each other through.

When a vampire died it was usual for their bodies to disappear to ash; nothing remained, and there was no sign of them ever having walked the Earth. But Lilith wasn't just any vampire—she was the first, the first vampire ever created. No matter what I thought of her, she was special and even in death she could surprise me. Staring up at me from the floor was a skull—Lilith's skull—with its elongated fangs still intact. She wasn't completely gone, she never would be really.

I picked up the skull and focused on it, allowing the fire of Hell to erupt from my palm. The skull was engulfed in flames—flames that only I could control and wield, but that nothing could withstand. Yet, Lilith's skull remained. I dropped the flaming skull to the floor.

She was gone, but a part of her would always remain. It served as a reminder that she was the first, born of my blood, born of the darkness. Lilith was gone, but her legacy of vampires lived on.

39

TESS

WITH THEIR QUEEN DEAD, the rest of the vampires had fled. They had witnessed first-hand just what Lucifer was capable of, and it had clearly scared the shit out of them. In all honesty, they weren't alone. His power had dominated the room, and everyone shied away from him in some small way; despite that, I knew he would never hurt me. I felt it deep within me. I couldn't explain why, but I just knew it.

I forced my eyes away from Lilith's fanged skull—the only bit of her that remained and was caught in an intimate gaze. Lucifer's eyes raked over every inch of my body. His eyes were filled with not just concern, but a level of lust I'd never seen him show. Bee was standing close to him, talking and gesturing to the skull, but he never once cast his eyes anywhere other than on me. Conrath and the giant of a man approached him and also began talking to him, yet he didn't reply to anything they were saying, still transfixed on me.

"Lucifer, are you listening? Did you hit your fucking head?" Bee asked. "We need to know what we should do with the skull?" She nudged it cautiously with her boot like it was a bomb waiting to go off.

Lucifer's gaze finally broke, focusing on the skull at their feet. "We should take it to Hell, see if we can destroy it there. If not, it should be locked away with the other artefacts." They were all staring awkwardly at the skull; none of them wanted to pick it up or touch it.

Aware I couldn't help, I gingerly walked back to the cells and pushed through the door to where Emma lay. I was amazed at what I saw. Unconscious, she lay on the concrete slab perfectly still. There was no trace of the bite marks on her, no sweat or shivers. Her skin had found its colour, losing all trace of the pale greyness that had settled in her. I held my hand to her forehead, and she was warm again, no longer icy to the touch. She looked asleep and peaceful.

Just to reassure myself, I checked her pulse and found it was strong. I moved my fingers and could see the flicker of her artery under her skin. She hadn't woken up yet, but I was just relieved that she was no longer close to death.

As I stared down at my friend, I felt a pair of strong arms wrap around my waist and pull me close to a firm, warm chest. He nuzzled my neck—the side that wasn't covered with blood and had an ugly wound on it—pressing feather-light kisses along my skin. His gentle touch made my skin prickle, and a fire ignited within me.

"Hey, Red," he whispered softly into my ear.

"Hey, yourself," I replied, turning on the spot, his arms still cocooning me. I stared up into his eyes, which had gone back to their usual desire-filled darkness but were no longer completely black. He stroked the pad of his thumb across my dry, cracked lips, and then moved his hand under my chin to tip my head slightly back.

He leaned in, his lips meeting mine tenderly. It was a soft, gentle, lingering kiss that conveyed just how glad he was that I was okay. He was savouring every second of it, licking and nipping at my lips, stroking his tongue against mine—it was a kiss that told me what he was unable to say. My arms wrapped around him, holding him tight, showing him I wasn't going anywhere.

I felt him relax into me, the hint of a smile playing across his lips as he kissed me. Then, he moved back slightly, resting his forehead against mine. "I thought I'd lost you, Red. I was ready to burn everything to the ground." I believed him, felt it through our link; now, though, relief flooded through, bathing me in it.

"Come on," he continued. "Let's go." He tried to pull me, lead me away from where Emma still lay in the cell. He once more tugged at my hand when I wouldn't budge, eventually turning back toward me.

"I'm not leaving Emma," I said, unflinching against his dominant stare. He gazed at me, his face softening and a slight smile on his lips.

"Levi," he shouted. At that moment, Bee and the hulking man entered the cell, both looking between Lucifer and me. "Please bring Emma with us. You can put her in one of the guest bedrooms." The giant, who I now knew was called Levi —nodded his head in Lucifer's direction and moved towards Emma. I observed him, hoping that he would be gentle with her. It was then that I noticed the briefest flash of something on his face—lust, familiarity, love. I wasn't sure, but it was gone as quickly as it appeared. He leaned forward and scooped Emma up into his arms, cradling her gently, even reverently. She looked tiny in his arms.

Bee was carrying some sort of sack, swinging it around in circles as she walked. I was pretty sure the bag contained Lilith's skull, but she didn't seem to give a fuck. The remaining demons and fallen headed back to the open door, and we watched them go through. I started to move once the last had made their way through, but Lucifer pulled me back.

He closed the door and then immediately opened it again,

ushering me through. Bee and Levi—who kept stealing quick glances at Emma curled up against his chest—followed us through. We were in Lucifer's place in Hell; I recognised the grand entrance from the last time I was here.

Levi moved past us, walking up the stairs. I followed him, since I wanted to make sure that Emma was okay, and Lucifer, not letting go of my hand, trailed behind.

"I'll go see what I can do with this fucking thing," Bee said, still swinging the bag containing Lilith's skull.

"Contact Gabriela, we need her here. She needs to check over Emma, and we also need to tell her of the new developments," he said with a glance in my direction. He likely meant whatever had happened with my glowing hands. Bee nodded and headed out the doors.

I aimlessly followed Levi, who made his way into one of the huge bedrooms and placed Emma on the large, plush bed, like she was a bird with an injured wing. He was so gentle with her, completely the opposite to how I'd assumed he'd be with his gruff exterior.

"Why hasn't she woken up? Did I make things worse with my fucking crazy, magic hands?" I was terrified that I'd hurt her, done some irreversible damage she'd never wake from.

"I'm sure she'll be fine, Red. Gabriela will check her over when she gets here." He turned to Levi and continued, "Might be worthwhile getting some form of illusion spell on the house, just in case she wakes up and freaks out. Not every day you wake up in Hell."

Levi nodded in agreement. "I'll stay with her. You two get cleaned up." His gaze slid to Emma again, like there was an invisible pull. I glanced at Lucifer and saw him eyeing his friend curiously, but he didn't speak a word.

"Thank you, Levi. I'm Tess, by the way. It's nice to meet you." I gave him as big a smile as I could muster with the little energy I had left.

He focused his grey eyes on me and gave me a genuine smile. "Pleased to *finally* meet you, Tess." He cast a sidewards glance in Lucifer's direction.

"Fuck off," Lucifer said when he pulled me from the room. As we walked down the hall, he said, "Levi will let us know as soon as she wakes up. Then we'll take her home. Now, though, I need to get you cleaned up."

Finally making it to an enormous door, he pulled me through, and I recognised we were in his bedroom.

"Lucifer, will Emma be okay?" I asked. I couldn't lose her, I'd lost too many people already—she had to be okay, she *had* to be.

"Whatever it is you did to her saved her life, Red, believe that. It's likely she's just sleeping it off and recovering. Try to relax." It was hard to relax, especially with the sense of uncertainty filling the link between us.

I knew he'd never ask, so I just blurted out, "I don't know *what* I did to her... or to Lilith. It was different, though. When I touched Emma, it was a loving, reassuring feeling that settled in me. But with Lilith... well, it was the opposite." I chewed my lip nervously, as I looked down at the floor.

He reached up, stroking my cheek with his fingers, tipping my head back to look at him. "I know, I felt it. It was powerful, Red, whatever it was. Hopefully, Gabriela can give us some answers." He didn't shy away from me, didn't blanch at the uneasiness I was emitting. Instead, he stayed next to me, holding me in a bid to calm the jitters that had set in at my apparent newfound powers.

I snuggled into his chest, trying to bury myself in his strong arms. "I'm scared. I don't know how to control it. Whatever *it* is." I tried to breathe in his smoky scent, hoping it would soothe my frazzled nerves.

He planted a gentle kiss to the top of my head and pulled

me closer. "I know, Red, but whatever this is, we'll figure it out together. I promise."

40

LUCIFER

I HELD her firmly against my chest, pouring everything I could into her to reassure her. I had absolutely no idea what she was, especially having seen her powers up-close and personal. But to me, it changed nothing. She had accepted me and the darkness within, who was I to walk away from her now?

I didn't want to—if anything, it made me admire her even more. When faced with a totally impossible situation, she had fought tooth and claw and came out on top. Not only had Tess healed her friend, but she'd also dealt a debilitating blow to Lilith, even after Lilith had drained her of so much blood.

Lilith had known. After feeding on Tess, she'd known what she was. She had known, yet I was in the dark. I brushed Tess's hair from her neck, studying where Lilith had clearly torn through her flesh. Her skin was stained with blood, and it had run down her neck and chest, soaking into her clothes. I wasn't sure how she was still standing, after everything she'd done.

I gently stroked my fingers up her neck and felt her

shiver at my touch. To my surprise, the wound had completely healed. Vampires could feed almost painlessly from humans when they wanted to—the initial puncture of fangs would be the only sting, then it would be euphoria. But Lilith showed Tess no such mercy. She'd torn her throat, caused as much pain as she could, so all Tess would feel was torturous, crippling agony.

"Is it okay?" she asked shakily.

Continuing to brush my fingers against her soft skin, I pressed a kiss to her temple. "It's fully healed, Red. Whatever you did to Emma must have healed you as well. Why did Lilith feed off you, did she say?"

I felt her muscles tense slightly, so I pulled her closer, resting my chin on her head. "She found out I was the one who killed Daniel. They said they couldn't just kill me because if they did then—"

"You'd end up straight in Hell… with me."

She nodded. "They said they'd have to turn me and then kill me. I think she was looking forward to it, and she wanted it to be as painful as she could—"

"It's over, Red. You're here now, and you're safe with me. Always."

"She knew. She knew what I am. She had answers."

"She never would have told us. Even if she had, I wouldn't have believed her. Lilith had manipulated people for millennia; it was another way to keep herself alive, to keep herself useful." Lilith was a sneaky bitch, and I'd never trusted her after what she'd done, so I couldn't trust she knew about Tess. Hopefully, we'd have answers soon enough regardless.

"No, she knew," Tess said adamantly. "I saw the surprise in her face, and she was *smug* about it. Smug that she knew what I was, even when I didn't. And now she's gone."

"Yes, she's gone. Which means she won't be able to hurt you ever again. It doesn't matter that Lilith knew, Red. We'll figure this out together. I promise." I hoped she believed me, because I meant every single word.

She tipped her head back to look at me, then nodded. Although her wounds were healed, she was still far from being one hundred percent. Her hair was matted and dirty, and her eyes were sunken with dark circles underneath them, showing me just how tired she was. Her lips were still chapped, and she was paler than usual. Her once-bright emerald eyes looked dull and weary, yet as I continued to gaze at her, I still thought she was the most beautiful creature I'd ever seen. Her beauty outshone even the most coveted of succubi I'd met over the years. She stirred feelings in me I never knew existed.

"Did you mean it? When you… said you loved me. Did you mean it?" I held my breath, waiting for her to reply. I wondered if she could sense my anxiety. The gentle stroke of one of her hands across my cheek told me she could.

"Of course, I did. I wouldn't say it otherwise. I thought I was going to die, and I couldn't go without telling you how I felt. I fought hard to convince myself I'd get over you, that I'd find someone else who makes me burn like you do, but… I was lying to myself." A slight blush filled her cheeks as she dropped her eyes from mine.

I couldn't contain the grin that spread across my face as I lifted her face and stared deeply into those beautiful green orbs. I pressed a tender kiss to her lips. "Say it again."

She blushed a little more, trying to dip her head so she was no longer looking at me, but I caught her chin and tipped it up. She once more met my gaze. "Say it again, Red."

"I love you."

"Tess, you make me feel like no one ever has. I've been around a *long* time, but I've never felt this way about anyone. Not even a fraction of this. You have me completely. You say that no one makes you burn as I do? Well, Red, you have me *ablaze.*" I kissed her again, pouring even more heat into the kiss to show her just what she did to me.

She pulled away, studying me. "I know who you are, Lucifer and I accept that, I accept *you*, but how is this going to work?" She looked worried at what the future might hold, how it would look. In all honesty, I hadn't even thought about it. I was so focused on getting her back, I hadn't dared wonder about the future.

"We can deal with that as we go. All that matters is that we're together," I answered as honestly as I could, hoping she would agree. But this was Tess, and she liked to plan and organise. That wishy-washy answer wouldn't fly with her, and I knew it.

"But you're the Devil. I'm… well, we don't know what the fuck I am, but things aren't going to be normal are they? It's not like this is going to be a regular relationship. We're going to have to plan our next move." She looked pensive, as if a million things were running through her head, flooding her with a mix of emotions and questions.

"Red, relax. We can work all that out later. For now, we need to figure out what powers you have and establish exactly who your father is. I'm convinced answering those questions will give us the answers we need. Before we do that, though, we have to get you cleaned up." I scooped her up into my arms and carried her through to the bathroom.

She loves me, that's what matters. The rest is meaningless.

41

TESS

He carried me gently through to the lavish bathroom and placed me onto a plush chair. He stepped away to turn on the huge shower, which immediately filled the enormous space with hot steam.

I was in desperate need of a shower—I felt caked in blood and grime and I wanted it gone. I longed for the feel of the water against my tense muscles, hoping it would alleviate the aches and pains that wracked my body. As I shrugged off my jacket and dropped it to the floor, I looked up to see him stalking back towards me.

"I'll do it," he said gruffly. I knew that tone well, and it was laced with desire and heat. He knelt in front of me, positioning himself between my thighs as he pressed a soft, but very heated kiss against my lips.

"I can undress myself, Lucifer. I'm a big girl," I protested, though I knew it was pointless arguing with him.

"I want to, Red. I *need* to." There was a desperation in his voice. I wouldn't normally agree so easily, but I could sense just how much he craved this. Nodding, I sat back on the chair.

He casually slid his hands down one of my thighs, stopping when he reached my boot. He unzipped it slowly; I wasn't sure how anyone could make taking off a shoe sexy, but he just managed it. The tension built inside of me. He was feeding my desire just as much as he was his own. He dropped my boot to one side, then removed my sock, tracing his fingers over the arch of my foot. Then he slid his hands back up my jean-clad calf and to my thigh.

I expected him to brush across the zipper on my pants, but instead he skimmed his hand to my other thigh, gradually moving it down to rest on my boot. He slowly discarded my other boot and sock before inching back up to rest his body between my thighs.

His hands rested on my hips as he looked me in the eyes. His eyes flickered with the embers of a fire, and it stoked the lust-filled inferno raging inside me. My body answered to his touch immediately. It became alive at the slightest caress from him. All he'd done was dispose of my boots, yet I was practically ready to come. The anticipation was too much.

He grazed his hands underneath my top, brushing his fingertips against my soft skin, which caused it to prickle and my breath to catch in my throat. A small smile played across his lips as he continued to watch my response. Standing and sliding his hands up, he took my top with them, and I held my arms up so he could slip it over my head. He released it to the floor as he studied my white lacy bra, that was now stained red with my blood. A slight growl escaped his lips as his eyes fell upon it.

"Hey, I'm fine," I reassured him with a gentle smile. He leaned forward, placing another desperate kiss on my lips. I felt his hands glance across my stomach and heard the sound of my zipper being tugged down.

"Stand," he said, his voice low and commanding. It sent a shiver down my spine, and I did a little internal swoon at his dominance. I pushed myself up, facing him, mere inches between us. I could feel his warm breath against my skin, and my nipples pebbled in my bra.

"So receptive," he said with a smirk. Before I had a chance to think of a quick retort, he placed his hands on the waistband of my jeans. He leisurely slipped my jeans down my legs as he lowered himself to kneel in front of me. I stepped out of them, and his piercing focus scanned every inch of my nearly naked body.

He smoothed his hands up the backs of my legs, brushing my ass and then hooking his fingers into my white thong. After that, he slowly lowered it to the floor. His hands then grazed back up the front of my legs; I tried to will him to touch me exactly where I wanted him to. Instead, the bastard skimmed past, caressing up my sides and round to the top of my back to undo my bra. He made quick work of it, once again throwing it to the floor to join the rest of my clothes.

He stepped back again, admiring his handiwork. The mischievous grin that graced his face told me stirring my desire was exactly what he'd been trying to do.

The steam in the room continued to build, and it wasn't just from the shower. I watched as Lucifer slipped his suit jacket off, letting it drop to the floor. He undid the cufflinks of his shirt, and threw them onto the chair before he lazily undid the buttons of his shirt. *The motherfucker is teasing me.* Once all the buttons were undone, he pulled it up, untucking it from his trousers and slowly slid it off, again letting it drop to his feet.

His muscular chest was free, and I could see no remnants of the battle he'd just participated in. I was distracted as he undid his zipper, and I bit my lip as his trousers tumbled to the floor.

"No need to bite your lip, Red. I'll be doing that in a minute." His voice was husky and filled with a craving that I could tell was driving us both. I let go of my lip and watched as he just stared at me. I could see through his boxers that he was rock hard, and ready to go.

He stood there for what felt like an eternity. Watching. He pushed down his boxers, freeing himself. Yet he did nothing beyond that and remained still—allowing the tension to build. I ached for his touch, and it was literally painful. So, looking him in the eye, I snaked my hand slowly down my breasts, further down, skimming my navel and finally finding my sweet spot. I moaned at the contact I'd needed for so long. It wasn't the same as having his fingers on me, but it would do.

"No," he growled out, but made no attempt to come to me. His eyes were so intense, and I could see the fire burning within them; they flickered between red, orange, and black.

"If you won't, I'll do it myself," I breathed, continuing to touch myself and causing my stomach to clench. I closed my eyes and let my head fall back—I ached for some form of fucking release. I was shocked when I felt his hands shackle my wrists as he wrapped them around his back, pushing his body against mine. He let me feel the scorching heat of his skin that made every nerve ending in my body stand to attention.

"Not yet," he rumbled into my ear. Then—sliding his hands around my back and cupping the back of my thighs—he lifted me, my legs wrapping around him to find each other and hooking together, so I was curled around him. He walked me into the shower with purpose and set me on my feet under the hot spray. He allowed the water to wash over me, and I couldn't help but notice the swirl of bloody water that circled the drain. He tugged my face up, stopping me from focusing on it.

He grabbed a bottle, and squeezed something into his hands, lathering it up. He settled his hands on my head and began to tenderly wash my hair. "I can do it," I said as I went to take over. Gently taking my hands, he moved them down to my sides and then slid his own back up to continue washing my hair.

"I know you can, Red, but you don't have to. Let me take care of you. All of you." His words were spoken with such reverence that I couldn't refuse him. I'd let him have this. I was so used to taking care of myself, but at that moment he needed it more than I did. I nodded, letting him continue.

He massaged his fingertips through my hair, lightly but with enough pressure to clean away the blood and grime. I wasn't used to being treated so tenderly, especially in such a vulnerable position. But I trusted him—plus his fingers were fucking magical, even when they were just tangled in my hair. He guided me back to the water, rinsing off the soap. Then he grabbed another bottle and again massaged the contents through my hair while making sure to touch me as sensually as he could.

I opened my eyes when I no longer felt his hands on my hair or body and saw he was grabbing a cloth and lathering some lotion onto it. He stepped towards me, tilting my neck to one side and stroking the cloth gently up and down my stained bloody skin. He was tender, his touch almost delicate. Like I was fragile. He smoothed the cloth down my arm, cleaning me but doing so much more. He brushed the cloth back up and across to the other side of my neck, repeating his actions, taking his time to cover every single inch.

Then, he skimmed the cloth over my collarbone and down over my breasts. He drew circles around them, and every time he grazed over my hard nipples, a tiny gasp crept out of me. He was showing my body all the care and attention it needed at that moment, but he was also teasing, building the desire between us that was already at a boiling point.

He turned me around, gliding the cloth up and down my back, then teased it down my ticklish sides as I squirmed away from his touch. He planted his hands firmly on my hips as he leaned forward, pushing his hard cock against me and whispering in my ear, "Be still, Red."

I obeyed, and stilled my body as much as I could. Then he continued, massaging my ass, squeezing and rubbing it. He turned me to him, and our eyes instantly connected as we gazed at each other, neither making an attempt to move. I parted my lips a fraction and ran my tongue over them; it was an invitation for him to take my mouth. He leaned forward slightly, and I closed my eyes in anticipation. But the fiery kiss didn't come.

My eyes snapped open, wanting to know exactly what he was waiting for. Then I saw him on his knees in front of me, staring up and giving me a look that shot straight to my clit. It made my insides clench when he stroked up my calf, even further up my thigh, and then back down again. He made long, teasing strokes, ensuring my body was clean, but that dirty thoughts were racing through my head. He moved to my other calf and did it all again, and the contact fed a torturous lust within me until I begged him.

"Please, Lucifer." I was aware I sounded desperate, but in that exact moment I craved more than what he was giving, I needed rough, and I yearned him to take me, possess me, show me exactly what I meant to him.

He remained on his knees but, dropping the cloth, moved his hands to my inner thighs. Then he gave little bites to the flesh there, but it wasn't enough. I was just about to plead again—when he bit harder and then swiped his fingers over me, circling my clit with his thumb. My head fell back in the spray, causing the water to cascade down my overly sensitive body.

He licked my sensitive clit, then nipped and sucked on it

until I convulsed in little spasms. "Lucifer, I need to feel you." He didn't reply, just continued his rhythmic swirling and licking. "Plea—" Then he speared two fingers inside me, causing me to scream with pleasure and clench my hands in his hair so I could pull him closer to me.

His fingers stroked and scissored inside of me, and his movements pulled me farther and farther under into a heady frenzy. I was close, so close, but I didn't want his fingers—I wanted *him* inside me. "I need more, Lucifer."

"Patience, Red." He seemed smug, clearly enjoying every second of sexual torment he was putting me through. He upped the tempo of his fingers and tongue, stroking my g-spot with expert precision. I quickly crashed into a powerful orgasm. My body spasmed beneath his touch, and wave after wave of pleasure surged through me. Finally, he stilled his fingers. I slumped over, resting my weight against him, unsure if I could even stay standing.

He stood slowly, and took me with him as he skimmed his hands up my wet skin until he reached my soaking hair and snagged it with his hands. He pulled my hair back, tipping my face to meet his so he could devour my mouth. The earlier reverence was gone; this was a desperate and consuming kiss, one that showed me just how much he craved me.

He tore his mouth away from mine, which caused a little frustrated groan to slip for my lips. "Turn around," he commanded in that dominant tone that made me squeal inside. I did as he asked, then planted my hands against the marbled wall and looked at him over my shoulder. He gripped my hips and pulled me back as he parted my feet with his own. He leaned over me, his cock pushing just slightly into me; his muscular chest pressed against my back as he growled into my ear, "I'm going to fuck you, Red. Fuck you till you can't stand anymore."

"There's a lot of talking, why don't you just do—" The breath caught in my throat as he slammed into me, stretching me, filling me. I was so full as his long, thick cock drove into me, finally quelling the burning need that was always there but had been stoked to breaking point. I planted my feet and pushed my hands into the wall to steady myself against the pounding thrusts that he drove into me. He clutched the flesh of my hips, and dug his fingers in to keep me in place as he pulled out, then slammed into me again. The bite of pain caused from the pressure of his hands made me nip my bottom lip. I had to fight back a heady moan at the possessiveness in each stroke.

"Fuck, Red. I love the way you feel, like you were meant to take me," he breathed out as he withdrew and thrust into me again. He leaned over me, releasing my hips and snaking one hand round to cup one of my breasts and tweak my hardened nipple. The other hand lowered to my clit, and he stroked and tugged, never once losing the rhythm of his feverish thrusts.

I arched my back into him, as his new position meant he drove even farther into me and rubbed against my g-spot, causing a cry to rip from my lungs. "Lucifer, I'm going to—"

"Not yet, Red," he replied in his low, commanding growl. The way he said it nearly sent me toppling over the edge. He maintained his movements but increased his pace, causing whimper after whimper to escape me, showing him just how desperate for him I really was.

"I can't… I can't hold on." I was at my limit. I could feel myself clenching him tightly, not willing to let his cock go, wanting it to quell the need he'd put there. Every nerve ending in my body was alive, and the slightest thing was going to force me over the edge.

"Come for me, Red," he ordered as he thrust harder. And then it overtook me; my orgasm ripped through me causing me to scream his name loudly and arch my back into him, pushing my nipple into his hand. My body quivered with release as he continued until I felt him throb inside of me, coming just as hard as I had.

My legs gave way from under me, causing me to sag; thankfully he was there to catch my body and pull me to my feet. He positioned us both so we were under the water, and he let the spray wash over us. He then guided us out of the shower and wrapped me in the fluffiest towel I'd ever felt; it cocooned me in its warmth. I grabbed another for my hair while he wrapped one around his waist, leaving his delectable chest on display. Despite feeling sated and utterly exhausted, I still had the urge to lick and bite his chest, then trace every muscle with my tongue.

"Easy, Red," he laughed. "I can feel your lust through our link. You need to rest first, and then we can have another round later on. We have time," he said with a genuine smile. He once more scooped me up in his arms and carried me to the massive bed I'd found myself waking up in before. He gently laid me on it and then moved next to me, pulling me to him once he was in position. I snuggled into his side, resting my head against him.

"I've missed you so much, Red. Now sleep. You're exhausted, and we have people we need to talk to soon. For now, though, rest." His voice was soothing, and I felt a wave of drowsiness wash over me.

"But there's so much we need to talk about," I said while stifling a yawn.

"We have time." He traced his fingers up and down my arm, causing my exhaustion to become too much. The last thing I remember before drifting off was Lucifer planting a tender kiss on my forehead as he whispered, "I love you."

42

LUCIFER

Tess had fallen asleep a few hours ago, but I still wasn't tired. I just wanted to watch her, drink her all in, memorise every freckle, every inch of ivory skin. She was perfect, and she was mine.

I smoothed my hand over her auburn locks—it was soft, like spun silk. I'd alternated between doing that and stroking my fingertips up and down her back, feeling her perfect alabaster skin under my soft touch. She'd released a few throaty moans in her sleep, clearly enjoying my touch.

Lying there with her, I felt a contentment I never had, not even when I was in Heaven. This was better than that—I was more at peace here with Tess than I'd ever been as an angel. Having her curled up against me, resting, entirely at ease with me—despite knowing exactly what I was... it was euphoric.

I knew it was impossible, but it seemed like she was destined to be mine. Her head fit perfectly into the dip of my shoulder, her hands nestled perfectly into mine, she took my cock with a hungry, greedy need, and I fit inside her like I never had with anyone else. When we were together, everything felt so… pure. I knew I couldn't explain it to her—no words would do my feelings justice—so I'd just keep showing her. Give her everything I had to give, love her as no one had before.

When I'd offered Daniel the deal, I'd never imagined it would lead me here. It had begun like every other deal, but as soon as I'd laid eyes on her, I'd sensed something was different, that *she* was different. She pushed back, made me work for the slightest little victory, and gave me attitude over the smallest thing—yet it made me want her even more. I'd convinced myself that once I'd fucked her it would all disappear, that the invisible hold she had over me would vanish and I'd be free to move on to the next attractive, lust-filled woman.

But once I had her, I'd forgotten what it was like before her. She did things to my body that no one had ever done before. Her touch ignited a fire inside me that only she could quell; she could subdue it, but she could never extinguish it entirely. I blazed for her, but it was more intense than that. I was hot all the time anyway, perks of being the Devil, but this was true intensity, and I knew she felt it too. It buzzed through our link, crackling furiously.

I'd quickly realised I could never hand her over to that sadistic bastard. I knew I had to keep her, and that she belonged to me—no one else could touch her. Now we had a different set of problems. She was human—for the most part—which meant she had finite time. I'd lose her eventually; she'd grow old, then wither before my very eyes until she died and passed over into Hell. I wasn't sure if I'd be able to free her from her eternal punishment. I ruled Hell, yes, but there were things in place beyond even my control.

I felt her stiffen underneath me and her brow furrowed in her sleep. She began to twitch slightly, and I wondered if she was having a nightmare. I pulled her closer to me, so she was pressed up against me and held her. "Shhhh, Red. Shhhhh, it's okay, you're safe." She stilled once more, and I resumed stroking her naked back.

We still had to answer so many questions about her powers and where she had gotten them from. And about our own next steps, in particular what our future would look like. I wanted her to be with me at all times, but I knew that was impossible due to her fierce independence. If I tried to wrap her in cotton wool she'd push back, resent me for it. However this was going to work, we'd have to figure it out together—it would have to be a joint decision.

As for her, what she was, and the powers she had, I hoped we'd have more of an idea about that when we figured out the questions surrounding her father. He had to be the key to figuring her out, and there was a whole side to her that she didn't know about—a side that had been buried away. Maybe it would never have come to the forefront if she hadn't met me; perhaps she would have always been in the dark about it.

My contemplation was broken when I heard Bee link me. *Lucifer, sorry if I'm interrupting anything, but we need to talk.*

No, go on, Bee. Tess is sleeping. What's up?

I got in touch with Gabriela, and I explained that we needed her to come and consult on a human with some unusual injuries and possibly to carry out some illusion spells. She said she was on her way anyway. She has news for you about Tess's father. Bee seemed off, not quite her usual composed self.

What is it, Bee? Did she tell you something? I'd be fucking pissed if Gabriela told my lieutenant before she told me, especially as she had been instructed to report to me directly.

No, No, it's not that. It's just something I picked up on. I've gotten to know her... fairly well—

Bee, I know the two of you are fucking, so just get on with it.

Whatever she's found out it's spooked her, and she seemed agitated. She's just arrived and it's confirmed my suspicions. What-

ever she knows has her wound tightly. She wants to speak with you urgently. She's pacing about here in Pride. Shall we come to you?

Yes, bring her here immediately, but wait in the main room. We'll be with you as soon as we can get ready. Call Levi down, Conrath can watch over Emma.

Of course, she said as I felt her slip away.

I looked down at Tess, really not wanting to wake her or tell her that it seemed we had answers. I wanted to stay here, in bed, ignoring the rest of the world and remaining oblivious in our bed. Oblivious to an answer that had the potential to change both of our lives forever. But, I had to do this—she deserved to know.

I tipped her head back and kissed her softly and repeatedly till she finally began to stir. "Red, we have to get up now." Clearly not happy with being woken, she turned away from me so her back was to me, burying her head in the pillow. I kissed up her back, starting at the two little dimples either side of her spine and working my way up. When she didn't move, I gave her a small nip with my teeth. Still nothing. I moved farther up to her shoulder and nipped again a little more forcefully.

"Hey," she scolded as she turned to face me, her nipples hard. "Careful."

"You were ignoring me, Red. We need to get up, we have a visitor."

"Who is it?" she queried, suspicion etched in her features.

"It's Gabriela. She's here to see Emma, and she also wants to talk to me about something else, so we need to go meet her."

"Why do I need to come? Can't I just go and wait in Emma's room with her?" She stuck her bottom lip out in a pout and pulled the sheets further up her body in defiance.

"She's here to talk to both of us. She… has an answer about your father." I tried to keep my voice as calm as I could, suppressing the uneasiness that crept over me and trying to stop it bleeding through the link for her to pick up on.

She blinked a few times, staring at me blankly. I was about to ask if she was okay before she said, "Right, well, let's fucking do this, shall we?"

43

TESS

THIS WAS IT. I was about to get the answer to a question that until recently, I didn't know needed asking. Who was my father? And more importantly, exactly *what* was my father, and in turn, what was I? A million possibilities had run through my head, each of them crazier than the last.

Lucifer hadn't really shared any of his own thoughts with me about who my father was. In that regard, he'd played his cards very close to his chest. But we were about to get answers. Up until the fight with Lilith I was convinced that he'd gotten it wrong and that I was human, just like my mother—and probably my father. But then my hands had magically glowed, and both hurt and healed, so I wasn't so sure I could agree I was *just* human anymore.

Fucking glowing hands.

Whatever this witch was going to tell me would ultimately change everything forever. My life was about to become something different, something I had no control over. I hated that, I wanted to be the mistress of my own fate. After I'd left Daniel, I made sure everything I did was my choice. It was all me, my path to pave. Now, to learn that something potentially huge could change my life so monumentally without me having any say in it... well, it left me at a complete loss.

I got ready slowly, trying to prolong the inevitable change that I sensed was coming. Lucifer was dressed and waiting for me, yet he didn't push. He would be eager to find out the answers too; instead he waited patiently. Maybe he clearly sensed the gravitas of the situation and didn't want to exacerbate matters, so he allowed me to do things in my own time.

I pulled on some casual clothes and tied my hair into a high pony. Looking at my reflection in the mirror, I gave myself a pep talk. *No matter what happens, no matter what the answer is, you're still you. That will never change. You fought hard to find yourself when you were seemingly lost. You did that, no one else. You were a shell of a person, and you found focus, found who and what you loved. You built a life for yourself, something to be proud of. You've already faced your demons; you can face the fact you might be one.*

I blew out a breath and readied myself, then walked back to where Lucifer sat still patiently waiting. "Let's go," I said confidently.

"I'll be right next to you the whole time, whatever the outcome. Trust in that." He pushed up from the chair, moving towards me with purpose. He took my hands and brought them up to his mouth, planting tender kisses on each one. "Come on," he urged as he led me from the room.

It was a short walk, but it seemed to take an eternity. My feet had turned to lead, and each step was a struggle. He stopped in front of a large door and moved his hand to the handle. I pulled him back to me and laced my hands around his neck. I kissed him, and I poured everything I had into that kiss. "What was that for?" he asked.

"I just wanted to kiss you one last time. One last time as just me, Tess Adams. A crazy girl who you hit on in a bar, who drove you crazy—"

"You *still* drive me crazy. It'll be fine, and I won't go anywhere, Red."

"I know you said that, but if this is bad, I mean really bad, then you should have the option to walk away." He went to interrupt, but I held my hand up. "Come on, let's find out what dear old Dad actually was."

I pushed my way through the door and saw Bee and Levi, lounging on high, wing-backed chairs. "Who's with Emma right now?" I asked Lucifer. I didn't want her to be left alone in case anything happened.

"Conrath is, I know you trust him." He was right, I did. I trusted Conrath with my own life, so of course, I trusted him with Emma's. I nodded at Lucifer, giving him a weak smile. I then continued into the room and saw a stunningly beautiful woman pacing up and down. She had to be Gabriela. She did not look at ease or calm, for that matter. Yeah, this definitely wasn't good.

Gabriela stopped her pacing and looked up, her eyes darting between Lucifer and me, but she didn't speak. "Gabriela, this is Tess." I smiled at her, she nodded curtly and once more returned her focus to Lucifer. "It's Tess's lineage you've been looking in to. I understand you have answers for us?"

"Sir, forgive me. I'm not sure it's appropriate she remain present while we discuss this." Gabriela said nervously, in a thick Spanish accent.

Oh fuck no! This was my fucking life, and I was damned sure that I wouldn't be made to wait outside while everyone was given answers. Before I had the chance to voice my opposition, though, Lucifer spoke.

"Tess deserves to know, more so than anyone else in this

room. She will not be cast out while we discuss matters pertinent to the future—*her future*. She has a right to know whatever it is you've found out. You can continue."

Gabriela nodded in agreement, but the uncertainty was still clearly visible on her face. Her mouth bobbed open a few times, evidently unsure of where to start.

It was Bee who finally ended the silence. "Start at the beginning, Gabriela." Bee shot the witch a reassuring look, one laced with emotion.

Gabriela nodded and took a long, steadying breath. "The investigations I have performed are absolute, and there is no room for error. What I have found is correct, no matter how absurd and unlikely it sounds."

Shit this wasn't good.

"I performed the test several times to make sure. It is dark magic, and it required sacrifice, which I paid multiple times to ensure the results were accurate."

Fuck me, just get the point.

"I truly can't believe the results myself. I have to make sure you understand I have not doctored the results in any way, I—"

"Gabriela, was it?" I interrupted, and she nodded. "I don't mean to be rude, but… can we just get on with it? We get it, the results are accurate. Any chance we can find out this century just *what* the results are?" My patience was shot. Lucifer strode over to me, and once by my side gently rubbed my back and pressed a gentle kiss to my temple.

It's okay, Red, He said through the link, doing his best to reassure me with little avail. The way she was talking, it wasn't good, but I needed to know whatever it was.

"Continue, Gabriela. Please just get to the pertinent information," Lucifer urged. She nodded at him, swallowing hard before continuing.

"I'm afraid I can't tell you *who* Tess's father is. That magic does not exist. It died years ago—as did the witches who used it. What I can tell you is *what* her father is and therefore, what she is." The more she skirted around the answers, the more agitated I became. Lucifer pushed a sense of calm through the link, but it did little to appease my mood.

"Tess is nephilim." Gabriela said it so quickly she stumbled through the words. Her eyes were fixed solely on me after she made her revelation.

I had no clue what she'd just said, so it meant very little to me. But everyone else in the room turned to stare. They all stared with an uneasiness about them. Like nephilim were not to be trusted; like they were a danger to everything and everyone, and therefore I was a danger too.

My eyes flitted between them all, trying to gauge some reaction, but they all stared back at me with shocked, blank expressions. I turned to Lucifer to see he had the same look on his face. He looked at me incredulously. "You're sure, Gabriela? One hundred percent sure?" His voice was thick with uncertainty.

Nodding her head, she said, "It's the truth, Sir. I came straight here with the findings."

"No one else knows? Answer me, have you told anyone else about this? *Anyone?*" His voice had begun to sound slightly panicked.

"No, I would never disobey you," Gabriela said earnestly, dropping her head in a bow.

"Bee, Levi, we need to come up with a plan. Tess needs to be safe, so it's probably best if she—"

"Hey," I shouted at the top of my lungs, causing all of their eyes to shoot to me. "You might all know what she just said, it clearly means something to all of you, but I haven't got a fucking clue. So can someone *please* tell me what this means?" I sucked in ragged breaths in an attempt to calm myself down.

Lucifer pulled me to the couch, sitting me down on it and taking a seat next to me. "Tess, listen to me carefully. You're nephilim. That means that your father was an angel, which means that you are part angel."

You've got to be fucking kidding me.

44

MICHAEL

I WAS LEADING DRILLS, and I loved it. Putting the new recruits through their paces was one of my favourite tasks. If someone wanted to be part of the celestial army, you better be sure they had to earn that spot with blood sweat and tears.

I was proud to lead, proud to have the strongest men who would follow me to Hell and back. I was their commander, and they never questioned my methods or my motives. That was why when I asked a couple of soldiers to monitor the Devil—and in particular, his new flame—they did so without question.

They were to observe and report back to me, and I especially wanted to know who she was and what made her so special to him.

I *despised* Lucifer. He was so self-righteous. Thinking he was better than everyone else. Thinking he was God's favourite, despite everything he'd done. He was an arrogant, egotistical, selfish bastard, and one of these days I'd rid the world of him. I'd take pleasure in watching the life drain from his body, knowing he would never be at peace.

But that's exactly what this *woman* had done: she'd given

him peace, and I hated her for it. He shouldn't get to appreciate those feelings, and he shouldn't get to be *happy*.

"Harder, you all need to work harder. If this is the most you have to give you may as well give up now, you pathetic bunch of pussies." I knew I was taking my anger out on them. I didn't feel bad about it, though—it would make them stronger in the long run. It meant they would have no weaknesses to exploit and nothing would be able to get to them.

Before this woman—whoever the fuck she was—Lucifer had been arrogant, took what he wanted when he wanted. He'd shown little regard for anyone or anything except Hell and the empire he'd built there. Now, he had a *weakness*.

In my peripheral vision, I saw soldiers loitering on the side of the training ground. "What the fuck is it? Shit or get off the pot, gentlemen." The pair approached cautiously.

"Sir, it's about the information you asked us to get. We have an update for you." He sounded surprisingly pleased with himself.

"Go on, then, spit it out. I don't have all fucking day." Contrary to popular belief, angels weren't sunshine and light—in fact, it was my job to be the opposite. As the commander of God's army I had to make the tough choices and dirty my hands more than any of the other angels. Not that I minded—Lucifer wasn't the only one who had darkness in him. I held my hand out and the soldier handed me a brown envelope.

"Everything we have is in there. I think you'll be pleased with the work, Sir," the older of the two soldiers said, his friend nodding along in agreement.

"Is that right?" I replied with a fake smile on my face. "I'll be the fucking judge of that. Now leave me." I turned my back on them and stalked away before they could reply.

I tore open the envelope, pulling the contents out. There was information about the girl, her name, place of birth, etc.,

etc. Nothing of interest to me. I carried on thumbing through the information. If this was the best of what they'd uncovered, I'd have them running double-length drills for an entire week. Maybe I'd block their teleportation abilities for a month too, make them do everything the hard way. *Fucking amateu—*

I stopped when I came to some photos. He had such a smug fucking face, one I was desperate to punch every time I saw it. I wanted to pummel his face till my hands bled and he wasn't so fucking pretty anymore. I glanced over at the woman who had turned the Devil into a "better man."

I gripped the photo tightly, stared down at her face, and studied it, taking in every inch of her on the photo. After a minute, I leafed through the rest of the shots, examining her carefully, pouring over every one of her features.

Fuck.

I knew that face, I'd seen that face before. *But that was years ago, so it can't possibly be the same person. How can it be? She's dead, so how come she's looking up at me from these photos?*

I found the first sheet of paper and reread it. Tess Adams. London. The early nineties.

Fuck.

It wasn't her. It was her *daughter*. I scanned the birth certificate and found the father section was blank.

Fuck, fuck.

She was *my* daughter, she was *nephilim*, and she was in love with the fucking Devil. I was utterly fucked. There was absolutely no way of talking my way out of this one. I'd broken the rules, and God would be pissed. He would make sure I would pay, in the most brutal way possible, in front of all of Heaven. He wasn't as merciful as everyone assumed; in this instance, there would be no room for forgiveness. Not for this particular sin.

No, this was my mess, and I'd have to put it right.

HELL'S ANGEL

DARK DESIRES BOOK 3

Tess has answers about the power she holds—an ancient power, one thought lost forever. However, that power comes with even more questions. Tess must learn to control and harness her new abilities, as well as discover the truth about her father.

Lucifer is painfully aware that everything is far from resolved. Tess is in more danger than ever before and he needs answers in order to keep her safe.

Tess is a threat to everything. Her existence threatens a balance that has been in place since the beginning of time. A powerful entity has decided he can't risk her existence being known and will do anything to keep her a secret... even if that means he has to kill his only daughter.

Buy Hell's Angel now...

MAILING LIST

To keep up with all the latest news and releases from author M.L Mountford, be sure to sign up to her mailing list.

You will receive regular updates on new projects, as well as information on deals and exclusive offers.

Your email address will never be used for spam and you are free to unsubscribe at any time.

Sign Up Now.

ABOUT THE AUTHOR

M. L. Mountford loves to read and write paranormal romance. She tries to make her characters interesting, sassy, and quirky, as well as creating whole other worlds hidden within our own.

She is from the North-East of England, where she lives with her husband and two young daughters.

Her busy life means she's fuelled entirely by coffee and sugar. When she's not writing she can be found eating everything in sight, binge watching whatever new documentary Netflix has to offer, swearing far too much, or with her nose buried in her Kindle.

For more information
www.mlmountford.com

ACKNOWLEDGMENTS

The first, and most important, thank you goes to my amazing husband Lee Mountford. Without you paving the way and sharing your knowledge and expertise, I would not have had the confidence to complete this book. I couldn't have done any of this without your support, thank you. Also, to my two wonderful girls. I am very lucky to have such an amazing family.

I'd like to take this opportunity to thank my editor, Josiah Davis https://www.jdbookservices.com for all of his help with this project.

Thanks also go to Dianne McCarty for being an additional proof editor on this project.

The amazing covers were designed by the talented, Raven Nordmann https://www.facebook.com/groups/ravenbookcovers Her work is beautiful, and she helped turn my ideas into an amazing set of covers.

A huge thank you goes to my wonderful Beta readers: Laura Holland, Amanda Lynn-Domanowski Mashburn, and Cheryl Gray. Thank you all for your keen eyes.

My final thank you, is to you for taking the time to read this book. I hope you had as much fun reading it as I did writing it!

Copyright © 2021 by M.L. Mountford

All rights reserved.

No part of this book may be reproduced in any form or by any electronic or mechanical means, including information storage and retrieval systems, without written permission from the author, except for the use of brief quotations in a book review.

❦ Created with Vellum

Printed in Great Britain
by Amazon